For Gerry —

My favorite

Sutter town

compadre!

Best,

Tim

ON HIGHER GROUND

A Postmodern Romance

Tim Holt

cover by Sandra Hood

Copyright 2000
Suttertown Publishing
P.O. Box 214
Dunsmuir, California 96025
1st Printing
ISBN No. 0-914485-19-9

*For information about other books from Suttertown
Publishing, see last page of this book.*

*Tim Holt is an avid bicyclist and hiker who has lived in the
Mount Shasta region since 1995.*

Dedicated To The Memory
Of Wayne Hultgren,
Whose Gentle But Powerful Spirit
Still Inspires Me

ACKNOWLEDGEMENTS

A number of people have made significant contributions to this work. My good and patient friends David and Kay Mogavero provided encouragement and helpful feedback in its early stages. Authors Ernest Callenbach (*Ecotopia* and *Ecotopia Emerging*) and Bill Pieper *(So Trust Me: Four Decades Of Lies And Deceit)* read and critiqued the entire manuscript at various stages. I am particularly indebted to Pieper for his very meticulous and professional textual editing.

Essential background information was provided by retired farmers Clifford Cain of the Capay Valley and Bill Kinnicutt of Chico, and by air quality specialist Earl Withycombe of Sacramento. Useful background material on global warming and other environmental matters was gleaned from *The New York Times, The Sacramento Bee,* and *The Auto-Free Times,* as well as Gale E. Christianson*'s Greenhouse*, published in 1999 by Walker and Company of New York.

I am particularly grateful to my dear partner Sandra Hood, who listened to each chapter as it was completed and whose laughter and tears, and, at times, quizzical looks, told me whether I was on the right track or not. Sandra also drew the cover and the map of the Shasta region.

All of the geographic locations in this book are real places. Readers who have not yet visited Captain Jack's Stronghold in the upper reaches of Siskiyou County are encouraged to do so. If you are at all sensitive to such things, you will find that echoes of the great Modoc Indian battles of the late 19th century still reverberate through its haunted and winding tunnels.

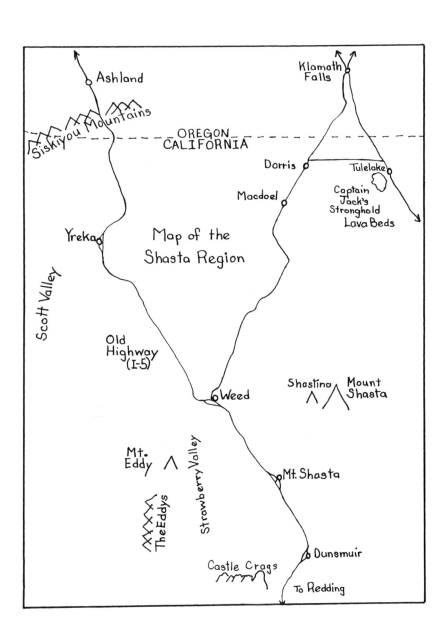

Map of the Shasta Region

CHAPTER I: JUNE 3, 2047 IN SACRAMENTO

*O*n normal days the six-lane freeway north of Sacramento accommodated moderate volumes of traffic in both directions. Today the traffic was in one direction, and all six lanes were jammed with vehicles piloted by panicked motorists. Cars disabled by accidents were strewn along both sides and had even piled up in the center strip.

Bill, like every other driver on the road, was frantically looking for openings in the next lane—the next lane always seemed to be moving faster. Switching lanes, as risky as it was on the crowded freeway, at least gave him the feeling he was doing something to get them to the airport faster.

Bill and Jess were both wearing face masks—the masks were connected to tanks affixed to a special belt they had hurriedly put on as they had rushed from the building only an hour ago.

They had left a city whose residents would soon die if they did not find some means of escape. The Sacramento dome was turning into a mass asphyxiation chamber due to soaring, out-of-control pollution and temperature levels.

When it was functioning normally, the city's air intake system sucked in outside air through the city's purification screening devices and ran it through a cooling system. The outflow system forced used air out of the dome through an underground network of radiating ducts. During a routine cleaning and maintenance operation on the main system, the engine that drove both inflow and outflow pumps for the backup system had failed. With the main system's huge central motor in pieces and the giant fabric screens that trapped particulate matter dismantled, there was no hope of getting the main system up and running in less than 12 hours. And no one, not even the plant's maintenance supervisor, had any way of knowing if or how long the reactivated main system could function with pollution and temperature levels soaring well above the normal range.

When Bill and Jess fled the telecommunications center where they worked, the temperature outside was already 115 degrees fahrenheit. And the ensuing traffic jams caused by people attempting to escape, coupled with the failure of the outflow system, was driving pollution to toxic levels.

The two young men had had the presence of mind to grab their emergency oxygen packets from their work stations before they fled the building. These were absolutely necessary since Bill's car was not equipped with its own air purification system. Fortunately, as a step toward making the car suitable for inter-city travel, he had recently had a purification system installed in the engine.

Their portable oxygen supply would last only two hours, and their only hope was to get to the airport, normally a 15-minute drive from the dome. From there they hoped to fly to another domed city, possibly Berkeley/Oakland or Los Angeles. They were fortunate that their building was near the city's perimeter. And by acting quickly, as soon as they learned of the system's failure, they had made it to the nearest exit module before gridlock occured on the city's main streets.

Jess had looked back as they left the chambers of the exit module that served as a buffer between the city and the heavily polluted valley air. These two environments were rapidly merging. Jess could see only the dimmest outline of the city's skyline. A dense gray fog was filling the dome as the city turned into one vast tomb.

As they emerged from the module, Jess saw people walking,

running, and stumbling along the side of the road. Although some had emergency breathing equipment, most did not. Some of the unfortunate refugees had already collapsed, lying alongside the road and gasping for breath. Some were no longer gasping.

Visibility outside the dome was, as usual, only about 200 feet. Only a narrow strip of dry, cracked, barren land was visible from the highway, but the travelers weren't missing much, since the land was similarly dry and denuded for miles and miles beyond the freeway.

As they inched along, Jess for the first time thought of Susan. Had she managed to escape? Would he perhaps see her at the airport? In his semi-panicked state, he could think of no other way she could escape. He reached over and pushed the button activating the car's microwave transmitter and punched in Susan's office number, but there were none of the usual ringing beeps—only dry, crackling static. So he did the only thing he could do: He prayed that she would somehow survive, and as he did he could see her—a frail, slender, gracefully beautiful woman with wonderful warm eyes. The thought that he might not see her again gave this awful tragedy an immediacy he had not felt until now.

He prayed for his parents and his sister and her family and for the rest of his co-workers and as he did so he was aware of the futility of what he was doing but it was all he could do, and it somehow kept him from completely breaking down. He could not afford to break down right now.

They arrived at the outskirts of the airport with less than half an hour left on their oxygen tanks. They saw people pulling over and parking their cars by the side of the freeway and soon learned that the airport's parking lot was completely filled, so they got out of their car and hiked in the last half-mile. Hordes of people were converging on the terminal, people stumbling along, holding handkerchiefs in front of their faces, few of them with emergency oxygen. People emerged from their cars and tried to move at a brisk pace—some almost jogging despite the crowds—hoping to make the distance before the foul air got to them. Most were staggering by the time they got to the terminal; some dropped by the wayside. Jess got a brief glimpse of one man lying on the ground as he passed by. The man's lips were silently moving, his bulging eyes staring directly upward. Farther along a pudgy, middle-aged man lay collapsed on the ground while a woman, perhaps his wife, struggled to pull him up. By the time Jess got up to them the woman too had collapsed on the ground. Jess turned away as he passed by.

Reaching the airport's vast terminal building provided only temporary relief. There was clean air to breathe, but all flights were booked for weeks ahead; the ones leaving in the next several days had already accumulated long waiting lists.

There were already rumors circulating in the crowded terminal that the airport would have to shut down by the end of the day or even sooner, since the fuel needed to drive its air purification system arrived by truck daily from Sacramento, as well as food and other supplies. Optimists in the crowd argued that surely fuel would be shipped on an emergency basis from the Bay Area or one of the other climate-controlled cities in the valley. As time wore on this argument seemed to have fewer and fewer adherents.

At one ticket counter a man was pounding on the counter with his fist, screaming at the agent on the other side that he absolutely must have—*must have!*— tickets for, if not himself and his wife, at least so his two children, aged 5 and 7 —*5 and 7, dammit!*—could make their escape. The man, in tears, was finally led away by a security guard. Frantic, tearful exchanges were going on at ticket counters up and down the length of the building. Had it not been for the presence of security guards, there would likely have been a mass storming of the gates every time a new flight began boarding. As it was, sullen crowds looked on as the lucky few boarded their planes.

At one gate, Jess and Bill saw one desperate man wave a checkbook as he approached the boarders, one by one, offering them whatever sum they wanted for one precious ticket.

The two young men, after waiting in line for over an hour, managed to get on a waiting list for a flight to Los Angeles in three days. As they gazed longingly out the window at the dim outline of a plane flying off toward the south, they wondered how they would hold out for the next three days. Both silently shared a vague sense of foreboding, that somehow the terrible disaster only a few miles away would engulf them if they stayed in this building much longer.

Just during the past hour, as they had waited in line, the mood of the crowd had deteriorated dramatically. Shouting matches and even fistfights were now frequent occurrences, and the security guards had had to wrestle with and physically restrain a number of people who'd tried to force their way onto boarding flights. The notion that there would be any semblance of order three days from now seemed ludicrous.

Out of desperation, Jess and Bill had come up with an alternative plan, but it would need to be carried out immediately. They headed toward a side exit. Once they stepped outside, with only minutes of oxygen left in their tanks, they had to act quickly. Donning their masks, they headed across what seemed like an endless stretch of asphalt to the hangars that housed privately owned airplanes.

The hangar doors were thrown open all along the row of cavernous buildings, and a steady stream of small planes issued forth, heading toward the runway. All manner of people were heading into the buildings—some alone, some in pairs, even a few families. These people had for the most part come prepared with emergency oxygen equipment, which is why Jess's attention was immediately drawn to one lone man holding a handkerchief to his face.

Instinctively Jess grabbed Bill's arm and headed toward the hangar the man had just entered.

By the time they caught up with him, the man was leaning against the side of a plane near the cockpit. He was short and heavyset and looked to be in his fifties. As they got closer, they could see that his face and hands were turning blue. He had pulled a set of keys from his pocket and was making a frantic but fumbling attempt to unlock the cockpit's door. As he did so he was slowly sliding down the side of the plane. By the time Jess and Bill got to him he had slumped down to the ground and was making aimless, pawing movements with one arm in an apparent effort to grasp the side of the plane and raise himself back up.

Jess wrenched off his mask and placed it over the man's head. He unbuckled the apparatus, handed it to Bill and grabbed the man's keys. Motioning to Bill to keep the mask on the man's face, Jess stood up, managed to open the cockpit door and clambered up and into the pilot's seat. He was gasping for breath—his lungs taking in huge quantities of air, trying to get enough oxygen—as he tried the keys in the ignition. Finally, on about the fifth key he heard the engine turn over, but the sound seemed to come from a long way away. He looked among the various switches and dials for some way to set the airplane in motion . . . *where?* . . . *what was he looking for?* . . . *having trouble focusing* . . . *chest heaving, can't get enough air* . . . *sleep, need to sleep* . . .

Just before he passed out he felt himself being moved. He was also dimly aware of something being placed over his face.

" . . . had to clear out so fast I forgot to grab my breathing stuff. If you guys hadn't happened along like you did I don't see how I could have made it. . . . "

The sound of the stranger's calm, reassuring voice was accompanied by the strange but welcome sight of blue sky and white clouds as Jess, regaining consciousness, slowly sat up and looked out the plane's window. But the lovely sight was in eerie contrast to what was coming in over the radio.

" . . . reports of the disaster in Sacramento are still sketchy, but deaths in the hundreds of thousands are anticipated. The city is one mass grave, as are all the exit routes near the city's perimeter. The city is now totally uninhabitable, except for some remaining pockets of filtered air in climate-controlled buildings.

"In fact what reports we do have are coming from people trapped in those buildings. There may be several hundred or even several thousand people still surviving in this fashion—it's impossible to say at this time. But with the pollution levels outside, it's unlikely the air in those buildings can remain breathable for more than a few more hours. And escape for these people would be difficult, if not impossible, since all the city's main arterials are choked with vehicles whose drivers have died attempting to escape . . . ."

Bill, unwilling to hear any more, turned off the radio. Beside him the pilot was quietly sobbing and muttering to himself.

"Sarah . . . Mindy . . . Tommy . . . too many cars . . . too many people trying to get out. . . ."

Bill quietly put his arm around the pilot. Jess thought again of Susan, and of his parents—his dad, no doubt trapped in his downtown office building when the sirens came on; his mom, who worked at the senior center in South Sac, far from any escape modules; his two little nieces and his nephew, who would have been in school; and their mother, his sister Gwen, who worked at the downtown hospital. Had any of them made it to a safe place, where there was breathable air? Or had they . . .

"Don't they ever check their backup systems?!" the pilot suddenly blurted out. "By God, you'd think in a city of 400,000 people, with their lives depending on these goddamn systems, they'd have made sure nothing could go wrong with the backup!" He was pounding his fist and shouting at the mute radio.

Bill, his voice quavering, managed a weak smile as he looked over at the pilot and said, "I'm Bill Juno. This is Jess Renfree. What with all the confusion, we never got a chance to get properly introduced."

With a sheepish sideways glance, the pilot gratefully took the rope offered him: "Name's Clement, Chuck Clement. I own—or I guess I used to own—a sporting goods store in town. My wife, she works . . . she . . . "

As Chuck Clement faltered, Bill jumped into the breach again. This time his voice was more controlled. "So Mr. Guardian Angel, also known as Chuck Clement, where are you taking us?" Jess couldn't help but admire the way Bill, who must be experiencing a good deal of inner turmoil himself—he had left his wife of six months back in Sacramento— was trying to maintain an atmosphere of calm in the closely confined cabin.

"Well, Portland is as good a destination as any. I've got relatives there. How about you guys?"

"Suits me. I didn't have any travel plans at all until a few hours ago, and I'm pretty flexible," Bill said with forced jocularity.

"Okay with me too," Jess said. Up until this minute he had only been able to think about what they'd left behind, not where they might be going.

"We'll have to refuel somewhere along the way. Should have filled up in Sacramento, but . . . Easiest stop I know of between here and Portland is Mott Airport, near Mount Shasta. If they've been deluged with planes because of this . . . this . . . this mess, we'll still have enough fuel to try a couple of places farther north."

The three refugees settled into a troubled calm for the rest of the ride. There was an unspoken understanding that they would speak of anything but the awful tragedy. So they talked of sports, of Portland and its attractions, and vaguely of other cities each might want to live in, and work they might do once they got there. But their minds were clearly not engaged in this small talk, which was halting and frequently broke down altogether.

After about half an hour Mount Shasta was visible on the horizon.

Jess peered out the window. For the first time since they left Sacramento there was actually something visible below. To the north, hills densely carpeted with dark green forests rose up out of the valley's haze. Snow-capped Mount Shasta dominated the horizon. After they had passed Redding, one of the smallest domed cities in the entire central valley, Jess could barely make out the broad expanse of Lake Shasta beneath the film of pollution, but by the time they had traveled a short distance farther the Sacramento River was clearly visible, snaking its way southward toward the lake. Running parallel to the river was the old interstate highway. The traffic headed northward was about three times the volume of that headed in the opposite direction.

They touched down alongside the highway on the football field-sized runway. The airport was on a small leveled-off plain surrounded by steep, forested hillsides. The three travelers ambled the short distance over to a little tin-roofed shack that served as the airport's office. Half a dozen people were clustered outside. One gray-haired lady in blue overalls, whose ruddy face was topped by a yellow golf cap, called out, "If you guys are lookin' for fuel you're gonna have to wait awhile. They drained the final drop outta the tank about half an hour ago." Shading her eyes, she peered at them curiously. "You guys comin' from Sac?"

Chuck ignored the question. "Any idea when it'll get filled?"

The lady, who seemed to understand Chuck's reticence, said, "Truck's on the way from Eugene. Maybe an hour, maybe two—traffic's not too bad comin' south, but nobody really knows how long."

"Well boys, might as well try our luck a little farther north, maybe Ashland," Chuck said. "That's about as far as I'd feel safe going. Sounds like they might get refueled there before this stop. At worst we'll end up waiting, same as here."

The three of them headed back.

When they got to the plane, Jess said, "I'm not going any farther." His companions were momentarily speechless. Finally Bill said, "Jess, you sure about this?"

"Not much up here other than a few farms and a lot of mountains," Chuck said.

"Yeah, I know, but yeah, I'm sure I want to stay here awhile," Jess said calmly. "I liked the look of the place as we were flying in. Guess we're all kinda homeless right now, and this place looks like it'll do for me for the time being." He reached his hand out to Chuck, who took it firmly in his. "Thanks . . . thanks for everything," Chuck said.

Jess turned and embraced Bill. "Good luck," Jess said. "Take care of yourself," Bill said. "I'll send you a message as soon as I find a transmitter." There were tears in both men's eyes as Bill stepped into the plane. Within seconds the plane's propellers were spinning. Jess watched it as it taxied down the runway, and he followed it as it soared upward over the trees, toward Mount Shasta and out of sight.

CHAPTER II: JUNE 3, 2047 IN THE
SHASTA REGION

*A*s William waited for the man to come down the gravel road, he had settled into an uneasy calm. For the moment, anyway, his thoughts were drifting rather pleasantly. Funny, he thought to himself, most of his friends back in Sacramento regarded him and Cheryl as pioneers, but he had never thought of himself as the pioneer type. In his old life his pioneering had never gone beyond baking his own bread and taking the occasional weekend walk through the wilds of Sacramento's William Land Park.

And both of them, really, were a little on the stout side to fit the classic image of the pioneer. Although—and here William patted himself in the mid-section with a sweet, self-satisfied smile—although the long days spent in the fields *had* trimmed him down quite a bit from his city days. . . .

William's musings were interrupted when Chester the goat butted up against him. Chester did not want William to forget that he was there, that he had a stomach to fill, and that it was very near his feeding time.

Was it Thomas Jefferson or Harry Truman—William couldn't remember which—who said that farmers make good philosophers, because they have lots of time to think while they're out working their fields?

Well, that was a good theory, all right, but the fact is that on a farm you spent a lot of time thinking about the practical, nuts-and-bolts stuff that kept your farm producing and your buildings and machinery from falling apart.

Right now, as he fed Chester and his two siblings, William had his eye on the barn roof, calculating whether it would hold up through another rainy season with a little patching or whether it would need to be replaced during this dry season.

And then there was the big gamble he was taking on the asparagus crop he'd planted last year. There was a lot of money, potentially, to be made from organic asparagus, and William had planted 15 acres of it—had, in fact, bet the farm on it. If it produced as he hoped, it would give him the means to pay off the farm's mortgage. The only catch was, it would take two more years for the newly planted seedlings to produce their first harvestable crop.

So there was the problem of getting through the next two years. For some time now he and Cheryl had been able to do little more than keep up with the interest payments on the mortgage. Here and there, they had chipped away on the principal, but not by much, and it had been five years now since they had taken out the loan. The bank, a cooperative formed by the farmers of the region, had been patient, but there was a limit. . . . That was essentially why Tom Griffiths, the bank's chief loan officer, was coming out to the farm today. They had had these little talks before, during the past few years, but this was the first time he had actually come out to the farm.

From where he stood, William could look out over the bare fields to the south of the barn. That brought up something else: Should he plant chard in the south five acres only two years after the last chard crop had been planted there, or go with a soil-enhancing crop like beans or even alfalfa? The deer fences also needed mending or replacing in a number of places where last winter's rains had caused the fence posts to give way. Where was he going to get the money for that?

With all this and more to deal with, this grappling with the age-old dilemma of how to wrest a living from land and livestock, he was often distracted from thinking about the bigger things. And there certainly were some big things to think about. Something new—no one was quite sure what, least of all William—was being created right here in this region without any real blueprint or plan of any kind, it seemed. Perhaps because, like William, everyone was just too busy with day-to-day living to come up with any kind of road map. Things kept getting patched together, improvised, as old ways were shed and new ways of doing things gradually became the norm.

Oh, every once in awhile a Conference On The Region's Future, or something of that sort, would be called, which would attract mostly new residents and the few officials who were paid to attend such events. And then an "action plan" or a "blueprint for the future" would be issued by the conference with great fanfare and a few speeches, and then just as quickly shelved and forgotten. And in the meantime, new ways of doing things kept evolving at their own steady, un-studied, un-confeienced pace.

The biggest changes were economic rather than political. Because of the skyrocketing prices for oil and the high costs of transportation nowadays, more and more goods and food items were being produced right here in the region: wood products (mostly furniture and building materials), pottery and many kinds of housewares, rugs, blankets, woodstoves, bicycles—all manner of simple, practical items, all of them handcrafted right here. As the competitive reach of the national chains had shrunk, the small-scale producers of the Shasta region had a chance to grow and prosper. And this, in turn, had spawned a thriving barter system.

William let out an involuntary grunt as he shoved the handcart, loaded with three bales of hay, in the direction of the sheep corral. It was enough for him right now that in this new, "pioneering" life of his and Cheryl's they were actually *producing* something—vegetables, eggs, sheep's wool, goat's milk—something *tangible*, un-like what he had "produced" in his old job: figures on a computer screen and endless reams of paperwork.

The sheep were in the upper meadow and had to be herded back to the corral, so William left the cart at the corral and tramped up toward the meadow. As he walked he called out "Sheeee-eeeep! Sheeee-eeeep! Sheeee-eeeep!" which brought the leaders, at first a little hesitant but soon quickening their pace, down the path to the corral. The parade of sheep soon became a mini-stampede, all 25 of them charging toward the corral, and William had only to lope down the path behind the last one and close the gate behind it.

That was the last of his late-afternoon chores, and William headed back toward the farmhouse. He gazed intently at the highway that ran along the farm. It was late afternoon. What had happened to Mr. Griffiths? Perhaps he'd gotten tied up listening to some other farmer's sad story.

The Shawntree farmhouse was a sturdy, two-story frame struc-ture that had been built at the beginning of the last century. The high, steep roof was designed for winters far more severe than those of the present age, but the thick walls, supported by beams a foot square, kept the interior cool in the blistering summer heat.

When he entered the kitchen he was treated to a sensory feast. Cheryl had gotten in from town an hour ago, and already the aroma of breakfast muffins baking in the oven mingled with this evening's vegetarian pie. The odors and the warmth wrapped themselves around him like a soft blanket, while Cheryl, paring apples at the kitchen table, sang along to the music on a country station.

Cheryl stopped singing. Her smooth face, as round and polished and shiny as the apple she was holding, was tilted up for a kiss. He gave her a nice, long, wet one.

"Mmmmmmm," she murmured, savoring the moment. Then she went back to the apples and William quietly moved around behind her and reached around and drew her to him as he kissed the back of her neck and slowly ran his open hands down her thighs.

"So," she deadpanned, "I take it things went pretty well today."

"Yeah. Griffiths is putty in our hands," he said as he slowly brought his hands up along the curves of her hips. "Old Tom says to me, 'I'll tell you what, if it wasn't for that beautiful, gorgeous, sexy wife of yours I wouldn't be doing this, but take as long as you want to pay us back. And tell her . . . '"

"No really, what happened?" she said, breaking free of his embrace and shooting him a look of mock-reproach. She went over to the cupboard to fetch a couple of wine glasses and a half-filled bottle of burgundy. She plunked them down on the kitchen table and sat down, pouring out two full glasses. William, already seated, took his first sip, rolling it on his tongue. After the tension of waiting for the bank officer, he was starting to savor the sensory pleasures of home and hearth.

Cheryl sat down next to him. "C'mon now," she said encouragingly, patting his hand, "be a good boy and tell me what happened."

William looked down at his glass. "Actually, honey, he hasn't shown up yet. Something must have held him up, maybe some other poor farmer explainin' to him why he hasn't paid up for awhile—sometimes those sad stories can go on forever, you know."

The two were silent for a few moments. Then William gave Cheryl's hand a squeeze.

"You and Kathy still planning to tackle the shearing next week?" A little over a year ago Cheryl and her neighbor Kathy Stillwater had opened a small shop in town that sold yarn and fabric and women's clothing.

"Yeah, we're psyching ourselves up for it," Cheryl replied, her perpetual smile, that quiet beacon of self-assurance, fading for just a moment. It was all very well to spin your own yarn, and weave fabric on a hand loom, and sell your products, but *shearing* sheep? Were she and Kathy perhaps carrying this hands-on thing a little too far? They had been taken with the simple purity of the idea, of being involved at every stage of the process. And the sheep were right there on the farm, after all, waiting to be shorn, and the two women had watched others do it many times, and it really didn't look all that difficult. . . . So they had armed themselves with several pamphlets and books on the subject and two electric shears. A little voice kept reminding Cheryl that it wasn't always a good idea to mix philosophical principles with the running of a business, that such considerations as the efficient use of one's time needed to be factored in, but they had already bought the books and equipment, so . . .

With a conscious effort, Cheryl recovered her smile. "So what's it going to be at the lower end? Chard, or another exotic experiment like those two acres of Portuguese peppers that even the goats wouldn't eat?" she teased.

"Oh, I dunno. Thought I'd talk to Ed. Chard that soon after the last crop of 'em might not be a good idea." Ed and Kathy Stillwater and their brood of four children lived on the farm just south of theirs. They were also refugees from Sacramento. The Stillwaters had settled on their 60-acre spread twelve years ago and had started in farming right from the beginning. They were generous with their time and hard-earned expertise and in the first years of William and Cheryl's residence had provided an informal, ongoing seminar on all aspects of basic farming. Ed also ran the six farmers' markets in Siskiyou County.

William drained the last of his wine and headed upstairs to check for messages.

"Supper in an hour?" Cheryl asked, tilting her head up for another kiss as he walked by.

"Sounds good."

Underneath the sharply pitched beams of the roof was a sizable attic, which served as the couple's office and work space. William's desk sat in one corner, and Cheryl's sewing table, sewing machine, and spinning wheel in another, while along the wall books, bolts of fabric, skis, snowshoes and camping equipment jostled each other for space.

William sat down at his desk and turned on the microwave receiver. As the screen began to flicker on, he leaned back in the chair and enjoyed the unimpeded view of the plush, ripening fields to the north that the picture window afforded. He could feel the tension draining as his mind and body began to relax for the first time since he'd gotten the call from Griffiths yesterday.

At the near end of the fields, before the new crop of asparagus, he could see the tomatoes, row after row of them, and then just to the east the squash plants—that would soon be bursting with their plump yellow and green bulbs—sprawled across another couple of acres.

Tangible, that was the word for it, the word that summed up the difference between their old life and this new one. The stuff you produced here on the farm you could hold in your hands, and it had a tangible value: it was food that nourished you, or clothing that covered and warmed you and pleased you with its colors and design.

In the climate-controlled city, everything had seemed so *intangible*. You were warmed and cooled by mechanisms you never saw. You put on a headset, and you traveled to Egypt or Mars, but you never touched sand or red earth. Living under that huge dome, you never saw the sun, or the clouds through the valley's heavy pollution. There were children in Sacramento who had no idea what rain felt like.

And you churned out reams of paperwork, and played for hours with figures on a screen, and at the end of the day you wondered who benefited from it and what was the purpose, other than earning you a paycheck.

Most days after work William had escaped these nagging doubts, for awhile, in the cool, dark bar he went to that was full of loud talk and laughter and where work was dismissed with a joke or a quip and where the important subjects were vacations, sports, and sex. Limping along behind when all other subjects had been exhausted was home improvement. The point was that, here in this cool, dark, pleasant haven from work, you talked about anything but your job.

You certainly could lead a very comfortable life in the city—as long as you stayed in the bubble. You always knew what the weather was going to be. The dome with those huge spotlights attached to the roof meant that it would always be clear and bright, or clear and dark (after the lights were turned off at precisely 10 p.m.). The temperature was always 70 degrees fahrenheit. (You could adjust that higher or lower with your individual climate-control unit in your home or car.) And the nasty, choking air outside the bubble was kept out by filters that screened out the worst pollutants before the outside air was sucked in and cooled.

Otherwise, life was as it always had been in the city: There were the usual array of restaurants for every pocketbook and palate. (Most of the produce for restaurants and stores was supplied from hydroponic farms and multi-story gardens right in the dome.) Sacramento still boasted one of the finest park systems in the country, an emerald string of lush urban oases, and there were golf courses, tennis courts, indoor and outdoor pools, everything one could possibly want in the way of recreation.

And it was all as safe and protected and constant as life in a bomb shelter. And, in a way—with no sun, no clouds, no rain, and with one's movement and panorama always restricted by the perimeters of the dome—just as claustrophobic. You very soon got to the point where the World Outside the dome, that dim, hazy, scorched and deserted landscape, was something to be feared, and you clung more and more to the predictable safety of life inside. You turned inward, and in so doing turned your back on the poor, cracked, barren earth outside. Outside was where you sent your waste and your polluted air.

And when life in the bubble got a little too confining, when you got the urge to escape, it was as easy as clicking a button on your computer, and you went anywhere in the universe you wanted to go.

Sacramento, the central valley city William and Cheryl had come from, had gone to climate-control mode in the year 2035, a decade after larger and more polluted cities like Los Angeles and Houston had done so. William remembered the days before the dome, the "O-days," when ozone levels were so bad that face masks were mandatory, and the days when the combination of O-days and tinderbox conditions in the forests kept the entire population of Sacramento indoors.

The Shawntrees had made their escape in 2042. They had abandoned their secure jobs   William in state government, Cheryl as the junior partner in a law firm—and a secure climate for one of the few habitable regions left—the high mountain region above the valley. They migrated to the northernmost end of California, to Siskiyou County, which, through climatic changes, was being transformed from a ranching to a farming economy.

You had to get to an elevation of at least 2000 feet simply to rise above the brown cloud of pollution that had settled in over the Sacramento Valley. At the 3500-foot level, where the Shawntrees had settled, you could finally enjoy clear, non-filtered air and blue skies. William and Cheryl were at first dazzled by the sight of blue sky, having gotten their last glimpse of it five years before on a bus trip along the coast.

Here, at 3000-plus feet, temperatures were generally at levels that would have been typical of California's central valley in the previous century, and ranchers with large holdings found there was more money to be made in lettuce, cabbage, grapes and a myriad of other agricultural products—all made scarce by the scorching heat of the lower elevations—than in cattle.

So now the icy pinnacle of Mount Shasta loomed over wheatfields and cornfields, and the men and women in the bars down below mixed in talk of crops and fertilizer and market prices with the standard barroom topics of love, lust, and divorce.

The Bubble People, that's how William thought of the people they had left behind in Sacramento. It was, to be sure, a smug, self-congratulatory term, and a little hypocritical, since he and Cheryl had spent seven years inside that bubble. But somehow they had found the will and the energy to pull up stakes, to leave the bubble and start a life up here. At first they had felt exhilarated, and at the same time frighteningly naked and vulnerable, to look up and see the stars at night and the sun and the blue sky and the clouds during the day.

Yes, they were pioneers in a way, but not because they bathed in iron tubs or scrubbed their clothes on washboards. No, their life for the most part was just as comfortable as it had been in the city. They were pioneers, in their city friends' eyes, because they had ventured into the threatening Unknown, into the world beyond the dome.

In their own eyes, they were pioneers because they were attempting to wrest a living from the land and from the sweat of their brows.

The Shawntrees had moved onto a former ranch, a 50-acre spread framed by the two imposing giants of the landscape—Mount Eddy to the west and Mount Shasta on the east. It was one big meadow when they moved there, with a small forest of trees in the northwest corner. It and the neighboring spreads had been used early in the last century as the setting for Western movies, starring a long-forgotten cowboy actor named Tom Mix, and when you looked out from the house across the fields, with those imposing mountains in the background, you could see why Hollywood had favored this mountain valley, known locally as the Strawberry Valley. The soft, inviting beauty of Nature, as well as her threatening, intimidating side, were combined in one magnificent vista. When the sky was laced with lightning during one of the frequent winter thunderstorms, and the trees undulated, one after another, marking the passage of the wind through the forest, and the grasses bowed down in waves before the force of that same wind, why, then you felt that Nature herself had taken over the direction and staging of her own spectacular drama.

It was, in all respects, as different a world as you could imagine from that in Sacramento.

When they had first moved to the ranch, William and Cheryl had no idea how to go about making a living. Somewhere in the back of their minds was the slowly germinating idea that they could make some sort of living from the land, but at first they, like other emigres before them, tried to replicate the jobs they'd had in the city. For Cheryl, that meant taking temporary office jobs that usually involved glorified secretarial work, and not always glorified at that. Government jobs were hard to come by, unless you wanted to commute long distances, so William got a part-time job teaching English at the local community college.

They had managed to keep a small garden plot in the city and had continued the practice up here, albeit in a space much larger than the city plot. The first year they had simply grown a small amount of green and yellow and orange stuff in the summer, but by the following year they had built a greenhouse and were trucking produce down to the farmers' markets in Dunsmuir and Mt. Shasta.

They had been able to scrape together the mortgage payments

in their first year, but with their gradual plunge into full-time farming the payments soon got whittled down to the bare minimum. And then the phone calls from Tom Griffiths started coming, every month or so. The difficulty lay in finding a good cash crop, one that would provide reliable and abundant harvests year after year and fetch premium prices at the farmers' markets and in direct sales to restaurants and other produce buyers throughout the region and down in the valley.

But as they struggled with the business side of farming, they were already reaping benefits from this new life that were not reflected in their bank balance. Slowly in the fresh mountain air and under vibrant blue skies they began to re-invent themselves and their lives. In the city, work had been something they did so that they could afford to do other, more enjoyable things, or so they could buy the things they thought they needed. Up here, as they gradually spent more and more of their time in the fields, work became not a means to an end but an end in itself. Work in the soil, the hoeing and the turning over of the earth, the sowing of seeds and the planting of seedlings, and then the reward of the harvest—all of this was recreation in the usual sense of the word, as their tanned and trimmer bodies attested, but it was re-*creation* as well, a central part of the ongoing evolution of their lives. And as the work in the fields became an end in itself, something to be enjoyed and savored, the Shawntrees found that they were willing to shed things from their past life that no longer seemed important. Their combined income, what they were able to scrape together after the bank received its minimum tithe, was no more than one-fifth what it had been in the city, but they saw their reduced circumstances as a fair price to pay for the joy of living in this beautiful area and the chance to do work that actually enriched their lives.

Somehow, despite the minimal mortgage payments, Cheryl had persuaded Mr. Griffiths to loan her and Kathy Stillwater enough money to start up their ambitious new venture, what Cheryl termed a "vertically integrated clothing business." The idea was to sell natural fiber clothing in the shop that they made themselves from yarn they spun themselves, that, ultimately, came from sheep they *sheared* themselves. (That part of the plan, at least, had a certain frugal logic—they already had a flock of sheep, inherited from the property's previous owner.) The new owners quickly found that they could not do it all themselves, not stock the store with the labor of their hands *and* run it at the same time. So they expanded their limited inventory by buying clothes from other seamstresses in the area. To the surprise of everyone, especially its new proprietors, From Ewe To You started making money soon after its first year of operation; this had no doubt contributed to Mr. Griffiths' patience about the mortgage.

William scanned the messages as they came up on the screen. Mostly routine stuff: Farmers Market board of directors meeting next week, Handcrafters Cooperative meeting tomorrow at the Olsons' (he'd have to remind Cheryl of that when he went downstairs). When he switched to the News Summary, there was a paragraph on another one of those outages in the purification system in Sacramento. Oh well, they had backups for that sort of thing, didn't they?

William clicked off the receiver and stood up. He gazed absentmindedly out the big window. In the dim light of dusk, a moving object caught his attention. *Finally!* There he was, at the far end of the gravel path, walking toward the house. As he rushed down the stairs, William wondered idly why Mr. Griffiths was arriving so late and why he hadn't driven his truck all the way up to the house.

When he reached the kitchen, he called out to Cheryl, who was taking the muffins out of the oven, "Well, better late than never, I guess—he's finally here." He reached for the screen door and was about to go out when Cheryl's voice stopped him.

"Who's here?"

He let the door bang closed. "Mr. Griffiths, of course. Who else would I be talking about?" William replied, a little testily.

"Oh, I meant to come up and tell you. Mr. Griffiths called a half hour ago. Said he'd gotten stalled at another farm all afternoon and would have to come by next week."

CHAPTER III: REFUGE

*W*illiam rushed out the kitchen door to see a young stranger, tall and sturdily built but haggard-looking, stumbling along the gravel path as though he might fall forward with every step. William waved, but there was no response from the young man, who was looking toward the ground. His face had a sickly white pallor. He had the look of someone who had traveled a great distance.

William walked briskly through the open gate of the picket fence and strode the few yards to where the stranger was stumbling along. He put his arm around him for support and guided him through the opening in the gate.

"Looks like you could use a good strong cup of coffee and maybe a little food, eh?" The stranger, without looking at William, nodded his head.

By the time they reached the door William was half-dragging the young man along. Cheryl's anxious face was visible through the kitchen window. As he threw open the door, William blurted out, "Pour a cup of coffee, honey, and cut him a slice of that pie." He deposited Jess in one of the chairs at the kitchen table and went over to cut a few slices of bread. He put them on a small plate and set them in front of the visitor.

Jess stared at the bread, not reaching for it or speaking. When Cheryl placed the coffee in front of him he picked up the cup and took a sip. Then, very deliberately, he slid the cup and saucer to the side. He had a splitting headache and felt slightly nauseous.

William, seated next to him, kept coming in and out of focus, and then he just vanished altogether.

Jess woke up on the Shawntree's living room sofa. It was dark outside, but there was a light on, and Cheryl was in the corner at her spinning wheel. She had brought it down from the upper story to work while she kept an eye on him.

"You must have been pretty exhausted. I'll bet you don't even remember us dragging you in here," she said softly.

"No ma'am, I sure don't." Somehow "ma'am," a word Jess had never used before, seemed right for the occasion. "I had kind of a long day yesterday." After he'd left the small airport, Jess had in fact walked for hours in a kind of half-daze, before he'd decided to head down the gravel road with the pleasant-looking farmhouse at the end of it.

"Did you come from Sacramento?"

"Yup."

"Well, we've got a spare bedroom down the hall. As soon as you're up to it, we'll get you into a real bed for the night . . . unless you'd like a little something to eat first."

Although he still felt exhausted, Jess's empty stomach was calling out for food. He and Cheryl headed for the kitchen, where he quickly dispatched two generous slices of vegetarian pie and four buttered slices of homemade bread. He ate so quickly that Cheryl barely had time to welcome him to their home, tell him he could stay as long as he needed to, and tell him a little bit about the farm. He was grateful that she avoided asking any questions about what he'd been through. And he was blessed that night with a sleep free of dreams or nightmares.

Jess's physical recovery took only a matter of days, bolstered as it was by plenty of rest, the congenial company of his hosts, and heaping plates of health-giving food. During the first few days in this temporary refuge he slept late, foraging in the kitchen for his breakfast—Cheryl had gone to her shop in town and William was out on the farm.

At first he had a little trouble adjusting to the Shawntrees' kitchen, which contained only old-fashioned, manually operated appliances. You could not simply say to the toaster, "medium brown," or to the stove, "boil, then simmer for 20 minutes." Everything had to be painstakingly adjusted by hand and the food watched constantly to make sure it didn't burn or boil over. And the cupboards and the refrigerator had to be opened by hand, too! It required every ounce of his patience just to navigate through breakfast that first morning, and after a few days he was starting to miss his own little, well-appointed kitchen . . . but, when in Rome . . . And it was kind of interesting to experience firsthand, in this museum-like kitchen, what his grandparents had had to endure just to put meals on the table.

After breakfast those first few days he spent some time browsing through the books in the Shawntrees' attic, and sat in a chair on the front lawn with a book in his lap, trying not to think much, still mesmerized by the sight of the clouds and the sky and the fields below.

The day after he had shown up at the farm, they listened to the news via microwave transmission. It focused exclusively on the Sacramento disaster. According to the report, a small portion of Sacramento's population, estimated at roughly ten percent, had survived the disaster either by flying out or by escaping to nearby domed cities in climate-controlled vehicles.

After the broadcast was over, he told them his survival story. He told it briefly and with little emotion and when he had finished neither Cheryl nor William made any comment.

Jess made repeated efforts to communicate with Susan and his parents and his sister's family via microwave computer links, but to no avail.

It took three days for the National Guard to get troops into the devastated city. They were accompanied by a few pool reporters, and these first reports told of streets choked with immobilized vehicles, their drivers slumped over the wheels; and of tens of thousands of carcasses—already beginning to swell and stink in the 130-degree heat—covering the sidewalks.

Many Sacramentans had remained in their homes and workplaces, surviving on emergency supplies of oxygen and no doubt hoping that the system would be fixed—right up to their last, suffocating minute.

There were a few miraculous cases of survival. A rescue team found a dozen employees in a central food warehouse alive and in reasonably good shape. They had survived using the company's copious supply of individual emergency oxygen tanks, similar to those that had saved Bill and Jess's lives. When temperatures in the warehouse had soared, they had fled to a freezer unit, leaving a note at the main entrance as to their whereabouts.

One family had managed to survive by carefully sealing all door and window openings until a rescue team arrived. Even so, their six-month-old baby died from heat prostration.

But the vast majority of Sacramento's 400,000 souls had tried to escape by any means they could—foot, car or bicycle—and had died in the attempt.

Gradually Jess became aware of how much he had lost. The life he had known was gone, most of those who had been part of that life were apparently gone forever, too. And with Susan gone, and his hometown an empty shell, his future was a blank. All Jess could feel was emptiness. He had landed safely, by some miracle, in a totally new world, a strikingly beautiful world populated by two warm, caring people, and he was drifting through it in a half-daze, reminded constantly by new vistas that the old world was gone forever. That this was not altogether a tragedy was one of the great revelations of the first period of his new life.

* * *

Sensing that Jess needed simple distractions once he had recovered his strength, William took him along as he did his chores on the farm and ran errands in town.

William was always eager to show visitors around the farm. He was particularly proud of his greenhouses, where warm-weather crops like tomatoes and squash and cucumbers were sprouted in the winter. The largest of the three greenhouses had been placed against the south wall of their house, so that you entered and left via the greenhouse. On the coldest winter days the greenhouse was heated simply by leaving the back door open for a few hours.

The other two greenhouses were heated using a passive system of William's own invention. They collected snow and rainwater in a wide gutter on their roofs.* The melting snow or rainwater drained through pipes into 55-gallon barrels in the greenhouses. The barrels, painted black, served as sources of heat and could also be drained to water the seedling beds. Two large compost piles in each greenhouse served as additional sources of heat.

William, tutored by his neighbor Ed, had learned the simple methods for testing the acidity and mineral content of his soil, and he explained these techniques and the necessary soil remedies at some length to Jess. Jess had little interest in all this, but he was grateful for the chance to leave his thoughts behind and to dwell, if only temporarily, in this bright new world of self-reliant husbandry.

They went into town one morning, and in the course of running errands stopped in at the local coffee house. In a bygone era, when such concoctions as lattes and cafe mochas were still exotic

---

*With global warming, and the resulting increased rates of evaporation of ocean and inland fresh waters, levels of precipitation in this mountain area were roughly 20 percent higher from September through April than they had been 50 years before.

beverages to most coffee drinkers, the coffee house (as opposed to the coffee *shop*), had a faintly bohemian flavor even in small towns like this one. In those days one typically encountered in the coffee house people who seemed to spend most of their waking hours discussing all manner of philosophical, political and literary matters and who appeared to spend little or no time earning a living.

At this time, and in this particular town, the coffee house was still a place for wide-ranging discussion, but the habitues were almost all working people—shopkeepers from down the street, farmers like William and Ed, and even, on occasion, some of the old-time ranchers whose roots in the Mount Shasta region went back countless generations.

Today there was the usual melange of town and country folk, each clustered around their customary table. Seated near the front window was Jonathan Brill, editor of the weekly paper. Jonathan, sitting by himself and apparently oblivious to everything going on inside, was glaring defiantly out the window at whoever happened to be passing by. Jonathan was beefy and muscular; looking at him, with his short-cropped hair and meaty hands, you wouldn't guess he was someone who juggled words for a living. You might guess he was in construction or that he plowed fields or drove a truck, and the bluejeans and checked flannel shirt would have added to that impression, except that they were a little too new and clean. And then there was the odd hat. It came from somewhere south of the border and was made of soft cloth and featured a repeating pattern of exotic birds embroidered around its rim. With the hat, Jonathan was a study in beefy originality.

"Mind if we join you?" William asked as he grabbed a seat on the other side of the table.

Jonathan waved a hand as if to say, "Who cares?" which was as close as he ever came to an actual greeting. Jess took the seat between them, facing the window.

"Jonathan, I want you to meet Jess. He just got here from Sacramento."

William let the introduction sink in, savoring Jonathan's slow transition from genuine to feigned indifference. Jonathan was not about to sacrifice his reputation for hard-shelled irascibility. But William could see that from underneath his protective shell Jonathan was now regarding Jess the same way his wife Cheryl might look at a fine piece of fabric or the way William might look at a patch of rich, fertile soil.

"I imagine," Jonathan said with forced casualness, "you've been through quite an ordeal."

Jess nodded his head and stared down at his coffee cup.

"He's staying with us a few days while he figures things out," William said.

Looking over at William and then at the editor, Jess smiled weakly. "Couldn't ask for a nicer bed and breakfast."

But Jonathan wasn't about to let the conversation drift into small talk. "How'd you manage to get out, son?" he asked.

Once again, in short, clipped sentences, Jess told his story. Jonathan had to restrain himself from asking a lot of questions to flesh out the tale. He could see the young man was reluctant to talk about it. Well, maybe he'll be more talkative next week, he thought hopefully.

When Jess finished his abbreviated account, Jonathan, as was his time-honored custom, delivered what he considered to be a definitive opinion.

"The whole thing was inevitable, you know. Unfortunate, but inevitable. I've been expecting it for years."

"Expecting what, exactly?" Jess asked; there was an edge to his voice.

"Well, the way I see it, the best systems are the simplest ones, especially when lives depend on them. Now I'm not familiar with all the details of how many wheels within wheels there are in your air purification system, but I know there are a lot of them. In the old days, even something as simple as a home air-conditioning system would break down periodically. And now you're trying to cool the air for an entire city, and you've added more complicated technology for purifying the air, so the way I see it you've added way more parts to the system, made it way more complicated, and you've made people's lives utterly dependent on it. A lethal combination, if you ask me. Heck, from what I've read there was a malfunction with some little escape valve that's supposed to keep the steam from building up in the system that drives the air pump. Do you have any idea how many little valves and pistons and flywheels there are in a system like that?"

"So how come the systems in other cities, like Los Angeles and Seattle and New York, haven't failed? They're bigger and more complicated, aren't they?" Jess asked.

"Sooner or later, sooner or later," Jonathan replied calmly. "I recall reading just a few months ago that Atlanta had to use its backup intake system after its main system broke down. The backup system only has the capacity to absorb a relatively small accumulation of pollutants, and if the main system hadn't been fixed in 24 hours—poof! . . . another Sacramento.

"You just can't sustain those artificial environments indefinitely—sooner or later some little wheel's going to fall off, and the whole thing'll come crashing down."

"So what's the alternative?" asked Jess, his face flushed, the words spilling out in a torrent. "Are we all supposed to move up to the hills and raise pigs and alfalfa? Make pottery and other little knickknacks?" Jess, in his anger, hadn't considered the impact his words might have on the farmer seated next to him. But the incredible tensions of the past week, the anger that had built up as he helplessly watched his world crumble, rose to the boiling point in the presence of this smug, know-it-all editor.

Jess couldn't resist one last shot: "And suppose we all were willing to move up to the hills. Wouldn't that kind of shoot your quiet little Eden up here all to hell?"

William, trying to avert a head-on collision, broke in: "Actually, Jess, this ornery guy and I are two of the people up here who *want* to see more folks like you move up here and settle. We need more bright young guys like you in this region. Isn't that right, Jonathan?"

"Yeah, more or less." Jonathan said reluctantly. As a matter of principle, he rarely out-and-out agreed with anyone about anything, and, besides, the phrase "bright young guys" was much too effusive for his dour nature.

As for Jess, the color had drained from his face after his brief outburst, and he lapsed again into a brooding silence.

But Jonathan, now on his third cup of coffee, was just getting warmed up.

"Simplicity, simplicity, simplicity! Just as Thoreau said, that should be the aim of any sane society. Don't be dependent on anything you can't fix yourself. That would eliminate computers, virtual reality, microwave broadcasting, and, yes, air purification systems. In my ideal society, there'd be nothing more mechnically complicated than a bicycle . . ."

"How in tarnation would you get out your gossip sheet, then, without all those doo-dads? You gonna use carrier pigeons and stone tablets?" The question came from a gray-haired, gray-bearded man who'd just walked into the coffee house. Rufus Pitbottom was an eighth-generation rancher whose great-great-great-great-great grandparents had settled in the nearby Scott Valley in the 1870s. He was Jonathan's match for spouting opinions, both in quantity and decibel level. Often their high-volume discussions precluded all others within the small space of the coffee house.

Without waiting for an invitation, the grizzled old rancher shoved a chair between William and Jess, where he could look directly across at his adversary.

"The trouble with you, Mr. Editor, is you never had to work for a livin'. If it were up to you, we'd still be threshin' wheat on the barn floor and tryin' to get our produce to the markets by ox cart, for Chrissakes. Livin' the simple life is just fine if you don't have to produce anything, but ask the guys who print your paper how they'd do it without computers and all that fancy equipment they use." Rufus, as usual, delivered his opinions with an impish grin, which reflected both his simple good nature and his childlike joy in tussling with an opponent.

Jonathan smiled condescendingly on hearing these arguments, ones he had heard many times before from his habitual sparring partner.

"Rufus, I hate to take advantage of someone like yourself, who's obviously a victim of brainwashing. But the thing is, Rufus, you're totally mesmerized by the razzle-dazzle, high-tech practices of a society still caught up in the dehumanized Dark Ages. You're so immersed in the outdated techno-value system of the 20th century that you reject anything that doesn't have a complicated, technical solution. But I'll cut you some slack, Rufus, since I know you're just parroting all the stuff that was crammed into your brain when you were a boy. Still, it's a shame that you never developed any capacity for independent thought."

"Oh, is that so, Mr. Smarty-Pants Editor?" said the old man, defiantly thrusting his bearded jaw out. "Well, have you tried delivering cattle on a bicycle? You gonna put your dang bicycle on a treadmill and power your printing press with it?"

By now, about half the crowd in the small coffee house had turned to listen to the two combatants.

"Well, Mr. Techno-Worshipper, would that be any sillier than creating domes with artificial environments? And thinking you're nice and safe in these jerry-rigged death traps, where one loose bolt can screw up the whole works? Reminds me of those nuclear power plants of the last century that were always breaking down.

"I'll grant you, Rufus, that my approach isn't as sexy or exciting as domes and computers and virtual reality, but the idea is simply that we humans need to figure out how to fit in with the rest of creation on this planet, not just do our own thing and screw up the planet for ourselves and everybody else. And the more people you cram into a place like Sacramento, the more important that idea is.

"And, yes Rufus, we need to get away from all that techno-gadgetry—a lot of which isolates people from each other. With those domes, they think they can seal themselves off in one big techno-cocoon from the environment they've ravaged all these years. Heck, they wrap everything else up in plastic, why not entire cities?"

There was scattered applause after this statement. William found himself in the familiar position of agreeing with the views of the editor, while cringing at his manner in delivering them.

Jonathan, basking in the crowd's applause, was moved to add a final jab: "All of this may not sink in right away, Rufus, but go home and think about it."

"Well, there's one thing you got right," Rufus said, ignoring this last dig. "A lot of the problem with places like Sacramento is too many people."

"Uh, Rufus . . . ," William tried to interject, watching Jess out of the corner of his eye. Jess showed no reaction, and Rufus, blithely unaware of his *faux pas*, kept right on: "Up here, on the other hand, there's room for everybody—people and nature both. That's what I say, Mr. Editor."

"So are you implying that awful tragedy in Sacramento was some cosmic correction of the population problem?" Jonathan asked with arched eyebrows.

"Oh, go to hell with your 'cosmic' crap—I'm just tryin' to *agree* with you for a change—if you'll just shut up for a second. Too many people on too little land just ain't a good thing, not for the people nor the land."

"So would you favor a similar occurrence in the other domed cities, Rufus?" (Oh, let *up* for God's sake, William thought.)

"Hell no. You have another thing like what happened in Sacramento and we'll have hordes of city folks on our doorstep." He let out a chuckle. "That's all we'd need, more arrogant bastards like you comin' up here and tellin' us what to do." This provoked a ripple of appreciative laughter from the fickle audience.

"You mean, like the folks that moved up here five years ago and lease out your south twenty acres? Or that fourth grade teacher, the one from Fresno that got your grandson to read something other than comic books?"

"All right, all right, you got me there, Mr. Smarty Pants, but this time it's *you* who don't get the big picture. I ain't sayin' every city folk who comes up here is a bad egg—they ain't all like you, after all. Why (glancing over at William and winking) this guy here isn't too bad, nor his hard-workin' wife either—but the point is that too many of 'em in the same place, all crowdin' each other, *and* your precious nat'ral environment, ain't good for anybody, man nor beast nor flower in the field. D'you get it?"

"Yeah, I got it Rufus, but you still didn't answer my question."

"Well, of *course* I'm not in favor of thousands of people being killed in those cities. Geez Christ, Jonathan, they can live as long as they like, as far as I'm concerned. I just don't want to see 'em hightailin' it up here, that's all. I just want 'em to stay right where they are." And with that the old rancher folded his arms and glared at his opponent, as if to say, "Oppose me at your peril."

After a brief silence, it was Jess who spoke. Looking at Rufus, he said quietly, "You know, I think you're absolutely right."

CHAPTER IV: EXPLORING

*A*imlessly but not altogether unpleasantly, Jess drifted from one day to the next. It was still a fresh experience, a little overwhelming, to be able to walk outdoors and see the sky and the clouds directly overhead. He liked to set out directly from the house and walk through mile after mile of fields and woods, exulting in freedom and endless spaces.

With his technical background, it wouldn't have been difficult for him to find another job, in another domed city, but he took no immediate steps in that direction. He had begun to help with some of the chores on the farm, and the Shawntrees seemed content to let him stay on indefinitely.

William found their visitor an interesting, even exotic, companion. It had been so long since he and Cheryl had left Sacramento that Jess seemed like a visitor from another world. It was hard to imagine how anyone, once he had been up here for awhile, could want to return to the closed-in, artificial world of the domes, especially after what Jess had experienced, but judging from some of his comments that seemed to be where he was headed.

And yet as Jess spoke about life—his former life—in the Sacramento dome, William was reminded of some of the things that had made that life bearable, even enjoyable much of the time: The fresh-baked bread from the little bakery down the street from his office; the cool, sweating glasses of ale from the microbrewery on the next block; the creamy blended fruit drinks they made in that little cafe on 16th Street and—oh yes!—speaking of sensual pleas-

39

ures, that endless parade of female joggers with their lithe, athletic figures that ran around and around the park in East Sacramento. If you knew how to pick and choose among a city's myriad offerings, it could be a good life, really, a universe unto itself full of sensual delights, good friends, plenty of things to do—you just had to find a way to forget that you were living in a kind of trap.

* * *

Borrowing a bicycle from the Shawntrees, Jess set out early one morning toward the little town of Dunsmuir, about ten miles to the south. He pedaled to the old interstate freeway that connected the town of Mt. Shasta with Dunsmuir. He headed up an onramp and was suddenly confronted with a varied and confusing array of travelers, each of them seeming to have his or her own unique mode of transportation. Some walked, some skated, some rode skateboards, and some, like Jess, bicycled. There were quite a few travelers on horseback and even some horse-drawn wagons. These, and an occasional slow-moving auto or truck or bus, occupied the center lanes, while the human-powered transportation moved along in the outer lanes. The hikers tended to stay on the very outer edges of the old freeway, to avoid the faster-moving traffic.

Jess soon found himself weaving in and out among the skaters and slower bicyclists. It was rather like being in the middle of a traveling street fair from the Middle Ages. All around there was the sound of chattering voices, clattering hooves, the occasional cry of an infant. Most of the horse-drawn wagons pulled some kind of merchandise. Often it was yellow or green or red produce of some sort, but Jess also saw what appeared to be handmade wooden toys in the bed of one wagon, and piles of thickly woven throw rugs in another. Another wagon was filled with round metal containers—probably milk, Jess thought—and another with bales of hay.

Some of the bicyclists even carried goods behind them in small trailers. Jess saw one bearded, middle-aged fellow with a heavy load of books, and a young woman with a colorful assortment of kites.

Jess realized after awhile that there was a crazy, patchwork pattern to the traffic on this highway. Those using human-powered, wheeled transportation—skaters, skateboarders, and bicyclists—tended to follow one another in narrow, winding rivulets, and these individual rivulets wound around and sometimes through one another, frequently adjusting their course to avoid stray pedestrians. The overall effect was like that produced by a kaleidoscope, with swirling, ever-changing patterns of motion and color.

Many of the bicyclists had attached long, colorful streamers of ribbons to the rear of their bikes and trailers. Bright, multi-colored jerseys were popular attire, and both men and women favored form-fitting leggings, or leotards in colors ranging from black to the brightest yellows and reds.

Perhaps because of the small number of motor-driven vehicles, few of the cyclists wore helmets. In their place, all kinds of headgear were in evidence: sunbonnets, beanies with propellers, berets and the more prosaic baseball or fishing caps. One fellow wearing a top hat and vintage 19th century garb, which included a long-tailed coat, sailed by on a big-wheeled bicycle. From his lofty perch he acknowledged greetings from the crowd below with a dignified nod of the head.

Only the center lane, with its heavier, lumbering vehicles, each traveling a straight trajectory, suggested the freeway of a bygone era. The rest of the thoroughfare, with its swirling and interweaving streams of traffic, bore more resemblance to the nearby river that meandered down the canyon it had carved through the mountains, the canyon the freeway builders had followed, and the railway-builders before them. The freeway, it seemed, was returning to its roots.

Following William's directions, Jess exited the freeway a few

miles south of Dunsmuir and parked his bike at the beginning of a
trail that headed up toward the jagged rocky outcroppings known as
Castle Crags. He started upward on the trail. The path was shaded
mostly by pine and fir trees, but there were also some recent
immigrants from the lower elevations: timid, tentative stands of ash,
mahogany, and hemlock that were creeping ever higher in these
mountain regions as the earth warmed.

Gradually the relatively gentle, tree-shaded slopes gave way to
steep, rocky cliffs, and he found himself looking straight up at a
cluster of soaring rocky spires that had once formed the guts of a
volcano. The rugged peaks spanned several miles from one end to
the other. While nearby white-capped Mount Shasta had a benign,
majestic presence, there was something malignant about this dark,
jagged range to the south, this mass of molten lava frozen on the
verge of eruption. No wonder the early pioneers had named it The
Devil's Castle. It was with a mixture of fear and awe that Jess
walked the path that skirted around the base of the crags. As he
looked up at the jagged spires, he could, with very little effort, see
the row of grim, hooded figures high up above, their faces distorted
through hatred and anger like the gargoyles on a medieval church.
They seemed to be glaring down at him with an implicit warning:
"Proceed at your own peril."

But as if to break this evil spell, there appeared in odd little
cracks and crannies of this rocky facade the most delicate little
waterfalls. They must have sprung from hidden patches of snow
tucked into crevices and pockets in the rocks high above. The little
silvery strands of water suggested, gently but insistently, that there
would be a day when these massive rocks, and the brooding spirits
that dwelled among them, would be no more.

* * *

Jess got back to Dunsmuir in the latter part of the afternoon. He
parked his bike on the main street and strolled down to the river,

settling down on its banks to eat his two sandwiches and his apple. There was an angler on the other side of the stream who, lost in his own quest, seemed oblivious to Jess's presence. He cast and re-cast his line with such purposeful intensity that the fate of the world seemed to hang on each cast. Upstream from the fisherman two boys and a girl, teenagers, lolled in a rowboat that had been anchored with a rope to an overhanging branch. One fishing pole hung over the bow of the boat, but none of the three paid it any attention. Not far from the fisherman a silver-bottomed fish jumped playfully out of the water, as if to say, "Here I am and there's nothing you can do about it!" Downstream from the fisherman a sleek-coated river otter splashed in the shallow water near the bank, searching for a late-afternoon meal.

The afternoon was drawing to a close as Jess got up from the grassy bank. The trees threw their shadows across the river, turning its waters dark green. Jess walked beside it until he came to a short residential street with modest homes on either side; most of them had high foundations in deference to the river. At the end of the row of homes a steep cliff rose up, towering over the street that snaked alongside the river.

Jess headed up a dirt path that started at the paved road and veered up along the edge of the cliff. It skirted between the cliff's edge and the steep, heavily wooded slope above. As he climbed higher on the path, Jess had a magnificent view of the river and a portion of the town. It was already growing dark, but he could still see pastel-colored homes, some with lights already twinkling inside, cascading down the opposite side of the river canyon. Far up against the darkening sky, high above the homes and the river, loomed the forbidding granite spires he had so recently explored, watching over the town like grim-faced sentries.

By the time he reached the end of the trail, night had fallen. Another paved road took up where the trail ended. It led to a small cluster of homes nestled on this forested hillside. The road only ran for a hundred yards before it joined another at a t-intersection, and right where the two roads joined was a big, two-story house. Jess could barely make out the figure of a man seated in front of the house, with an empty chair next to him. The house had no front yard; the man was seated within a few feet of a stairway leading up to the first floor.

As he got closer, Jess could see that the man was black and that he was a very old man. In the dark his eyes shone like two white beacons, glowing with an almost supernatural luster. Jess's first instinct was to keep walking. But when the old man, without speaking, gestured to the empty folding chair, Jess walked over to him and sat down.

The two men were silent for awhile. Even though the old man stared straight ahead and seemed to be avoiding Jess's gaze, Jess could feel himself relaxing in his presence.

Finally the old man spoke. "Come a long ways from here?"

"Yes."

"Where from?"

"Sacramento."

"Lord almighty, that *is* a long ways from here."

"Yes."

"Where you headed?"

"Don't know yet."

"Well, you better sit here and rest awhile. You got a lot of travelin' ahead of you, 'cause it don't look like you're goin' back where you came from anytime soon."

"Yeah, I know."

"You know, travelin' ain't such a bad thing. Sometimes it's good for a man to pick up and leave and start out new. My father, he set out from Mississippi 100 years ago 'cause he didn't like the way things were there. In those days, if you were black, they put you in a kind of box from the day you were born, and there was no way you could get out of it, no matter how smart you were, no matter how hard you worked to get out.

"So as soon as he could get out, he *got*. Came out here and got himself a job workin' for the railroad, cast his first vote for the President of the United States—that was a big deal in those days—started himself a family, built this house."

The old man's eyes, as he looked over at Jess, had grown even brighter than when Jess had first seen them shining out at him from the end of the road.

"Heck, boy, this whole Siskiyou County's traveled a long ways since I was a boy. It was in a kind of a box, too, I guess. Seems like only the past couple of decades that we've been able to break out and find our own way. Hell, we *had* to, what with them cities like Sacramento goin' the way they have. *Had* to find our own way. Now we're makin' things and doin' things for ourselves and not havin' to ask permission from anybody in Washington or New York or Sacramento.

"No, suh, we're *travelin'* now, gettin' out of that box and stretchin' our *wings*. . . ." The old man fairly sang out the last few words.

While he said all this the old man had been staring off into the distance with his beacon-like eyes. He was quiet now. This last outburst had either tired him, or he was lost in thought, Jess couldn't tell which. He got up to leave.

"Where you plannin' on goin' from here?"

"Don't know yet."

"Well, keep in mind what I told you—about travelin', that is."

"Yessir."

Jess offered his hand to shake good-bye. The old man kept his folded in his lap.

"Good-bye," Jess said. "Good-bye," the old man said quietly.

Jess hadn't gotten very far down the road before it dawned on him that the old man was blind.

* * *

Jess spent the next few days aerating the soil on a five-acre patch where William planned to plant a fall crop of beans. Soil aeration was done by hand, as were many of the tasks on the farm. Jess used a tool called a broadfork, which is like a pitchfork but has two long handles. There is a five-tined fork on the other end, which is pushed into the soil. After embedding the fork, Jess pulled back on the handles to lift and aerate the soil. Then he lifted the fork out, moved back about half a foot, and repeated the process.

It was light work, and Jess was in a relaxed mood as the sun warmed his back. He absentmindedly listened to the calls of birds and the muted sounds the awakening earth made as it stretched and groaned under his feet. His thoughts drifted to the events of the day before—the dazzling color and swirl of movement on the old freeway; the languid afternoon spent by the river; the imposing, fearsome presence of the crags; the sudden, specter-like appearance of the old man at the end of the day, and his emphasis on that word—"travelin'." Jess's first impulse was to dismiss it as the ranting of an old man, but his words kept running through Jess's mind as he worked the soil. If there was a deeper meaning to the old man's words, it eluded him for now. If "travelin'" meant anything to Jess, it was the idea of getting on with his own life, which of course meant leaving the Shasta region for a job in one of the domes.

As he headed toward the house that afternoon, Jess felt himself moving in that direction. He was ready to stop drifting, ready to take the first steps toward getting control of his life once again. Tomorrow he would start checking with the personnel departments of some of the major communications companies. He'd start with the Bay Area branch of the company he'd worked for in Sacramento. Fresno was also a possibility, since according to recent news reports state government offices were going to be locating there on an interim basis. It would be awhile, perhaps a good long while, before the survivors of the Sacramento disaster, or anyone else, felt that it was safe to move back there.

As he was heading into the barn to put the broadfork back, Jess saw something near the house, a dazzling flash of color and form, that stopped him momentarily in his tracks. The first thing he noticed was a swath of long, dark hair against the bright blue of a summer dress. All of this resolved itself, fleetingly, into a woman's form, full and well-shaped, before disappearing through the kitchen door of the house.

When Jess entered the house a half hour later he learned from Cheryl that this fleeting vision was a young woman named Rachel, the oldest daughter of their neighbors, the Stillwaters. She had come by for a costume fitting for a play that was going to be produced that summer in the community hall. He also learned that they were expected at the Stillwater house for dinner that Saturday evening.

CHAPTER V: A THEATRICAL EVENING

The little room is spilling over with life and color. In the center is the long dining room table, adorned with two vases of pink and red roses. There had at one time been bowls and platters heaped with yellow summer squash, green salad, brown rolls, and lasagna. These colorful contents have since disappeared into the nine folks seated around the table.

Four of these are young people, and their faces are glowing with good health and high spirits. Your eyes might first be drawn to the oldest, Rachel, her pretty face framed by cascading waves of dark hair, almost-black hair, tinted ever so slightly by the sun—rich dark hair that, by contrast, makes her bright green eyes even brighter.

Next to her is impish-faced Ted, whose thatch of tousled brown hair sits precariously atop an eleven-year-old mind whirling with visions of faroff galaxies and fiendish space villains. Across the table is the youngest and also the quietest, eight-year-old Lucy, taking it all in, never missing a word, so that she can report every last detail that very evening to Panda before she falls asleep. Lucy, like her brother Ted (and her friend Panda), also has brown hair. Another quiet presence at the table is Tim, the second oldest, dark-haired like his older sister, seated between his father and the new young man who's barely old enough to be his older brother. Tim, already nearly six feet tall, broad-shouldered and slender, serious and thoughtful.

The walls of the dining room are wood-paneled. On one wall is hung a richly colored tapestry of burgundies and deep purples. On

49

the opposite wall is a large oil painting, done in bold swatches of color, of a farmhouse set against fields of green and gold and red. At one end of the dining room is the white swinging door to the kitchen. At the other is an off-white muslin curtain, hung in two pieces drawn together at the center in makeshift fashion on a cord, looking rather incongruous in this otherwise carefully appointed room. Beyond the curtain is what appears to be a spacious living room.

At this stage of the evening, amid the ongoing conversation, two important events are still expected. One is the imminent appearance of two fresh-baked blueberry pies, the anticipation of which no doubt adds to the general good humor pervading the room. The other upcoming event is an original play, written by Rachel and Tim and to be performed by same—hence the makeshift curtains.

If eight of those seated around the table could be described as well-contented, the ninth—little tousle-haired Ted Stillwell—was soaring to heavenly heights. All the past week he had been bursting to tell the incredible story in *Space Blasters #27*, but had been thwarted at the dinner table by discussions of crops and other dreary farming minutiae, the latest boring bulletins on the progress of Rachel's costumes, and a lot of other forgettable news that the rest of the family somehow deemed more important than the blasting of entire galaxies to smithereens.

But now he had his chance, and before an expanded audience, too! Ted's chance had come when the new person, Jess, had innocently asked him what he liked to do around the farm. That was all the opening that Ted needed; it hardly mattered what the question was as long as it gave him center stage for a brief moment or two. Ted seized the opportunity for all it was worth. What did he like to do around the farm? Why, read *Space Blasters*, of course! (And sketch his own versions of the *Space Blasters* heroes and their incredible intergalactic spaceships.)

For the reader unacquainted with the *Space Blasters*, it is a series that pits highly evolved humanoid space explorers of the 26th century against a series of extremely powerful and evil intergalactic villains. No sooner has one of these been dispatched by the heroes in one novel than another set of villains, if anything more powerful and meaner and uglier than the last ones, pops up in the next.

In *Space Blasters* #27, the heroes (from the planet Oneraymon) were up against the evil robots from the planet Xer-Rayon. The robots were under the control of Xer-Rayon's evil dictator, Dr. Zed, who was a lizard-like creature with slimy green scales and three big heavy-lidded, protruding eyes.

"Shhhhrooom! Shrooom! Phhhhhhhht! Phhht!" Ted filled the room with the sounds of the atom-splitting fission lasers used by the evil robots from Xer-Rayon. "Bwom! Bwom! Bwom!" was the response from the atom fusion lasers used by the heroes from Oneraymon to undo the mess wrought by the evil robots—the hardworking heroes had to reassemble three whole galaxies using these fusion tools. Then Ted patiently explained that the heroes had their own brand of fission lasers—"phwoooot! phwoooot! phwoooot!"— to finish off the dastardly robots, whose every movement was controlled by the evil Dr. Zed. *Then* there was the final, climactic battle between the heroes and Dr. Zed on Xer-Rayon itself. . . .

Normally Ted's narrative would have been interrupted long before by one of his siblings or even Ed or Kathy, since his immediate family had long ago learned all they wanted to know about the *Space Blasters*. But the presence of guests, particularly a well-intentioned stranger who kept prompting Ted with polite, encouraging questions, made it difficult to bring the narrative to a halt.

So young Ted continued to spread his narrative wings as he basked in the dinner table spotlight. He reached new heights in his descriptions of the carnage in the final confrontation with Dr. Zed, which included gripping images of his dismembered, lizard-like body parts flying off through outer space. After this performance, how would anyone dare bring up subjects as mundane as the weather or crops at the dinner table again? Certainly not on this particular evening.

Jess bravely stepped into the breach. He patiently explained to these somewhat out-of-touch country folk how technological advancements had made science fiction novels like the *Space Blasters* totally obsolete. Through the latest technology, cameras mounted on interplanetary space vehicles enabled viewers on Earth to travel right along on the frontiers of space. And computer users could tap into a vast library of stored videos from these unmanned probes. When these film records were combined with a technique called "virtual reality enchancement," you could actually land on Jupiter or Saturn or Uranus and "smell" the gases that made up their atmospheres while exploring their mountains and valleys. No life beyond the tiniest micro-organisms had ever been discovered on these planets, so these "empirically based" excursions featured mainly rocks and dirt, but "fantasy enhancements" were available that enabled the cyberspace explorer to mingle with the creepiest extraterrestrials that the human mind and advanced computer graphics could create. And of course all sorts of computer-generated weaponry, more advanced than even that found in *Space Blasters*, had been created for interactive users of these programs, so that they could blast away at and destroy and dismember these monsters to their hearts' content.

The level of interest in this high-tech discourse among Jess's listeners tended to be in indirect proportion to their age. Ted himself was a study in slack-jawed fascination, with Lucy and Tim running a close second. Rachel, alone among the younger set, seemed a bit bored by the whole thing, as if it were not much different from her eleven-year-old brother's endless plot summaries.

Ed had been listening politely to all this talk about space travel with about as much interest as Jess reserved for the techniques of farming. Finally he broke in: "You sure know a lot about this space stuff, but that's not your field, is it? William said something about you doing some kind of communications work in Sacramento."

"Yeah. I worked for the company that maintained the communications equipment—the central microwave transmitter and receiver—for all the state buildings. Any communications, voice or visual, between Sacramento and anyplace else went through our equipment. I was part of the support crew that handled repairs and maintenance on all of it. As far as I know, me and a guy named Bill were the only ones who survived from that whole crew. There were about 20 of us. Bill headed up to Portland. Said he'd get in touch with me when he got settled."

"So what are you going to do now?" Ed asked.

"Oh, I'll probably look for something similar in the Bay Area—shouldn't be too hard to find."

"Have you thought about staying up here?" Kathy asked. There was an expectant silence around the table.

"Yeah, I sure have," Jess smiled. "You folks have a lovely setup up here, and William and Cheryl have been real kind." He paused. "But this just isn't the life for me. I'm a techie, and I'm used to the city, you know, the hustle and bustle (*and the money, the money*). I just don't know what I'd do with myself up here."

"Oh, it takes awhile to adjust, that's true for all of us, but a smart young guy like you could find plenty to do up here, don't worry about that." *Oh boy,* Kathy thought to herself, *here we go.* Ed, in a typically expansive mood, was just starting to get revved up on Topic A: The Booming Future Of The Siskiyous, and when he got revved up like this his enthusiasm could consume everything in its path, including, on this occasion, this young man's future. She shot Ed a warning look, but he blithely ignored it, plunging full-speed ahead.

"I tell you," he enthused, "every day we get more and more folks comin' up here from the cities. They've all got their fancy microwave gear, 'cause they want to keep in touch with the folks they left back home—only it breaks down every so often, and there aren't a lot of folks up here know how to fix it. A guy like you could do all right repairing that stuff"—and here Mr. Revved-Up came up with an inspired, creative stroke— "and, heck, Jess, why not set up a central transmitting and receiving station, just like the one you kept running for the state! You could charge everybody a monthly fee to hook into it in exchange for guaranteeing that they can talk to the folks back home with no interruptions. Hell, you'd have it made." Ed beamed on the young man, clearly pleased with himself at having worked out his future in this booming region.

"Well, sir, I dunno. As I said, I'm a city kid . . . ."

But Ed was not about to be dissuaded. "Oh, I know how you feel, son. You've been through a heck of an ordeal, and the last thing you want to think about is somethin' like this. But just keep it in mind. This region's gonna need all kinds of talents, and there'd be a place for you, son, don't worry about that.

"Heck, I was just sayin' to William the other day, wasn't I William, that I'm gonna need an assistant to help me with these farmers' markets, the way they're growin'. New people keep comin' here, as I said, and it's for darn sure they all *eat*. Way things are goin', what with tryin' to run this farm *and* run the markets, I'm gettin' spread pretty thin, I'll tell you."

As Ed spoke, Jess could feel himself being lifted and carried along by the older man's enthusiasm; it took a major effort to resist being swept up by this tidal wave of energy.

"I'm sure there are great opportunities up here, Mr. Stillwater, but I'm a city boy, and I just don't see how I'd fit in here."

"Okay, okay, son," said Ed, finally responding to the series of winks and grimaces coming from his wife. "Sorry if I got a little carried away. I'm so big on the future of the region I just want everybody to have a part of it—and recruit an up and comin' fellow like yourself if I can." Ed said this with a wink that was part apology.

While this discussion had been going on Kathy had served the pies around the table. By the time Ed was finished speaking his was the only piece lying cool and untouched. As he applied himself to this bit of unfinished business, Kathy tapped on her glass and announced with mock ceremony, "Ladies and gentlemen, for your entertainment and edification the Stillwater Acting Company will present the premiere performance of the new play by Rachel and Tim Stillwater entitled 'Real People.'"

Two innovations in the Stillwater family since they'd moved from Sacramento were the punctual gatherings of everyone around the dinner table at 6 p.m. and the production of home theatricals. The latter had begun with after-dinner charades. Rachel, who had eagerly participated in every school play since the 4th grade, was the inspiration behind the home theatricals; they featured, for the most part, she and her siblings, with Ed and Kathy occasionally playing supporting roles but for the most part serving as a captive but highly receptive audience.

As the children matured, so did the content of the plays, culminating in tonight's presentation. Its two co-authors, who doubled as the cast, had spent two whole evenings conceiving, perfecting and rehearsing the play, which Kathy, who had watched the rehearsals, described as "the cleverest thing ever to grace the Stillwater stage." She noted that it was loosely based on a few encounters the children had had with visitors from the city.

While the two actors got into their costumes, Kathy told Jess about her daughter's latest theatrical coup: Rachel had landed the part of the ethereal goddess-narrator in the community theatre's upcoming production of "Our Town Revisited." Written by the local newspaper editor, Jonathan Brill, it was a rather daring endeavor: the characters, Kathy explained, were thinly veiled caricatures of some of the more prominent figures in town, including the irascible editor himself.

Radiantly beautiful even in work clothes, Rachel in her role as the sublime goddess would wear a lavender robe trimmed with gold, and a diamond tiara over her braided hair. It was for that role that she had rushed over to Cheryl's the other day for a fitting.

There was a nervous cough from behind the makeshift curtain, and hands reached up from behind to draw it open, revealing Rachel in bluejeans, t-shirt and work boots. To emphasize the rustic nature of her character, she was chewing on a piece of alfalfa straw and wearing a battered straw hat. She was making motions as if hoeing weeds.

TIM (*entering; his voice is flamboyantly dramatic; he is wearing dress shoes, carefully pressed dark pants, and a white shirt.*): Oh my God! This is it! This is the place!

RACHEL: Huh?

TIM: A Real Place with Real People! Oh God, you can't imagine how it feels, after all these years in the urban wilderness! Touch me, pinch me, do *something* to let me know this is really real! Really, really, really, really real!

RACHEL (*affecting a slow, rustic drawl*): Uh, you ain't by any chance the new cook dad hired, are you? The one who said he could make home-fried grits and onion rings?

TIM: Home-fried grits? Onion rings? (*dramatic pause, while he gazes upward*) Real Food for Real People! Grits! Onion rings! (*looks down again, grasps her by the shoulders, locking eyes with her*) All these years *I've* been immersed in one vast onion ring . . . the vast, stifling onion ring of so-called civilization. And not just *one* onion ring, but ring after ring after ring after ring . . . choking me, stifling me, cutting off all air and light.

But it's all changing. I can feel it. As soon as I walked in here, I could feel ring after ring just . . . (*with a light-hearted, self-consciously careless laugh*) . . . ha, ha . . . fading away . . . (*he releases her, flinging up his arms heavenward, and as he does so she stumbles backward a few steps*) . . . ha, ha . . . . Suddenly, everything seems so new, so fresh, so . . . so . . . so *real*!

Tell me, you dear, sweet beacon of light, by what shall I call you?

RACHEL: You mean, what's my name?

TIM: In more prosaic terms, yes.

RACHEL: Darlene.

TIM (*extending hand*): Spencer. (*She offers hers. He suddenly drops down on his knees while kissing her hand rapturously.*) Oh, I suddenly feel so young, Darlene. I was born just today, when I walked down the path to these fields. Darlene, I know so little of this world as it really, really, really is. Tell me about it, show it all to me, be my teacher, my guide. (*He drops her hand, raises both of his as if in prayer, speaks hesitantly, timorously.*) Won't you?

RACHEL: Listen, mister, I'm not sure exactly what you're drivin' at, but I should tell you before things go any further that I got a boyfriend.

TIM: A boyfriend?

RACHEL: Yeah, name's Ben. Treats me real good, too. Kinda the jealous type, if you know what I mean.

TIM: My dear, dear Darlene, how could I possibly even *think* of being your *boy*friend when I'm just one day old, a mere infant in this new, real world of yours. A *boy*friend? (*the affected laugh again*) ha! ha! . . . I'd be content to sit at your feet, begging for a chance to *learn*, to *live*, to learn to live, and yes, maybe one day, to really, really *love*.

RACHEL: Well, I dunno. I still don't get what it is you're drivin' at, but whatever it is, I don't think Ben's gonna go for it.

The play continued for awhile longer in this vein, with the citified, histrionic stranger talking past the prosaic country girl, all to comic effect.

Jess was impressed with the clever content of the play, written as it was by two young people still in their teens, and especially by Tim's acting; he had played his part with a flair not apparent from his quiet manner at the dinner table. Rachel's part hadn't demanded much from her, and Jess wondered idly what she could do with something more challenging.

"Anybody for a walk?" Ed asked after the play was over. The two youngest children, for reasons of their own, jumped at this suggestion. They were just as proud of the small patch of ground they tended, and anxious to show it off, as Ed and Kathy were of their acres and acres of lush fields.

So as soon as they were outside, Jess found himself being separated from the rest of the group and eagerly guided by the two youngest Stillwaters to a garden patch near the house. There, in a small raised bed measuring perhaps 20 feet by 20 feet Ted and Lucy had planted every type of vegetable they could get their hands on, and with successful results for the most part. They proudly pointed out the wispy green tops of sprouting carrots, the more robust leaves of tiny young radishes and beets, the tender shoots of onions and garlic, and short rows of chard and lettuce. And, they informed Jess, they would soon be putting in the family's Halloween pumpkins.

In one corner, there was a patch of exotic mushrooms. Last season the mushrooms had earned the two children just over $40 at the Mt. Shasta growers market, half of which the two entrepreneurs invested in seeds and a serious little booklet entitled "The Professional Grower's Guide To High-Yield Mushrooms." (The other half of the mushroom proceeds had been spent on some of the pleasures of life.)

While Ted went to fetch their pet goat, Agnes, to show Jess, Lucy took the opportunity to confide in Jess, whom she had immediately sized up as a trustworthy and sympathetic person. She told him a secret she had told only to her mother. The mushroom patch, she whispered, was the nighttime gathering place for certain Little People—whom adults might call "elves," but certainly not Lucy, who thought of her friends as smaller versions of herself. Like herself, they were secretive and shy but really quite playful once you got to know them.

Lucy confided to Jess that she would often come out here in the evenings, ostensibly to check on the garden, but really to chat and play with her friends. She was even called on frequently to mediate disputes between Maud and Claude, a married couple who were always quarreling. It taxed her patience "to the utmost limit," she confessed, to try and find some middle ground between the warring pair, but (with a sigh) she did her "utmost best."

Lucy quickly clammed up when Ted appeared with the goateed and lively Agnes, but there were knowing looks exchanged between Lucy and Jess as they went to visit the children's other pet, Flossie the milk cow, whom the children took turns milking every morning.

Then it was time for the adult—and, to Jess, much less interesting—portion of the farm tour. While Lucy lingered behind near the small garden for her own mysterious reasons, the rest began a walk that skirted along the periphery of the fields. This was accompanied by a running discourse on the crops growing, or scheduled for planting, in each section, together with information on the diseases that plagued each crop, which of its varieties did best in this climate, a short history of how frosts, drought and other weather vagaries had affected crops in the past, etc., etc. To his credit, Jess did manage a few polite questions. If nothing else, it was inspiring to listen to folks like Ed and Kathy and William and

Cheryl who were so knowledgeable and enthusiastic about farming. Still, as the tour continued, all the crops with their various characteristics seemed to Jess to blend together. As the small group headed back toward the house and a promised side trip through the Stillwaters' elaborate complex of greenhouses, he found himself longing for anything other than this seemingly interminable seminar on husbandry—even another *Space Blasters* episode.

Mercifully, Rachel came to his rescue. Perhaps sensing his *ennui*, she detoured him from the greenhouse expedition by blurting out, as she headed purposefully toward the barn, "You can't leave the farm without meeting Pilot—he'd be really offended if we didn't stop by and say hello."

With a shrug of his shoulders and a bemused, what-else-can-I-do look back at his hosts, Jess caught up with Rachel with a few energetic strides. They headed out to a small, adjoining stable next to the barn. Pilot, a black stallion, was one of three horses sheltered there. Rachel grabbed a large brush and a halter from their pegs on the wall, opened the door to Pilot's stall and led him out to the corral. Once they were inside the corral, she threw the end loop of the halter over a fence post and began brushing the horse, who snorted with pleasure.

Jess patted the horse gently on its rear flank, feeling the otherwise hard and unyielding muscle twitch ever so slightly at his touch. The horse jerked its head back to see who this interloper was.

"It's okay, Pilot, he's a friend. He's a city boy, but he's all right," Rachel said in a soft, soothing voice with a wink at Jess. She had changed to shorts after the play, and Jess couldn't help but notice the abundantly graceful curve of her calves as she reached up to brush the horse.

"From what you said in there, it sounds like you're gettin' ready to get outta here. How much longer do you think you'll be staying with the Shawntrees?" she asked.

Just as long as you'd like. "Well, I guess until I can line up something in the Bay Area or LA or maybe Portland. Don't think it'll take too long."

"Well, I hope Dad didn't scare you off. Once he gets going on the boundless opportunities of Siskiyou County, he's like a steamroller—there's no stopping him."

"Nah, that's okay. It doesn't bother me that he's big on this area. It *is* a wonderful place. But, as I told him, I'm a city kid. I'd go crazy here."

"Do you really think so?" Rachel asked, a little defensively.

"Oh, definitely. No doubt about it. It's been proven by all the tests."

"All the tests?"

"Yeah. See, I've always scored at least a 750 out of 800 in science and technology and maybe 400 or 500 on all the other stuff. I mean right from the first grade on . . . " Jess paused, noting the puzzled look on Rachel's face. "Don't they test you up here?"

"Not a whole lot. What are these tests for?"

"Basically to see if you should be on the science and technology or the humanities track in school. You know, what you have an aptitude for."

"But you were saying that the tests proved that you definitely belonged in the city."

"That's a different test. The fact that I'm cut out for a technical job, of course, makes it pretty unlikely I'd ever live in a place like this, but there's another test called the PIS that tells you just about everything else you'd ever want to know about yourself."

"The PIS?"

"The Personal Inventory System. They give that one to you every year from the time you're ten years old. By the time you're 18 they can give you a complete rundown on all your strengths and weaknesses. It's a complete inventory, you might say, of who you are—intellectually, socially, morally and emotionally."

"Who's 'they'?"

"Oh, the school districts have a whole team of people that go around to all the schools and give the tests. It's a state program; I'm sure kids in the Bay Area get tested. I'm surprised you didn't know about it."

"There's a lot of stuff we don't do up here that they do in the cities. The schools up here kind of go their own way, I guess, just like folks do generally around here. 'We piss and kiss where we want,' as the saying goes. Heck, a lot of folks, when a relative dies, just plant the body right in the ground. I'm sure the folks in your government down there . . ."

" . . . what's left of a government . . ."

" . . . would just love to know about *that*. Had an old farmer not too long ago wanted to be buried out in his south 40. They got him planted just before they put the corn crop in. Had a record harvest that year." (This was actually a joke that had been going around the county for several years now.)

"So, Mr. City Boy, who tells you you have to take these stupid ol' tests? What if you told them to take their old personality inventory test and stuff it?"

"Well, for one thing, you can't get a job, at least not in a city like Sacramento, if you don't have your PIS to show them. It tells them whether you work well with others, if you're a creative type, and all kinds of stuff employers want to know.

"And—here's the most important thing—it's pretty hard to get a date, at least with the kind of person you'd *want* to date, if you don't have your PIS results."

"Huh? You've got to take a test to get a date?"

"More or less. Well, not everyone you ask out is gonna want to see 'em, I guess, but nowadays most of 'em do. For one thing, women are kinda paranoid. Maybe one of their friends tells 'em about some weird guy she went out with, or they see something in the news about an ax murder on a first date—I mean, I'm exaggerating a little, but something like that. They see the tests as a way to weed out the bad seeds.

"But it also has a more positive side. You see, when you take the PIS, every possible trait you might have is rated on a scale from 1 to 1000. I mean they really fine tune it, so when two people's scores mesh really close, it's almost like they're the same person, you know, really compatible.

"So let me get this straight. The object of this test is to find your perfect mate, who is essentially *you*."

"Nah, it's not quite that simple. Of course that would be ridiculous. For one thing," he said, looking at her rather pointedly, "I'd want my perfect mate to be prettier than me. . . . And, to tell you the truth, I don't know how they come up with all the formulas, but, say, you get an aggressive, domineering type on a test result—well, of course you're not going to match that person with someone who scores 1000 on that also. In fact, you probably want that person's mate to score about 100 on that. But then it's okay, say, if they both score around 800 in the aesthetic appreciation areas—you know, they like to enjoy the beauties of nature and so forth.

"It gets pretty complicated, but they've got this formula they feed into the computer, and its parameters change with the test results of each person, in terms of who they should be matched with." He smiled in a self-deprecating way and added, "In other words, as I said, I don't really understand how it works, but I do know it *works*. It's how Susan and I got matched to each other."

"Well, I think it's all totally, absolutely ridiculous, that some test is gonna practically run your life, find you a perfect mate . . ." Rachel stopped her outburst in mid-thought. She had stopped brushing Pilot during her tirade, but now resumed with deliberate calmness. "Who's Susan?" she asked quietly.

"I guess you're not gonna believe this, but we were a perfect match. Perfect. You know how they say that if people have been together long enough each one knows what the other is thinking? Well, we had that from day one. We're both kind of analytical types, both like to take things apart and see how they work, only she was more an idea person—'symbolic analytical,' they call it—while I'm what they call a 'thing-handler.' But we both scored high in the aesthetic area; we love music, art, being out in nature—of course, where we were you had to experience nature through virtual reality.

"And we were pretty unusual as a couple in that neither one of us scored high on the domineering or submissive part. We're both kinda in-between, pretty accommodating types."

"Were you living together?"

"Nah, not yet. Would have been, probably, in a year or so, but . . . I haven't been able to contact her since the Sacramento disaster."

There was silence for awhile. Rachel had stopped brushing. She looked thoughtful.

Finally she frowned and said emphatically, "I can't think of anything more ridiculous than being tested to go on a date." She resumed her brushing.

"Aw, it's just 'cause it's something you've never tried, Rachel," Jess said patiently, "but I'm telling you from my own experience that it *works*."

"Yeah, but I *like* dating, getting to know a bunch of different guys . . ."

"This isn't dating Rachel, it's finding your perfect mate using proven scientific methods."

"Well, that's what I'm doing too, I guess, only I'm going about it differently. First off, Mr. City Boy, I don't have to test anybody around here. I've known most of 'em since I was in second grade.

"And another thing which maybe you and your scientists

haven't thought of. . . . No, make that two things. First off, *I* want to decide who's gonna be my mate, not have some computer tell me. Second, who says I wanta go out with my perfect mate from day one anyway? There's something to be said for tryin' out different sizes and styles of clothes to see which one really fits you. Your method reduces everything to a bunch of numbers. It kinda takes the fun out of it, don't you think?"

"Oh yeah, I don't totally disagree with you on that. You can definitely have a lot of fun with someone you're not totally compatible with. Only, as I said, that's not the way a lot of people, especially members of your sex, look at it nowadays. I guess they'd rather have the sure thing, the scientifically proven thing, than take a chance on making a big mistake. Playing it safe is what you'd call it."

"Pretty boring, if you ask me. You were saying you couldn't live up here. Well, I don't see how I could live down there if you had to show some dumb old test scores to go out with someone. That's just plain *weird*."

With that she got on the stallion and rode him bareback at a leisurely pace around the corral. Jess thought of that first glimpse of Rachel, a few days ago, as he watched her long tresses sway with the gentle rhythm of the canter, and her muscular legs press against the horse's sides. Rachel had wrapped her arms around the horse's neck and was leaning forward into the canter, as the two of them, horse and rider, merged in a beautiful, fluid symmetry.

After a couple of turns, Rachel slowed the horse down to a walk. She looked down as she passed Jess and said, "You know, I kinda like you despite some of your weird ideas." With a toss of her head, she added, "And I didn't need a test to tell me that, either."

Jess was smiling to himself as he walked alone back to the Stillwaters' house. *She's got spirit, all right. Must be these wide open spaces.* And then he thought: *She'd be easy to fall in love with.* And with that alarming notion he instinctively quickened his steps toward the farmhouse.

Later that night, when he got back to the Shawntrees, there was a message waiting for him. It was from Susan. She was in the Bay Area.

CHAPTER VI: THE REUNION

Susan was waiting for Jess at the bus terminal in Oakland. With a few quick strides they were in each other's arms. He whispered her name as they held each other close. Susan's soft sobs while her head rested on his shoulder spoke of relief and sadness and joy.

When they drew back, Jess could see the signs of weariness and stress, the deeper lines around her mouth and the sadness in her eyes that hadn't been there before. Susan had always been on the slender side, attractively so, with lovely blond hair that framed blue eyes, a delicate, upturned nose and full, sensuous lips. She had always carried herself with an understated, serene awareness of her physical beauty. Now there were cracks in that facade, a fragility and vulnerability that hadn't been there before.

"It's wonderful to see you," Jess said.

Susan smiled, her face suddenly radiant, her eyes no longer sad but glowing with the sight of him. She looked down at his two suitcases and said, "We can stow these here in a locker for awhile. There's a little coffee house on the next block where we can talk."

They walked in silence to the coffee house, hand in hand, frequently turning to gaze in wonder at each other, joyous at this simple but incredible miracle of walking down the street together, but also needing, after all that had happened, to reaffirm with a squeeze of the hand or a sidelong glance that this *was* really happening, that it was flesh-and-blood reality.

After they had gotten their coffee and sat down, Susan told her story. When the air purification system gave out, she had been trapped in her building, the CalBank's Sacramento headquarters. Her office was on the eleventh floor of a 60-story highrise. After a couple of hours the air began to get noticeably worse in the building—"you had to take in big, deep lungfuls; some people, I remember Lucy from accounting, were gasping for breath and sobbing at the same time, and you could see some people's skin starting to turn blue." Panic began to set in. Most of the 20-odd people in Susan's unit made a run for it, either heading down to the basement garage for their cars or going directly outside, headed God knows where.

"They knew they'd die if they stayed in the building—they just wanted to get out."

Susan and five of her co-workers had remained behind, thinking that their best chance of survival was in making it to the nearest building with a long-term emergency oxygen supply: the county courthouse, five blocks away. One of Susan's co-workers had rummaged around in a storage room and found five individual oxygen units (IOUs). Since there were six of them, they had to work out an elaborate system of IOU-sharing to get from their building to the courthouse.

"It was just horrible; I don't know how to describe it. There were already a lot of . . . bodies . . . all over the place. We were stepping over them . . . or trying to. One poor guy who was still alive grabbed my leg, tried to pull me down, I guess thought somehow he could get at my mask. . . ."

She stopped for a moment, looking at the busy street scene outside the window.

"I just tried to keep going, keep going those few blocks and try not to think about what was happening. We were all right on the edge of panicking. It's just the most horrible, the most totally horrible thing to be surrounded by air you can't breathe. Something you've always taken for granted, the air around you, and now if you take a few breaths it'll kill you. . . .

"We were about halfway there when Brad lost it. As I said, we had to take turns with the masks, and Brad at that time was the odd man out, and I guess he couldn't hold his breath any longer or something, but he just grabbed at Nick's mask—you remember Nick, Nick and Karen? Had dinner with them at that little Italian place last December?— Well, Nick and Brad struggled for the mask and Brad, who probably outweighs Nick by about 50 pounds, finally just punched him hard in the stomach, and Nick went down and . . ."

Again, Susan stopped, unable to continue.

Taking a deep breath, she finally forced the words out: ". . . so we finally got to the courthouse, the five of us, that is. . . . There were maybe a hundred people in that big open area on the first floor. Everyone just sort of milled around, and it was pretty quiet. You could look out through those big windows on either side of the building and see the air outside getting murkier and murkier. It was like being in the middle of a firestorm—after awhile you couldn't see more than ten feet past the windows—and there we were, huddled together, just glad to be alive and breathing but feeling horribly trapped at the same time.

"The five of us stuck together for the most part. Nobody said anything to Brad about what had happened. We were just trying to stay calm. I remember we talked about whether they might be able to get the purification system going again. At that time, of course, nobody really knew what had happened to the system, so we were just speculating, just looking for something to talk about and keep our hopes up.

"Finally somebody came up with the idea of a van caravan to the Bay Area. A couple of the employees at the courthouse figured we could get out of there in the prisoners' transport vans, which are all equipped with Air Purification Systems. I volunteered to be one of the drivers."

There was another pause, and again Susan had to force herself to continue: "It was awful, getting out of Sacramento. . . . all those bodies . . . there was no way you could steer around them . . . you just had to . . .

"And then when we got out of town the freeway was littered with abandoned cars. . . . But we made it, we made it. It took six hours, but we made it."

Looking down at her coffee cup, Susan took a deep breath and sighed.

"You went through hell, Susan."

"Yes, it was a living hell," she said slowly, still looking down at her cup. "There's no way to really describe what happened that day." She was still avoiding Jess's gaze. "I guess it's what war must be like, being right in the middle of a battlefield, only this time there were no sides or causes—just victims, hundreds and thousands of them dying in the streets for no reason. . . ."

She smiled faintly, having surprised even herself with this little speech. Then she told him in a flat, lifeless monotone that her parents and her only sibling, her older brother Tom, had perished in the disaster. Her expression, as she looked at him across the table, was as flat and lifeless as her voice—not from lack of feeling, but the opposite, the numbness of overwhelming grief. In the silence that followed, Jess wanted to tell her that he, too, had learned in the past week that he had lost everyone—his parents, his sister, his little nieces and his nephew—but he couldn't get the words out.

This time, when Susan spoke again, it was with a kind of relief. She had gotten past the hard part, and now she could talk about rebuilding her—*their*—shattered lives.

"When I got here, I tried to get things back to normal as soon as possible. I found a nice little one-bedroom near the Berkeley campus. You'll like it. You can walk to just about everything; things aren't as spread out as they are . . . were . . . in Sacramento.

"I got hired by the bank at its Oakland headquarters; my new job actually amounts to a promotion, since I'm just below the bank's chief financial officer. I'm actually overseeing the accounting departments in all the branches. The people I'm working with know what I've been through, and they've been great, just great. They all seem to understand, even the big guy upstairs, that I just have to go off every once in awhile and be alone. All of a sudden I'll see Nick and . . . and everything . . . and it just blocks out anything else, and I have to go off somewhere until I've calmed down and my mind clears."

"Yeah, I know. I'll never forget that day. It was like being wide awake in the middle of a nightmare."

Somewhat reluctantly, Jess recounted his own experience. To minimize the pain and the awful memories, he told it, once again, in short, clipped sentences, with one exception: He couldn't resist telling Susan, in some detail, about the dramatic, cliffhanging escape in the private plane.

And he told her of seeing, on the official published casualty lists, the names of all those who were dear to him—except, thank God, her.

But as he went on with his story and got past the horrors of that awful day and began to tell Susan of his brief sojourn in the Mount Shasta region, he became more expansive. He described the wonderful scenery—the mountains, the river, the forests. He spoke, as to a fellow prisoner, of a glorious world where you could look up at the blue sky and the clouds and breathe pure, unfiltered air. He told her of the Shawntrees and the warm, unquestioning hospitality they'd provided when he'd shown up on their doorstep, bedraggled and weary.

He told her of the old blind man he'd met in the hills above

Dunsmuir and the word he kept repeating, "travelin'," that had been running through his brain ever since, and his visit to the awesome crags and his trip on the old interstate with its varied and colorful modes of transportation.

"It's a lovely little paradise up there, Susan. But it's like going back a hundred years or more in a lot of ways. You oughta see their kitchens—*every* single appliance is *manual*, if you can believe that. And they make a lot of their own stuff—oh, I forgot to mention that Mrs. Shawntree, Cheryl, and her neighbor, Kathy Stillwater, sell handmade clothes in town, even spin their own yarn—anyway, these Shasta folks make a lot of their own stuff by hand.

"It's like they've gone back to the old rural-based economy, which has its good points. I guess there's something to be said for making do with less, and either making it yourself, or getting it from your neighbor. And they do a lot of bartering. A dentist'll take a basket of tomatoes for a filling, for God's sake.

"So you've got this back-to-basics society, which, as I said, has its good points, but these people are *so* out of touch. I mean, there's nothing wrong with going back to the land, but that doesn't mean you have to go back to the 19th century at the same time, does it?"

"How do you mean?"

"Well, neither one of the families I met had a television. They do have microwave transmitters for communications, like everybody else on the planet, but otherwise they're kind of cut off from the rest of society, you might say. For information, they mostly rely on an old-fashioned hardcopy weekly newspaper that this oddball guy named Jonathan—who also writes plays, I'll tell you about that later—puts out.

"And they make their own entertainment, I guess you could say. I had dinner at the Stillwaters one evening, and after dinner two of their kids performed a play they'd written themselves—pretty good, too, but can you believe that? It's like something out of an old

Charles Dickens novel.

"Ed Stillwater was trying to convince me to stay up there and set myself up with some kind of microwave transmitting service. But, like I told him, I'm a city kid, and, besides, I like working for somebody that can guarantee me a regular paycheck. And I didn't put it this way to him, but up there I felt disconnected, like you're in your own little Shangri-La. I guess that's part of being a city person, you want to feel like you're in the middle of everything, like you're *connected*."

Jess noticed the distant look in Susan's eyes and smiled apologetically. "Sorry for rattling on like that."

"Oh, that's okay, Jess. It's not you or what you're saying, really—it's me. When I start thinking about that day, I mean, it's why I just have to walk out of the office sometimes. It's impossible to focus on anything that's going on around me."

"I know, I know. But I didn't mean to go on and on about all my little adventures when what's important is that we're together again," he said, taking her hand. "That's it, isn't it?"

Susan responded by giving his hand a squeeze. She didn't say anything, but her eyes, those now-sad eyes, sparkled again with the glimmer of a smile. Something about that look stirred feelings in Jess he had never felt before in their relationship. He didn't really understand what it was at this moment, but it had something to do with seeing that look in her eyes and wanting very much to see it again and again.

The rest of the afternoon was spent talking, Susan doing most of it, chatting about her new job in the West Coast office of Cal-Bank, then growing expansive about Jess's prospects in this bustling metropolitan area. There had been so many new developments in the field of long-distance communications, interspace communications, and the Bay Area, with its intellectual, technical and academic resources, had become a national—no, a *world*—center in this growing field.

As Susan talked, Jess drifted in and out, thinking at times about the incredible good luck they'd had getting back together, thinking about the changes he saw in Susan as she spoke: the new lines around her eyes and mouth, and the sadness—and the fear that he could see just below the surface. He was touched by and drawn to this new Susan. Somehow there seemed to be more of a place for him with her than with the Susan of old, the crisp, self-assured, sharp-looking professional of Sacramento.

They both took it for granted that they would be moving in together. There were obvious practical reasons for doing so, given Jess's currently unemployed status, but he also felt a new emotional undercurrent in their relationship, a mutual need for a stronger, deeper bond that hadn't been there before.

So they chatted away, happy just to be sitting across from each other like any normal couple enjoying each other's company, their happiness drawn from the shared knowledge that they had cheated fate, that they had a second, unexpected chance to build a life together.

Out on the sidewalk people were already hurrying home from work. Jess noticed the predominance of the new single-unit, unisex, form-fitting clothing that had just been coming into vogue in Sacramento. The cosmopolitan denizens of the Bay Area, particularly the younger ones, had apparently adopted this new style with a vengeance. It attracted younger wearers because it fit the form of the wearer perfectly. To be fitted, the customers donned a thin protective shield made of some sort of durable plastic; then a softer polyethylene plastic was literally poured over them, creating the perfect form-fitting outfit. The particular type of plastic used had been chemically treated to breathe on warm days and repel water on rainy days. It could be colored however the wearer wanted by dipping it in special dyes. Right now the popular pattern consisted of two bright colors arranged in alternating quadrants—kind of a court jester look, Jess thought to himself. Susan, who'd left work to meet Jess at the bus station, was wearing more traditional garb, a two-piece gray suit and an off-white blouse with a trim little bow at the neck.

The two took their last sips of coffee and headed out into the multi-colored office crowd parading down the sidewalk. They were going back to the bus depot to pick up Jess's luggage.

" . . . it's a small place, on the north side of campus," Susan was saying. "Great view of the bay from the west window, though."

Suddenly the wail of emergency sirens pierced the air. As soon as they heard it, most of the pedestrians broke into a trot and started heading in one direction. Motorists stopped their cars, got out, and started running in the same direction.

Susan grabbed Jess's hand, and they moved along with the others—having little choice, really, other than to move with the surging crowd. Over the siren's wail, Susan shouted that they were going to the main post office. Jess observed that while people were hurrying, none seemed in any way panic-stricken. In the crowd near him, there were even a few teenagers playfully jostling and shoving each other.

When they got to the building, which was only two blocks from the coffee house, monitors were standing at the entrance directing wave after wave of people to the second floor.

As the crowd squeezed up the broad stairs, Susan was finally able to explain to Jess what was going on.

"Nothing to worry about, really. We have these at least once a week now. Ever since the Sacramento disaster, they've been staging these drills to make sure people know where the safe buildings are if and when the Air Purification System does blow. The only reason people are rushing is because there's a big fine if you're not in one of the designated buildings within 15 minutes of when the sirens start. They actually do spot checks of offices and stores, as well as the streets. Money from the fines is supposed to go toward making the APS even more foolproof . . . or so we've been told. Who knows? Maybe just more pabulum to calm the masses."

There was actually a festive air among the crowd of several hundred people crammed into the upper floor. Had there been alcohol generally available, it might have turned into a full-fledged happy hour. As it was, these jaded urbanites of the 21st century, who lived every day surrounded by poisonous air, used the drill as an opportunity to unwind after work.

One man near Jess and Susan joked to a companion that he was getting more exercise from these drills than from his weekly jogging routine.

"Damn, left my VRU (Virtual Reality Unit) at the office," one man muttered.

"Hell with the VRU," said a very stylish-looking young woman dressed in a pastel-colored single-unit outfit. "Who brought the pizza?"

This barracks-room camaraderie continued for another half hour, the repartee starting to grow flat and the chatter in the hall to subside, as people began to yearn for dinner and the comforts of home. Finally a monitor called out "All clear!" from one end of the big hall.

"You'll get used to it," Susan said matter-of-factly as they left the building.

* * *

Over the next few weeks, Jess gradually settled into a quiet and temporarily leisurely life with Susan in Berkeley. For both of them, it was a time of opening doors—starting from the very first day, when Susan ushered him in to their very first shared home. In the ensuing weeks doors were opened to secret spaces within themselves that they had never shared before. At times Jess felt that he was falling in love with someone new, someone he'd never known before.

When they were making love, there was something joyful, even rapturous, in her eyes that had never been there before. Jess had the new and wonderful feeling of bestowing something precious on this beautiful, fragile woman, and her joyful acceptance of it only deepened his love for her.

During the early stages of job-hunting, Jess had plenty of time to explore his new surroundings. He had finally been able to tap into his small savings account through a branch of his bank in Oakland, and this gave him a little financial breathing space.

He spent a great deal of his free time, while Susan was working, simply wandering around Berkeley. Compared to Sacramento, Berkeley was a town where people tended to do a lot of walking, and the streets were consequently full of life and activity. They were lined with small shops with brightly decorated front windows, and it seemed to be the custom of the natives to walk from one to another clutching large, durable shopping bags. For Jess, this little pocket of hands-on, real world shopping (as opposed to the e-commerce variety that had been the norm in Sacramento) was a pleasant trip through a time warp, and he admired the Berkeleyites for doggedly hanging on to this 20th century practice. If nothing else, they got some exercise out of it, and there had to be some other benefits, he supposed, from dealing with real people—shopkeepers and clerks and fellow customers—as opposed to sitting at home and manipulating symbols on a computer screen.

These 21st century Luddites, with their string bags, were treated to live music from guitar-strummers, classical instrumentalists, and just about every other kind of street musician you could imagine. And the level of talent displayed was just as varied. On one afternoon at the bustling intersection of Channing and Telegraph Jess encountered a man and woman playing flute duets who could just as easily have been featured performers with the Oakland Symphony. Two blocks away, a scruffy, shirtless young man was singing and banging on a guitar at the same volume, and with about the same sensitivity, as one of the air alert sirens.

The clothing worn here was very different from what he'd seen that first afternoon in Oakland. In Berkeley it was mostly natural-fiber clothing, or at least natural-*looking* fiber clothing. Greens and browns and grays were more popular than the pastels and almost fluorescent colors favored by Oaklanders. (Speaking of time warps, there were even a few tie-dyed t-shirts and blouses.) Berets were popular for both men and women. Jess—who considered a well-shaped leg to be evidence of divine intervention in human af-fairs—was pleased to see that women's leggings, the kind that fit a little looser than a leotard and stopped at about mid-calf, were going through another revival in popularity.

As he looked down Telegraph Avenue on the same day he encountered the flute players, Jess was reminded of the colorful crowd that had swirled around him on the old freeway near Mount Shasta. These Berkeleyites generally opted for more subdued colors than the mountain folk, but they displayed the same zestful indi-viduality. Bicycles were also much in evidence here, and many had been customized by the addition of extra wheels, extra seats, extra handlebars and all manner of trailers for carrying goods, children and pets. One fellow on a recumbent bike was even *pushing* a trailer ahead of him—for no other reason, Jess assumed, than that no one had ever thought to do such a thing before.

Everywhere he went in Berkeley he saw street people. Most were young; their daytime haunts were the commercial streets where they could panhandle passersby. He would see them in little clusters outside the coffee houses or the markets. Sometimes one of them would be playing a guitar or a harmonica, or a blanket would be spread on the sidewalk with trinkets of some sort, but mostly they just engaged in straight, unadulterated panhandling. This was usually done in a detached, laconic style—accompanied by blank, joyless looks, no effort being made to ingratiate themselves with their would-be benefactors—*whether you cough up or not, Jack, it's all the same to me.*

It was a hard life, as evidenced in those grim, joyless faces. Living off the streets had always been hard, but it was more so now with the almost constant arrests. Liberal, reform-minded Berkeley had finally run out of patience with the street kids. A booming street culture had resulted from escalating school dropout rates and declining entry level jobs (the kitchens and front counters of most fast-food outlets were now robotized). Berkeley had long been a mecca for the young and footloose, but it had gotten to the point where the street kids were sucking the life out of Berkeley's quaint, old-fashioned string-bag economy. With their panhandling and their dirty faces and their off-putting demeanor they were jeopardizing the livelihood of the people who worked in all those charming little shops, particularly with the alternative of shopping in the comfort of one's home now readily available. And as the subculture of the streets continued to grow, so did its attendant problems, including shoplifting, deranged behavior from drugs and despair, and violence.

So the theme of "taking back the streets" became an oft-heard one around election time, and as the arrests increased and the jails became wretchedly overcrowded, work camps were established for young misdemeanor offenders. (By the time of Jess's arrival in the East Bay, one in five young people between the ages of 15 and 23 were either in a work camp or in jail.)

Some of the kids that Jess observed, the ones who hadn't been on the street very long, were still fresh-faced and relatively clean. Most, however, were covered with the telltale grime of the streets that seeped through their skin and clothes; it was this street grime, and the apathy and fatigue borne of their hard life, that aged them into a kind of hybrid between young and old. You looked into eyes sunken with fatigue and bordered with premature lines and it was as if you were looking into an abyss, a bottomless void where there was no past and no future and no hope. Then there were other times when a glimmer of light, like a beacon from a lighthouse, shone out of weary, sunken eyes.

When Jess saw such a ray of light, he instinctively reached into his pocket and pulled out some change. One young man with unusually bright and intelligent-looking blue eyes was out in front of the parking lot at the nearby supermarket nearly every day. He said his name was Chester, and Jess occasionally stopped and gave him a small contribution and exchanged a few snatches of conversation.

Chester's physical assets were his eyes, a thatch of curly brown hair, and a round, open face—but, still, the grime had settled in, and his bright, blue eyes seemed, to Jess, more like a cry for help from an entrapped spirit than shining beacons of energetic young life.

Through Chester, Jess learned more about the city's work camp program. It was an alternative to jail for those picked up for loitering, drunkenness—or panhandling.

Chester hadn't minded the work so much—cleaning rain gutters, picking up litter, raking leaves in the park—mostly outdoor work, for which he received a small daily stipend. What Chester didn't like about the work camps was the grub, "rabbit and squirrel food," as he called it. The good, liberal voters of Berkeley, via their elected representatives, had wanted to ensure that the undernourished waifs who entered the work program came out in better physical condition than when they went in—hence the emphasis on a healthy diet. There was an unintended side benefit to this since most of the street kids who went through the program, like Chester, hated the daily diet of greens and nuts and grains, and this acted as an additional deterrent to a life of crime, or at least one of loitering and panhandling. Chester told Jess of one young man who escaped the prospect of more "rabbit and squirrel food" by promptly applying for and securing a cleanup job at Dunkin' Donuts as soon as he was released.

Chester also hated the all-male barracks that work program detainees were housed in. With his last arrest, this had meant being separated from his girlfriend, a stringy-haired, beanpole-shaped waif named Adele who sometimes joined Chester in front of the parking lot.

Chester and Adele currently squatted in an abandoned bungalow on the Berkeley flatlands and were squeezed in there with, as near as Jess could tell, about twenty other people. Their main ambition in life was to stay out of the work camps, so while cadging for change they always kept a wary eye out for cruising patrol cars. (One little trick they'd learned was to never stick their hand out; that way the cruising officer couldn't tell if they were panhandling or just trying to start a little friendly conversation with passersby.)

Jess happened on Chester and Adele's "squat" one afternoon when he was taking a stroll toward the bay. He had reached the Berkeley flatlands and was walking through a desolate neighborhood of rundown bungalows. He was about to detour over to the more cheerful and bustling commercial strip on University Avenue when he saw Chester and another young man leaning against the chain-link fence in a weed-overgrown yard.

Chester saw him and waved. The other young man, who was tall and wore his greasy brown hair shoulder length, gave him a blank look.

"Hey Jess," Chester called out cheerily as he approached. What brings you to our charming little neighborhood?"

"Just out for a walk. This your place?"

"Well, I wouldn't call it *my* place, but, yeah, this is where we stay for now. Little crowded, but you can't beat the rent. Right, John?"

"Yeah," his companion said listlessly, with the barest trace of a smile.

Chester chattered away for awhile on the eerily deserted street, where even auto traffic seemed to be non-existent. He acted as a kind of spokesperson for his non-verbal companion, explaining that John had just been released from a work camp and was holing up here to escape the unwanted attentions of his mother, a UC professor.

"If mom finds him, we're talkin' *major* guilt trip," Chester said, putting his arm around John, who just rolled his eyes. Giving him a playful squeeze, Chester teased, "My, my, my, we had *such* big plans for our little boy, didn't we? Graduation from work camp wasn't exactly what mommy had planned, was it?" John rolled his eyes again and looked away.

Jess wondered how Chester himself, who seemed bright and capable and full of life, had ended up in squatters' quarters.

Those quarters were, if anything, more squalid than Jess had imagined. He got an opportunity to take a look inside when Adele popped her head out the door and announced that dinner was ready. No formal invitation was extended, but none seemed necessary, so Jess just followed Chester and John inside. The otherwise bare front room was filled with blankets and sleeping bags, some with bodies still inside them; they had to step over three to get to what had been a small dining room adjoining the kitchen. Here about ten more young people lay in or on sleeping bags along the walls; most of these were awake and some were already sitting up expectantly, waiting for the evening meal.

Jess recognized a few of them from the streets, particularly one young dark-haired woman with strikingly pretty brown eyes, and a slender, graceful figure. When he tried to meet her gaze, she continued to stare blankly at the opposite wall. The room, for being so crowded, was eerily quiet. Little by little, people from other rooms straggled in and squeezed themselves between the others along the wall. The atmosphere in the small room was oppressive with the stale smells of food and unwashed bodies.

One figure sitting in a corner stood out from the rest. He was an older man, at least 30, with a haggard face, scraggly beard, and clothing more grimy and tattered than the rest. He was speaking, or rather chanting, to himself as he slowly rocked back and forth. Jess couldn't make out what he was saying, since most of the words were mumbled, except for a stray word or two—"light" and "dark" were repeated several times. The chanting was punctuated with his gut-wrenching, hacking cough. With his constant movement and mumbling and coughing, he was easily the most animated person in the room.

"That's Scratchy," Chester said, gesturing toward the corner. Scratchy acknowledged the introduction with a slight nod of his head as he continued chanting and rocking.

Adele and a rather stout young man with a full beard emerged from the kitchen with a large, steaming cauldron of what appeared to be stew or soup. The repast had been prepared on a camping stove propped up on one of the kitchen counters. Another young man emerged bearing a tall, tottering stack of bowls. Before he could place them on the floor, the two top bowls slid off, landing with a crash and littering the floor with debris. No effort was made to sweep it up.

Everyone served themselves, grabbing a bowl and dipping it in the cauldron and then retreating to their spot to consume it. Most didn't even bother with utensils, but drained the contents of the bowls by simply raising them to their mouths. Jess took about half a bowl's worth; he found the contents, which consisted of bits of meat, carrots, potatoes and some other unidentifiable ingredients, to be fairly tasty. He was not practiced in back-to-basics dining, however, and had to use his handkerchief as a bib to keep his soup from dribbling all over his shirt. There was no electricity in the house, and as the room grew darker the group huddled around the cauldron brought to mind a gathering of tribal cave dwellers.

As the cauldron was drained, the energy in the room began to pick up. The constant mumbling and coughing from Scratchy's corner was soon drowned out by the sounds of laughter and excited chatter. Most of those in the room were making plans to hit the streets, and Jess gathered that it was an after-dinner ritual to share their recent experiences in different parts of town—the likelihood of encountering cops being, of course, a primary topic.

As it turned out, the nightly exodus to the streets began sooner than expected. "Raid! Everybody ditch!" someone called out suddenly from the front room. After hearing a car door slam, the young woman who gave the alarm had gone to the window and observed two beefy men, very likely plainclothesmen, heading up the walkway. This, Jess gathered, was a common occurrence, and the evacuation was accomplished with a minimum of panic or wasted energy. Within less than a minute, everyone in the house had filed quietly through the kitchen and out the back door. Once outside, some even paused to relieve themselves in what was clearly their *al fresco* bathroom. Others immediately began clambering over the back fence. Jess was one of these; he followed the pretty brown-eyed woman and the full-bearded young man as they maneuvered their way through the adjoining backyard and along the side of a house, and through a balky fence gate that was on the verge of coming unhinged.

When they got out to the street, the young man whispered over his shoulder, "It's better if we split up." Jess followed his advice and was soon lost in the after-dinner crowd leaving the restaurants and heading for the night spots along University Avenue.

Jess was later able to learn from talking to Adele and Chester that these raids were, in fact, common, but that by posting sentries they were able to avoid being arrested and sent off to work camps. But a raid meant the almost certain confiscation of all their sleeping gear and food and what few cooking and eating implements they'd managed to accumulate, so their already spartan existence was rendered even more so until they could find another "squat" and start pooling their limited resources.

Even this brief glimpse into the interior of their lives helped Jess understand why people like Chester and Adele spent so much time on the streets. The streets weren't much grimier than their "squats," for one thing, and there was certainly more elbow room out there.

Whenever Jess tried to get either Chester or Adele to talk about their plans beyond their next meal, or the free concert that weekend in the park, he would get the same bored, even sometimes hostile, look. *Planning and working for a future, Jack, is for suckers.*

Jess wandered all over the East Bay during his weeks of leisure—westward through the flatlands, south toward Oakland's Lake Merritt, and north toward the suburban enclave of Albany. The East Bay dome was on a smaller scale than the one on Sacramento's valley plain. For one thing, there were the geographic constrictions imposed by the bay to the west and the hills to the east. And nature-loving Berkeleyites had lost their bid to have the East Bay dome extended up into the hills above the University of California campus. In an earlier day, this lush, wooded region had offered grand views of the bay and a myriad of paths and dirt roads for hikers and joggers. Now, these same slopes were gradually being denuded as the moisture-loving vegetation—from elegant cypress trees to the lowly coyote bush—was exposed to a warmer, drier climate and greater levels of pollution.

The direct impetus for the construction of a Berkeley-Oakland dome was a cataclysmic event that occurred in 2024. The two polar caps had been melting since before the turn of the century, but in 2024 the massive Ross Ice Shelf broke off from the Antarctic cap and fell into the sea, causing what historical accounts later referred to as "the splash felt 'round the world." Huge tidal waves swept over the coastlines of five continents, and ocean levels rose an average of 30 feet worldwide. (A similar event had occured, scientists speculated, during another warming period 130,000 years ago.) This had the immediate effect of forcing partial evacuations of U.S. coastal cities and rendering portions of the country's coastline uninhabitable.

The cities of the East Bay occupy a gently upward-sloping plain that rises about 1000 feet above the bay, so only narrow strips of Berkeley and Oakland along the bay felt any real impact from the catastrophe. But it was a wakeup call of the first order, and within six months a bond measure was on the ballot to raise funds for construction of a bi-city dome. Another important, though not as dramatically obvious, reason for building the dome was the steady increase in pollution levels. As global warming continued, both the Sacramento Valley and the East Bay were being transformed into vast open-air ovens for the baking of pollutants; levels of lung-clogging ozone, in particular, rose in proportion to the increase in ground-level temperatures.

As plans for the East Bay dome were being developed, the Berkeley proposal to include the lovely wooded area above the campus was rejected by Oakland voters as adding unnecessary expense to the dome's cost. To their gritty neighbors, it was another example of Berkeley's often impractical, frou-frou environmentalism. (San Franciscans chose not to dome their city for a number of reasons, including the cost, the obstruction of their glorious views of the ocean and bay, and the fact that ocean breezes blew their dirty air eastward toward Berkeley and Oakland. However, as ocean levels rose, they had to gradually abandon low-lying neighborhoods and head for the city's hills. Many simply fled the city altogether.)

Once the dome was in place, Berkeleyites had to seek recreation and a tenuous link with nature in the parklike Berkeley campus, and in the lush parkway along their previously buried Strawberry Creek. And after they had availed themselves of what now passed for outdoor recreation, they could, at least, comfort themselves over steaming cups of coffee in one of the establishments that beckoned, it seemed, on every other block.

Jess's first visit to a coffee house in his northside neighborhood was a little disconcerting. Some aspects of it were familiar: the pastel-colored flyers on the front window, the cluttered bulletin board just inside the front door. And behind the counter a couple of attractive, slender young women—"cappucino babes," as they were called in the trade—mixed and steamed coffee drinks over coffee-splattered steel counters, trading banter and gossip with their regular patrons.

But beyond the front counter was a scene very different from that of any coffee house Jess had ever entered. True, there were the usual small tables, each one of them having a voice-activated computer embedded in its center. But more than half of the two dozen or so patrons were sipping their coffee while wearing portable Virtual Reality Units. Each VRU was shaped like a bicycle helmet, except that it extended down all the way over the eyes and ears. Inside the helmet, where it covered the face, a small screen enveloped the wearer with three-dimensional imagery, and headphones on either side bathed the wearer in sound. A small speaking unit located at the very bottom of the front side of the VRU allowed the user to interact with whatever program was running in the unit.

These VRU people sat by themselves. Some were engaged in what was termed "passive" VRU use and others were in an interactive mode. One young man, a passive user studying for a Russian literature class, was looking over Prince Andrey's shoulder as he asked for Natasha's hand. Later, he would mingle with the troops under General Kutuzov. A young woman, using voice commands, dissected a cadaver while sipping her latte. An archeology student, between bites of his carrot cake, unearthed artifacts from an ancient Mesopotamian civilization near Ur in Iraq. A computer sciences major was taking a break from her studies by going on a short hike on one of the moons of Jupiter.

The range of experiences was breathtaking in its scope, but something that the students seemed to take for granted. Theirs was the subdued enthusiasm that you might have found among a group of young novitiates perusing the books in one of the early medieval libraries. Occasionally they would trade headsets if they found something they thought would interest their neighbors, or they shared their experiences in subdued conversations. But like the youth of every age, they seemed to take the cutting-edge technology of their era for granted.

Jess sat down with his coffee. His neighbors were absorbed in their VRUs, so to occupy himself he dictated a message to his computer, giving it the Shawntree's address. He told them that he was settled in Berkeley with his girlfriend and that he was about to start serious job-hunting. "Good luck with the harvest," he added. As an afterthought, he also dictated a similar message to the Stillwaters, adding a note to Rachel that he hoped her opening night performance would be "dazzling."

A young man with a curly brown beard showing under his VRU was sitting at the table next to Jess's. He had been chanting something unintelligible in a low, deep voice. He took off the high-tech helmet and, with a gentle, wordless smile, offered it to Jess, almost as if he were passing along a joint of marijuana. Jess graciously accepted the gift, positioning it carefully on his head.

He was dimly aware that his neighbor was making some adjustments on the outside of the helmet when, all at once, he found himself seated in the middle of a group of chanting monks. They had Asian features and were wearing burgundy robes. They—Jess and the monks—were all in a large room, presumably in some ancient temple. The walls were grimy from centuries of burning incense and candles.

The chanting, the incessant repetition of deep base notes, was overwhelming. Inwardly, Jess shrank from its frightening intensity. The chanting seemed to be drawing him into this alien world, and at the same time sapping his will.

Abruptly the chanting stopped. The silent monks around him stared ahead impassively. A large, well-fed monk with an air of authority strode into the room, right up to the front row of seated monks. He bowed low and said a few unintelligible words to the monks nearest him, and this started a wave of murmured comments that gradually rippled up to the rows where Jess sat, until the entire room was filled with the monks' excited chatter.

The monk in front raised one hand and the monks were silent once again. Extending that same hand to arm's length, he pointed a finger at Jess. The general murmuring began again, and Jess felt himself being lifted up by firm hands from either side. The two monks led him down through the rows to a position a few feet behind the lead monk, who, after Jess was brought down, started walking back in the direction he had come.

With the two monks still at Jess's side and the head monk in front, the small entourage walked through an archway at one end of the large room, crossing another large but empty room hung with ancient, crumbling tapestries. From there a door led to a spiral staircase dimly lit by flickering candles on its walls.

The small, solemn procession mounted the steps slowly. The lead monk was murmuring something in a low, guttural voice, but the sound echoed up and down the staircase. Once again a sinister, controlling force seemed to envelop Jess. As they mounted the stairs, he was dimly aware that he was in an alternative reality, that there was a larger reality beyond this one, but he had no clear idea how he could get back. When he made a conscious effort to raise his arms, he found they were still in the tight grip of the monks.

The lead monk opened a door at the very top of the stairs. After the little procession had filed through, Jess found himself in the glare of midday, on the small, spare rooftop of the temple. It was circular in shape and surrounded by a low wall that rose no more than three or four feet from the rooftop floor. Beyond the wall, far below, Jess could see the adobe huts and the irregular pattern of curving streets of the village. Far off on the horizon, looming high over the village, were mountains, dark and menacing below their snow-capped summits.

Jess was led to the very edge of the rooftop. The chanting of the monk grew louder; it was accompanied by an insistent low droning from the other two monks. This grew louder as they moved to the edge. When they reached the wall, the leader looked up toward the sky. Jess looked up to see a large hawk soaring directly overhead. The leader looked down at Jess and smiled an odd, crooked smile; he looked at the two monks and nodded, and Jess could feel their grip tighten on his arms, and he felt himself being lifted up, and then he was looking directly down on the street below. The chanting was loud now; it overwhelmed him; it sapped him of his last ounce of willful energy. He could see the tiny figures of people on the street below, and gradually, inch by inch, he could feel himself drawing closer to them, until he was completely over the wall and falling, falling toward them. . . .

"No-ooooooooooh! No-ooooooooooooh!" Jess screamed at the top of his lungs. Then everything went black, and the next thing he saw was the unexpected sight of the interior of the coffeehouse. About a dozen patrons, those not wearing VRUs, were staring at him, as were the two young women behind the counter.

He felt a hand on his shoulder. His neighbor had placed the headset on his own table and was now looking at him with a mixture of concern and amusement.

"Gets pretty intense toward the end, doesn't it? I should have warned you, but if you just kinda look at it as part of the whole experience, the freefall is like the big thrill at the end. I mean, how often do you get to fall six stories and live to tell about it?"

"Live to tell about it?"

"Oh yeah, I guess you didn't get to that part, but down below there's a bunch of monks holding several lengths of silk tapestry to catch you. They're Buddhists, you know. It's against their religion to let you get splattered all over the sidewalk."

"But it's okay to scare you to death?"

"I don't think they see it that way. It's some sort of initiation ceremony. Something to do with transcending earthly cares, soaring above them like that hawk. . . . But, anyway, next time you get caught up in a program you want to get out of, just yell 'Stop!' That's a universal command for any system, and the system, whatever mode it's in, will immediately shut down."

"Thanks, I'll remember that."

Jess knew it would be a long time before he accepted one of those headsets again. His hands were shaking as he brought the coffee cup to his lips. The coffee was tepid. He got up to leave and found that his knees were weak, but he forced his legs to work, and slowly he made his way to the door. He even managed to wave and mumble "next time" to the two women behind the counter, who silently watched him stumble out the door.

When he got home late that afternoon, there was a message waiting for him on the screen: "Good to hear from you and that you've made a safe landing. Let's keep in touch. Our communications may be a little spotty in the next month or so with the start of harvest season. —William & Cheryl"

There was no reply as yet from the Stillwaters, and he was surprised to find himself feeling disappointed that Rachel hadn't responded to his message about her opening night. Oh well, maybe there'd be something tomorrow.

CHAPTER VII: SEEKING WORK

*A*s Jess was leaving the apartment the next morning, there was a young man sitting at the top of the steps leading down to the sidewalk. Jess said hello as he walked past him, but the young man continued to stare vacantly out toward the street. His scraggly hair and faded, tattered clothing marked him as a street person. Something about him looked familiar, and when Jess turned around to take another look he saw that it was John, the taciturn young man he'd met at Chester and Adele's "squat." Jess had not paid much attention to this unobtrusive young man before, but now he noticed that John did not have the thoroughly begrimed look of a veteran of the streets. Perhaps it was because they made you take baths in the work camps.

As he headed down the street, his thoughts lingered only briefly on the quiet young man. His stride this morning was purposeful, his thoughts directed outward to the world of work and commerce. Unlike the other mornings, he had a real destination; he had his first job interview.

The interview was only a few blocks from the apartment, with a company called X-Cell-O-Ray. The company's main product was a memory-enhancing device sold to the medical profession. Using laser technology, information could be transmitted directly to a patient's cerebral cortex—a poem, the names of grandchildren, even the entire Oakland/Berkeley phone book or the Encyclopedia Britannica—all this could be embedded in the patient's memory within seconds. This technique was popular with students as well as their professors.

When he arrived at X-Cell-O-Ray Inc., Jess was ushered into the office suite of no less a personage than Mr. Roland Jeffries, the company's co-founder and head of its research unit. During the interview, Jeffries lounged on a spacious sofa in a corner of his office. He wore a white lab coat over his single-unit black stretch outfit. His dark hair was combed straight back. That striking feature, coupled with his pale face and sharp, aquiline features, reminded Jess of old black-and-white photos he'd seen of movie stars from early in the last century.

The "interview" was really a stream-of-consciousness discourse by Jeffries on the history of the company and its contributions to brain modification technology. Right now the company needed "new talent," Jeffries explained, for research and development of two new applied technologies, both of which would involve the physical modification of brain tissue. One application, which was being developed primarily for use in the public schools, would be used to treat students with severe learning dysfunctions. Essentially, the subject's brain tissue would be altered to conform to a template copied from the brain structure of high-IQ subjects.

The other application was being developed primarily for large corporations. Currently, Jeffries noted, these companies spend large sums of money trying to instill loyalty in their employees, through perks and such questionable methods as motivational retreats and seminars. Why not take a more direct approach, one with guaranteed results? What if company loyalty could simply be implanted in the cerebral cortex of new employees, either through laser techniques similar to the one X-Cell-O-Ray used in its memory implants, or through some sort of re-configuration of brain tissue?

Oh, this was controversial stuff, no question about it, Jeffries admitted, even though X-Cell-O-Ray stressed that these techniques would only be used on *willing* subjects. In the case of implants for poorly performing students, parental consent would likely be required.

"I'll tell you one thing," Jeffries said toward the end of their session. He leaned forward on the sofa, tapping Jess on the knee for emphasis. Jess, whose face was now within a few inches of Jeffries', found himself staring at the small black hairs sprouting randomly out of Jeffries' prominent nose.

"I've got people, highly qualified people, UC faculty some of 'em, lined up outside the door wanting to get in on these projects. And I can guarantee you I don't have to artificially motivate *my* employees on these projects. I mean, how often do you get to push the boundaries of science *and* at the same time make a major contribution to society?"

When Jess left Jeffries' office, he was left with two distinct impressions: that Jeffries enjoyed the opportunity to extol the company's—and his own—accomplishments to a captive audience, and that he really ought to take a tweezer, or perhaps a laser, to those nose hairs.

Oddly enough, Jess had no clear idea what job he was being offered, if in fact he was being offered a job. He had applied to work there at the suggestion of Jason Griffin, a former co-worker from Sacramento who had transferred to a job with X-Cell-O-Ray six months before the disaster. Jason had smoothed the way for him—the two had become friends while playing on the company softball team in Sacramento and sharing drinks after games. Within two days after calling X-Cell-O-Ray's personnel office, Jess got his appointment with Jeffries.

The idea of transferring information via laser intrigued him; it was, indeed, a push-the-boundaries form of high-tech communications, and the challenge of learning this new field appealed to him, as well as what he assumed would be a generous salary.

But . . . well, Jess had some doubts about how the new technology would be applied, despite Jeffries' assurances. How did

Jeffries or anyone else at X-Cell-O-Ray know that it would always be applied to *willing* subjects? Wouldn't it be tempting not too far down the road to try the motivational stuff out on, say, prisoners, or perhaps the kids in the work camps? Suppose all you had to do was zap them with a laser while they were asleep, or tranquilized. . . .

He'd definitely have to think a little more about this, although he knew, realistically, that his ethical qualms would diminish at about the same rate as his bank account.

Jess had another interview that same day with a company called Robo-Remote. Robo-Remote supplied highly sophisticated robots for work in dangerous or remote locations not accessible to humans. When an earthquake had occurred a few years ago in eastern Nevada, its epicenter near a nuclear waste dump, Robo-Remote had supplied the crew that had cleaned up the mess and re-buried the radioactive waste. For the past several years they had also been involved in space exploration.

The Robo-Remote building in Oakland was only two stories, but, with the addition of a sprawling robot construction and repair shop in the back, the whole facility covered an entire city block. The first sign that Jess's prospects were improving came in the form of a very attractive, 30-something woman who met him at the reception desk and identified herself as "Ms. (Miss?) Schoenwald, Director of Personnel." Ms. Schoenwald was very crisp and professional as she welcomed Jess to Robo-Remote. At first Jess tried to look past the creamy complexion, the cascading locks of blond hair, the sensuous curves of her calves and upper thigh, and, with a supreme effort, to deal solely with the corporate entity known as Ms. Schoenwald, Director of Personnel. Had Jess been blind, this might have worked.

"I thought you might enjoy a brief tour of our facility, and it might give you an idea where you'd fit in," Ms. Schoenwald said with a tight little corporate smile as she led Jess away from the reception area and down a long corridor. The corridor had many doors on either side, and on every other door there was a name on a brass plate and another brass plate below that with the person's title. None of the doors opened as they walked down the corridor, and no one entered the corridor from either end as they walked down it.

Ms. Schoenwald opened one of the double doors at the end of the corridor, and they went into a very large, high-ceilinged room which was completely ringed with video monitors. The monitors were positioned about eight feet from the floor and arranged in clusters, six monitors to a cluster, and each cluster of videos was aimed at a work station, where someone sat pushing buttons and manipulating small color-coded levers on a large console.

Jess and Ms. Schoenwald stopped at one work station where a middle-aged woman monitored the construction of a research station on Jupiter. Ms. Schoenwald explained some of the procedures as they watched. Each robot, she noted, was programmed to accomplish one or two simple tasks. At one point the woman at the console had to switch a construction robot from auto-mode to direct control to guide the robot in re-positioning a wall panel that had not been placed flush and airtight.

When that task was accomplished, she swiveled around to acknowledge her visitors. Ms. Schoenwald introduced her as Mabel Gillis. "Mabel runs one of the tightest construction crews this side of Pluto," Ms. Schoenwald noted with a dry little chuckle.

Ms. Gillis smiled at the compliment. "Oh, they're a pretty good crew as long as they haven't been out on one of their all-night binges."

Jess chuckled. Ms. Schoenwald managed another tight little smile. Evidently this was one of Ms. Gillis's standard witticisms.

They left the main building and walked across a narrow open space into the cavernous building that housed the robot shop. There was an assembly line for new robots near the entrance. Ms. Schoenwald stood by as Jess watched, fascinated, as the robots were assembled. Each robot started out as a compact electronic console the size of a laptop computer. This was sandwiched between the two curved titanium sheets that formed its torso. Then the thin, articulated rods that formed the arms and legs were attached, and finally the cylinder-shaped heads that contained compact radio receiving and transmission equipment and visual and aural sensory detectors. Visual information was taken in through a clear plastic orb implanted in the robot's head. Wires snaking out of the bottom of the head were spliced to those sprouting out of the torso. All of these components—heads, electronic guts, metal skins, and appendages, were stacked neatly along one wall, ready to be moved to their proper place on the assembly line.

Toward the rear of the building was the repair shop, and as they walked toward it Jess was struck by the sight of a small mountain of robot limbs, the thin arms and legs all jumbled together. Some of the metal pincers that served as hands twitched spasmodically, like newly severed insect appendages. Beyond these was another mound of robot heads, each with its big plastic eye, and yet another of torsos. On a nearby wall a handwritten sign said jocularly "Believe In Us And Ye Are Reborn."

Most of the worker activity in the repair section involved testing and repairing the circuitry of the inner consoles. There was another unit in the very rear of the building where five workers were engaged in metal repair work and the final reassembling of the resurrected robots.

Finally, another large space was devoted to testing both the repaired and the newly manufactured robots. There, technicians sat at consoles similar to Ms. Gillis's and monitored the robots as they performed their simple tasks. The walls echoed with the noisy clatter of rivets being driven into titanium panels. At one point there was a thunderous sound as one of the 4'-by-4' panels toppled to the ground. As Jess and Ms. Schoenwald watched, the robot who'd dropped the panel was placed on a stretcher and carried back to the repair unit.

"Better to find that out here than a million miles away," Ms. Schoenwald commented.

They headed for the exit, and on the way they passed several rows of robots—hundreds of them—silently and patiently awaiting transport to another planet, or possibly a less glamorous posting to a toxic cleanup site.

As they walked by them Jess, on a sudden impish impulse, saluted briskly. Ms. Schoenwald smiled, this time with genuine amusement. The smile lit up her whole face, and she chuckled softly, tossing her head ever so slightly, shaking her golden curls and then reaching back to smooth her hair. In that moment, Ms. Schoenwald the Personnel Director dissolved altogether.

Yes, he had a deep attachment to another woman, but this was here and now, and during the short but intense moments that he was beside this lovely blond goddess with her shimmering hair and her beautiful, luminescent smile, his mind, functioning on hormones, drifted through visions of Ms. Schoenwald on their first date in a sexy evening dress, cut to mid-thigh; of Ms. Schoenwald stretched out on the sofa, looking at him dreamily, invitingly; and—oh my yes—of Ms. Schoenwald lounging on the beach next to him, all tanned and curvy and sensuous and smiling up at him. To his annoyance, these visions were interrupted several times by small talk from Ms. Schoenwald herself as they proceeded toward the office.

His pleasant daydreams received a severe blow when they got to the office. For there, on her desk, prominently displayed, was the photo of a handsome, square-jawed fellow whose neck was nearly as wide as his face. Jess had noted with satisfaction that Ms.

Schoenwald's fingers were ringless, but this photo suggested that she was by no means unattached.

Actually, the photo was of Ms. Schoenwald's dear younger brother, and she displayed it on her desk partly out of affection for her sibling, but mainly for exactly the message it was sending to Jess and to all the other amorous young men she guided through the interview process. Ms. Schoenwald, of course, never lacked for suitors, and in her first years as Personnel Director it had been a nuisance to have every other male job applicant ask her out. The photo of her brother had done wonders in stemming the tide of applicants for her personal favors.

However, on this occasion Ms. Schoenwald, *Jessica* Schoenwald, as the sign on her front door said, was thinking that she just might make an exception and explain her relationship to the man in the photo to this rather attractive young man—if he had the boldness to ask.

However, Jess did not ask. He *thought* about asking, to be sure, but he did not. Ms. Schoenwald, Jessica Schoenwald the Love Goddess, was still very much present in the room—how could she not be?—but she beckoned to him from a distance. She had faded into the background, was standing in a faroff corner, in the shadow of that photo.

So by default Ms. Schoenwald, Personnel Director, came to the forefront. But remarkably, even in that role, at *this* particular moment in time, she captivated Jess. It was not only what she said to him, but the *way* she said it. She was animated—no, more than that, *radiant*—as she spoke of the company's future plans.

The company's role, Ms. Schoenwald noted, involved it heavily in communications technology. That is why she had called Jess in for this interview, because of his experience in that field. The company anticipated continued expansion of its role in space exploration. Specifically, it was about to begin the preliminary research that would eventually enable Robo-Remote to staff deep space explorations with its robots. These would be trips to other stars, involving distances measured in light-years, that were out of the question for human space travelers (pending future progress in cryonics).

Ms. Schoenwald the Personnel Director became downright lyrical on the subject of robots and their uses in the farthest reaches of the known universe. They could truly venture where no human dared go. They would be the bold space pioneers of the future. But there were a few basic problems that had to be solved first.

How were the robots to be repaired and maintained over the long period of time these explorations would take? Should the company send ten or twenty or a hundred times the robots needed for the mission, so that there were adequate numbers of replacements when the original robot crew started malfunctioning? Or could sophisticated robot "doctors" be developed?

And what about the communications links with the robots and their ship, which would become increasingly tenuous the farther they went into deep space? How account for the seemingly random interference from planets and their moons in other solar systems, from asteroids and other space debris? Would tech support on Earth have to develop complicated space-and-time projections of the trajectories of all these objects during the period of exploration? Or could they send multiple transmissions of the same signal, perhaps numbering in the thousands or millions, each of them on a slightly different trajectory, bouncing off a different combination of objects in space, so that at least one of the transmissions was guaranteed to reach the robot-manned spaceship?

Jess listened, fascinated, as Ms. Schoenwald discussed these options, and offered the delicious prospect of his own participation in these pioneering deep-space efforts.

By the time she had finished her rapturous discourse on deep

space, Ms. Schoenwald *was* positively radiant; her blue eyes burning with an energy that seemed capable of lighting even the darkest
reaches of deep space. Jess found himself swept up by her enthusiasm; her energy-charged aura seemed to wrap around him as she
spoke, and when she had finished they were both aware that
something exciting and pleasurable had passed between them. Yes,
it was all very serious and purposeful, but there was *passion* in it as
well, something sensuous that reached all the way down to his loins.
Jess had just learned firsthand the intimate relationship between
power—power in this world, power over the whole universe!—and
sex, and that only a thin, almost irrelevant, line divides the corporate
takeover and the orgasm.

And as Jess left Jessica Schoenwald's office he had the implicit
understanding that he would be hired to work at Robo-Remote, and
that his relationship with Jessica Schoenwald would be some sort of
blending of the professional and the physical.

When he got back home John was still there, sitting at the top
of the steps, still staring listlessly out toward the street. Jess's first
impulse was to ignore him, to leave him to his private reveries and
go on upstairs, but a sudden impulse—perhaps from pity or curiosity—checked him.

Jess had already passed the young man, but he turned and
asked, "Waiting for someone?"

There was no response. Jess walked back down the steps so that
he was at eye level with the young man.

"John, you, uh, seem like the quiet type." *Hey, you gotta start
somewhere.*

"Uh-huh." *Success! Well, at least a start.*

"We might as well get acquainted. Am I gonna see you here
every day?"

"Dunno."

"Are you kinda, you know, at loose ends? I mean, it looks that way."

"What do you mean by 'loose ends'?"

"Well, generally speaking, if you're not going to school and you don't have a job . . ."

"Then I guess I'm at loose ends."

"Do you have a place to stay? I mean, since that raid?"

"Oh yeah, we found another place. You can always find another place." There was a short pause after this laconic response, and then the words came tumbling out. John practically spit them out. "Okay, okay, and here's a few more things before you ask any more of your *questions.* I had an okay childhood, but my dad's dead, okay? And my mom's real disappointed in me, okay? She teaches at UC, and she wanted me to be, I don't know, a genius, I guess, only it didn't turn out that way—*okay?"*

There was long pause this time, and John seemed to cool down a little.

"But that's okay, that's cool, you know." He looked up at Jess and asked, "Ever hear of a guy named Hemingway?"

"Yeah, I think so. Wasn't he some kind of writer a long time ago?"

"Yeah, long time ago. I think it was my dad first told me about him. I read one of his books, I think it was called *Sunrise* or something, 'bout a buncha people in Europe who drink and screw a lot . . . anyway, he had this saying: 'There's always a way out.' Okay, so his way out was he blew his brains out with a shotgun when he couldn't take all the shit anymore.

"So that's the way I look at it. People shit on you, they laugh at you, they're *disappointed* in you, but it doesn't matter, 'cause there's always that door at the end of the hallway with a big Exit sign. And what a lot of people don't realize is, you can open it anytime you want. You just walk outside the dome, that's all. I've heard of guys who've done it. Takes half an hour maybe, at most.

You just keep walking until you can't walk any more, then you just sit and wait."

Jess listened with a sick feeling in the pit of his stomach. What made it so awful was that the young man was smiling, he actually looked happy as he was saying all this. He spoke of the prospect of an easy, peaceful death the way a young girl might talk about her first boyfriend, or a young woman about her upcoming marriage, as if death were, in fact, the most wonderful thing he could possibly imagine.

Then he was silent again, staring out at the street. Jess couldn't think of anything to say, and John seemed completely tuned out anyway. As Jess opened the door to the apartment and mounted the stairs, he tried to think of something he could say or do to turn this poor kid's life around, to bring him back from the brink. Even as he did so, he instinctively realized that this was very likely a futile notion, that, as much as he might want to, he was not going to light up an otherwise bleak life with a few words. That was the sensible, realistic approach, and he spent the rest of the evening, off and on, trying to convince himself that it was the best one.

CHAPTER VIII: YOU CAN TAKE HIM ANYWHERE

They were out on the big blue lake, just drifting, Susan perched at one end of the small boat in a pretty yellow summer dress and a smart straw sunbonnet with a dark blue band. Over it all was the dark gray menacing sky above the dome, hovering over the yellows and the blues and the greens around the lake, the dark gray world outside kept so nicely at bay, and on a pleasant Sunday like this seeming to exist solely to provide a swatch of contrasting color against the bright pastels below.

Jess had fleeting thoughts of the blue sky over Mount Shasta and the truly vivid greens and blues in the pure mountain air, but it was no more than a fleeting thought, easily erased by a straw sunbonnet, a pretty yellow dress, the lovely, fragile face of his lover, the blue miracle of a lake in the middle of a teeming city.

After the vistas of Mount Shasta faded away, all that was left, occasionally surfacing from the recesses of Jess's memory, was the image of an old black man, looming over him from the hills above Dunsmuir.

Drifting, just drifting, on that quiet afternoon. Pleasant enough, pleasant not only because of the peace and beauty of the day, but because this peaceful afternoon was the prelude to his daring plunge into Deep Space.

They rowed to the north shore of Lake Merritt, near the old boathouse, and, tying up the boat, settled on a grassy slope removed from the crowds. Their only neighbors were a few scavenging ducks. Jess and Susan spread out their blanket and emptied the contents of their picnic basket. They took out glasses and a wine bottle, and spread out plates of bread and cold cuts and a bowl of salad.

"To us," Jess said as they clinked their glasses.

"To your new job, and fame and fortune," Susan said.

"Oh, to hell with fame and fortune. To *us*," Jess said gallantly, and drew her to him.

That afternoon they daydreamed together, walking through, room by room, the little home they would buy as soon as Jess had gotten settled in his job. They were, indeed, much like any other young couple on a pleasant Sunday afternoon with a bright future ahead of them—only, of course, for them this was still part of a miraculous second chance. To be planning a life together, just like any normal young couple!

When they got home late that afternoon there were two messages waiting for Jess. One, which Jess had been expecting, said, "Please check in with me sometime this week re your first assignment. —Jessica Schoenwald" The other caught Jess by surprise: "Opening night a triumph (of course). Sorry you missed it. —Rachel Stillwater"

* * *

A week later Jess was in the Robo-Remote robot shop with two other new employees. Sylvia Richardson had been hired as part of the research team that would be developing the deep-space robot "doctors." George Marsano had been hired as an assistant to the company's Vice President for Public Relations, Winston Birdwick.

Three copies of a thick, stapled manual were spread out on a large work table in front of them. At one end of the table were the component parts of a robot. At the top of each manual a warning was emblazoned in bold red letters: "Confidential Material—This Manual Not to Leave Company Premises Under Any Circumstances." The title of the manual was "Configuration of the Robo-Remote Robot."

It was standard procedure at Robo-Remote for all new employees hired, no matter for what position, to assemble the company's main product from scratch.

The three of them had been carefully studying their manuals for the past week in the company library and had watched the company video that showed, step-by-step, how a robot was assembled. Still, it was pretty daunting, this God-like task of turning a pile of metal poles and plates and electronic circuitry into an animate creature, and there was a palpable sense of shared anxiety and excitement around the work table.

Sylvia was a light-skinned black woman in her 30s. She had a quiet, intelligent and intense manner about her that Jess at first found a little off-putting.

Sylvia and George were temperamental opposites. George, also in his 30s, looked like a cleaned-up version of Chester, having the same open, round face and thatch of curly brown hair. He turned out to be the chatty member of the trio. That first morning it was George who broke the ice. He was not at all reticent about expressing his own perceived shortcomings and his anxieties about meeting the challenges of the new job. With his openness, George brought to the surface the anxieties they all had, and Jess and Sylvia breathed their own quiet sighs in the knowledge that their worries were shared.

With his constant stream of chatter and voluble sense of humor, George provided much of the glue that helped merge them into a working team. Toward the end of that first week he and Jess were already trading good-natured insults, while Sylvia, smiling her bemused, quiet little smile, occasionally threw in a quip of her own.

Sylvia's previous job had been in the research and development department of a company that designed and sold computers to banking institutions. She undertook the task of properly splicing all the wires from the "guts" of the robot—the laptop-sized computer console—to the receiving unit in the robot's head.

Transmissions received from a human operator, after being transferred down to the electronic "guts," had to be converted to action-producing impulses to the robot's appendages. (Usually it was simply a matter of the order from Earth activating an already existing program in the robot, such as that for riveting panels in a wall.) Here again, Sylvia took charge of connecting the circuits between the central console and the appendages.

While Sylvia fussed over the circuitry between guts and head, Jess and George began the laborious task of assembling pistons and rods, all made of titanium, into bendable legs and arms. Neither of them was particularly handy with a soldering iron, and they found themselves taking frequent breaks as they struggled to connect joints and the robot's piston-like "muscles."

During one break, George asked, "What'll we name him?"

"Rob, of course," Jess replied.

"Rob . . . Rob. Yes, I like it. Good solid name, Rob. Yes, a 'Rob' is definitely someone who can boldly go where no man or robot has ever gone before."

"Absolutely."

"Oh Jess, I just *hope* our boy Rob will grow up to be big and strong and make us *so* proud of him."

"Well, I dunno George, considering his parentage . . ."

By the end of the week, George had carried the joke about as far as it could go. He worked up a tune that began with the line "My boy Rob . . ." and sang it in a loud, operatic voice choked with ersatz emotion.

And by Friday of the following week, having met their two-week deadline for assembling a robot from scratch, the team of Sylvia, George, and Jess was in high spirits as they awaited the appearance of Ms. Glynnis Welbourne, chief of Robo-Remote's Design and Development Department, who would observe "Rob's" performance as he was put through his paces.

After a short, suspenseful wait Ms. Welbourne entered the building just a minute or two after the appointed time. A shaft of sunlight lit her from the rear as she opened the warehouse door. She was a stout woman of mid height and she was wearing a traditional suit of dark blue. Jess noticed that she was wearing a pair of black, thick-soled, no-nonsense orthopedic shoes. She strode briskly across the warehouse floor, past the construction section and over to where the three anxious robot parents were standing.

Eschewing any small talk, Ms. Welbourne, in the brisk manner of someone whose time is extremely precious, said, "Good morning, everyone. Let's see what we've got here."

Sylvia went over to the console and sat down. She had one hand under the console, her fingers crossed, as she pulled the activation lever. Then she moved another lever and the robot started to walk in slow, jerky steps toward a modular wall about 30 yards away.

"Excellent limb movement," Ms. Welbourne said, almost to herself, in a half-whisper. George, standing next to Jess, flashed a surreptitious thumbs-up, nudging Jess playfully with his elbow as he did so.

That, unfortunately, was the high point of young Rob's performance. In the next few moments Jess and George watched in helpless disbelief as the robot veered off its proper trajectory—only slightly, to be sure, but enough so that it missed the wall by about six inches on one side and continued walking toward the wall of the building, which was another 20 yards farther.

Syvia, trying to turn the robot around, was frantically pulling levers on the control panel right up until the moment the robot reached this far wall, which it began to climb by punching its v-shaped, titanium feet into the plaster. Still climbing, it had successfully grasped a rivet from a pouch at its side and had started to drive it in when the section of wall beneath its feet began to crumble, sending the poor, misguided robot tumbling to the floor. There, lying on its back, it continued to punch the air with its riveting hand, occasionally pausing while its feet punched into and climbed an imaginary wall. The poor robot resembled nothing so much as a turtle, or a very large beetle, trying to right itself. Finally, Sylvia had the presence of mind to pull the activation lever back, and the frantic movements stopped.

There was an awkward silence for a few moments.

"I'd say it needs a little work," Ms. Welbourne commented dryly, then turned on her thick soles and marched away just as briskly as she had come.

"And *I* say we put it up for adoption," George said. No one laughed.

* * *

The disastrous debut of their robot, it turned out, stemmed from a minor, easily fixable problem. The robot's right leg was one-half inch shorter than the other, which caused it to veer slightly to the right from the direction its laser-radar homing device was pointing it in.

Once the leg had been adjusted, the robot performed admirably in its next wall-building demonstration. Even Ms. Welbourne was impressed with the robot's agile movement as it climbed the wall—the correct one this time—and deftly drove rivet after rivet into the wall's titanium plating.

The three teammates decided to celebrate by treating themselves to lunch at a Chinese restaurant in the neighborhood—and it seemed only fitting that Rob should join them, aided by a portable robot control device.

As they strolled down the sidewalk, their robot lurching alongside them, they acted as if this were the most normal thing in the world. And they soon found themselves playing to an audience of delighted spectators—drivers were even slowing down in both directions to watch the strange entourage. Playfully getting into the spirit of the thing, the three co-workers threw in a few deft theatrical touches, slapping the robot on the back and pretending to point things out to him (a particularly attractive mannequin in a shop window, for example) as they walked along.

It was a delight to watch the expressions on the faces of the other pedestrians, who simply stopped in their tracks and gawked as the odd quartet passed by.

"I feel like Dorothy in the Wizard of Oz," laughed Sylvia.

Heads turned when they walked—and lurched—into the restaurant. But the waitress who brought them their menus and water was stoically imperturbable—acting, to all outward appearances, as if she were in on the joke.

As their fellow diners looked on silently, George asked the waitress in a loud voice where the restrooms were. When she pointed them out, Sylvia activated the compact control panel she was holding under the table, and, as the other diners watched in stunned silence, George and the robot got up, walked across the room, down a hallway and into the men's room.

As the days rolled by the robot became a kind of mascot to the three freshmen employees. They took him to the company cafeteria at lunchtime. There he soon ceased to be a novelty; their co-workers simply nodded, or greeted him with a perfunctory "Hi Rob" as they walked by. Sylvia installed a circuit that enabled the robot to salute executives of the company as the quartet passed them in the hallways.

The robot, this tangible symbol of their camaraderie and *joie de vivre*, also brought them to the attention of the company's top executives. George in particular was able to take advantage of the instant celebrity Rob had bestowed on them. Even as a new employee, George was not shy about speaking up, and from his post in the public relations department he pushed the idea of an official company mascot similar to Rob—something that could be used as a kind of logo in company advertising, but that could also make appearances at conventions and be trotted out for presentations at schools.

The idea was one that gradually gained acceptance at the upper levels of management—after being discussed and analyzed by two top-level working committees. Once the idea was implemented, "Project Rob" helped raise the company's profile and was an acknowledged success, jump-starting George's career at Robo-Remote. To a somewhat lesser extent, both Jess and Sylvia shared in the glory. Although it was not in their job descriptions, Jess and Sylvia received special dispensation from the company to go out with George to the school presentations. Rob, of course, was a huge hit with the kids, and they listened with fascination as Jess, to the accompaniment of three-dimensional visual effects, described the wonders of deep space and the ambitious plans for its exploration by the pioneering firm of Robo-Remote.

So it was with an understandable feeling of satisfaction that Jess returned home each day from the research lab. In his previous job, fresh out of college, he had been a kind of glorified electronics repairman. That was all well and good; the job had certainly had its challenges and had paid well, but now he was being treated as a colleague by researchers who, in some cases, had formerly been on the faculty at Berkeley. At this point he was only a junior partner in deep space research, to be sure, but the few minor successes he'd already had—not least of which was leaping that first hurdle with George and Sylvia—gave him the confidence to believe that he had a bright future ahead of him. And why not? He was still quite young (only 25), he was good-looking, and he had a certain kind of quiet charm that complemented his handsome face and manly figure. So that under any circumstances—whether he was an athlete, a carpenter, or a space researcher—the future was bound to look bright. That's why most evenings he was humming or whistling as he bounded up the stairs to the apartment—content with himself, his prospects in life, and life in general.

There was really only one little thing that disturbed his cheerful mood on these occasions. For several weeks now, there had been no one sitting at the top of the stairs.

CHAPTER IX: THE RETURN

Now that Jess was making a comfortable salary again it seemed that doors were opened and lights went on for him and Susan all over the city. They had their choice of the best restaurants now, and they went to plays or concerts virtually every weekend. (With rising ocean waters inundating San Francisco, the region's cultural center of gravity had shifted across the Bay, to the point where the cultural life of the Oakland-Berkeley axis had come to rival that of New York and Los Angeles.)

The two of them were faced with a bittersweet dilemma posed by their rising incomes: Should they buy a house now or wait a little longer and purchase something bigger and in a better neighborhood than they could afford now? This gave rise to their first serious disagreement, Susan favoring an immediate purchase, having dreamed since she was a little girl of having a home of her own, and also wanting the home as the tangible sign of their shared commitment.

Jess wanted it too, more for Susan's sake than his own, knowing how much she yearned for it. But, since his emotions were not as deeply involved, he had the luxury of stepping back and taking a longer, and (in his opinion) more practical view. What was the rush? Why not wait until they could afford something better? They were together again, that was the important thing. As long as they were reasonably comfortable, where and how they lived was of secondary importance, it seemed to Jess.

That he was having an affair with Jessica Schoenwald was

really not a factor in his favoring such a delay. Jessica of course knew that he was living with someone, that they had a very close and long-term relationship.

His affair with Jessica had begun, really, that very first day in her office and gradually grew into something physical in the course of long discussions, sometimes in her office and sometimes over lunch at a nearby bistro.

When Jessica spoke about the company and its great mission on the frontiers of space, a mission that now linked the two of them, she fairly glowed with passion and energy. Looking back on it, it seemed inevitable that this passion, as Jess came to share it, should eventually find some physical expression. And when that did happen, when their relationship *was* consummated, so Jess told himself, it was not just physical lust, nothing as common or banal as that, that brought them together, but that sense of a grand shared mission.

This was a convenient way of looking at the affair, for it tended to assuage whatever guilt Jess might have felt regarding Susan. It put the affair with Jessica in an entirely different sphere from his relationship with Susan. In simple terms, Susan was the woman he loved; Jessica was the flesh-and-blood embodiment of a cause, a shared mission.

Jess was by nature a romantic, and there was some validity to this high-minded interpretation of his affair with Jessica. But the fact is that Jessica Schoenwald was a beautiful woman, her lips were full and sensuous, her nicely rounded, full breasts rose above a trim waist, and her legs were beautifully tapered and curved, so there were certainly times—just before or during a climax, for example—when the company's great mission in space had little to do with their relationship.

And Jess was perhaps a little too wrapped up in that relationship and in the new challenges of his job to see that, for all the fancy talk about faroff galaxies and the company's great quest in space, he,

Jess Renfree, was really just drifting through life right now. The fact that he was drifting was further obscured by the glamorous trappings of his job. Jess now worked right alongside some absolutely brilliant men and women, and they, this Deep Space *team* that he was part of, were designing the sophisticated spacecraft and communications equipment that would reach into faroff galaxies and solar systems, possibly discovering new life forms in the process. Think of it!

In fact, Jess hadn't thought much about it at all. In those private moments when he might have reflected on the larger meaning of his work, he contented himself with little more than a soothing repetition of the same buzz-phrases: "Deep Space," "expand the frontiers of knowledge," "unexplored galaxies," "new life forms," and so on. It was a kind of magical incantation that he had first learned from Jessica Schoenwald and that they still employed in their conversations. It was essentially mindless and it kept them motivated—much as a church litany does for the faithful.

Some people are content just to drift, to let events and circumstances and the people around them be the current that moves them along and determines their direction. But Jess was not one of these. There was an undercurrent running in him, just below the surface of his life, an undercurrent that churned inside him and produced vague feelings of uneasiness. It was at those times that the image of the old blind man on the hill would surface, and Jess would puzzle over this, try to figure out what the old man had to do with these obscure, troubled feelings. Having no success, he impatiently and characteristically moved on to the tangible, to thoughts of robots and asteroids and Jessica's smooth, tapered legs.

But the undercurrent was always there, and so the following winter, nearly two years after Jess had fled to the Mount Shasta region, he suggested to Susan that they take their three-week vacation up there. There were obvious reasons for this choice: Both of them had advanced cases of "dome fever" from too many consecutive days spent under plastic. Both had grown up under Sacramento's hazy, polluted skies, but there had been times in both their lives when they had seen blue skies and clouds and breathed pure, unfiltered air, and they still had a deep-down yearning for them. Once at Mount Shasta, they could explore the landscape at will, and Susan could meet his friends and benefactors, the Shawntrees.

The more Jess thought about it, the more it seemed the perfect place for their vacation. Susan, caught up in his enthusiasm and wanting a respite from the dome, readily agreed. They received a quick response from the Shawntrees after sending them a message about their plans: "Come on up, love to have you and Susan. Don't mind us if we're a little distracted with the asparagus harvest, but at least there'll be plenty to eat! —William and Cheryl"

So one Saturday morning they flew in a small, 12-seater plane to Redding, and from there took a bus to the town of Mt. Shasta. They could have tried to hitch a ride from Redding on a private plane small enough to land at Dunsmuir's airport, but Jess wanted Susan to experience a gradual unfolding of the forests and mountains.

It wasn't until they reached the 1500-foot level that they left the valley's haze behind and the forests began to take on, to a city dwellers' eyes, their almost blinding, vivid green hues. From time to time, as the bus wound up through the mountains, they could see the river, its dark green waters flecked with glints of silver, following its snake-like path down below.

Susan, who had never been in this region before, was transfixed by the unfolding panorama. She said little, but kept her eyes fixed on the scenes outside her window. That first half-hour of unfolding mountain scenery was, it seemed now to Jess, the fitting prelude to the dramatic appearance of Mount Shasta—"starting up sudden and solitary from the heart of the great black forests of Northern California," a phrase he remembered from a musty old book in the Shawntrees' library.*

Susan gasped when the awesome, snow-capped mountain appeared on the horizon against a crystal-blue sky. Against that backdrop, with a few wispy clouds clinging to her sides, the mountain seemed to dwell in some ethereal world of its own between heaven and earth. Susan could not have put the idea into words just yet, but she sensed that the looming mountain was a kind of gatekeeper to a world vastly different from the one she had left.

With so much to dazzle them outside their window, they were actually pleased when the bus was forced to squeeze into one, slow-moving lane of vehicles on the northbound side of the old freeway. Bicycle and pedestrian traffic swirled on both sides in increasing numbers. This, too, was a novelty for Susan, and she watched the gaily dressed travelers, and the variety of loads the cyclists pulled behind them, with the same fascination as Jess had on his first trip.

They were dropped off on Mt. Shasta's main street, and strolled the few blocks to Cheryl's shop. On the way they passed the town's manufacturing hub, reminiscent of something out of the medieval era—rows of shops that displayed goods crafted on the premises: shoes, furniture, pottery, a wide variety of clothing items, breads, candies, and all manner of delectable pastries. Some, particularly the food shops, were quite clean and presentable, but most of them lacked the fresh, gleaming sparkle of the little shops in Berkeley. Some, indeed, had a rather grimy appearance, reflecting the priorities of their owners. Jess and Susan peered through one unwashed window and saw, sitting at a cluttered workbench, an old man stitching a sole onto an elegant, high-topped woman's

---

*The quote is from the first sentence of a 19th century novel set in Siskiyou County, *Life Amongst The Modocs*, by Joaquin Miller.

shoe. Working under the light of a little bulb dangling from the ceiling, he seemed an island unto himself, oblivious to anything but his work. A potter farther down the street had set her wheel right at the shop window, and they watched in fascination as she fashioned a bowl out of a whirling mass of clay. Although she was in the public eye, she worked with the same quiet preoccupation as the old shoemaker.

Each shop had its own little story, its own little drama of patient, careful work in the pursuit of some modest little dream. Had they not felt the frenetic pace of the city still pushing them forward, Susan and Jess could have spent several hours browsing among the shops and learned something of these dreams, from shopkeepers who loved to show off their skills and their carefully crafted products.

Walking briskly past the newspaper office, they saw Jonathan Brill seated at his desk near the window, alternately glaring out at passersby and frowning at the papers on his desk.

"My, he looks like a friendly sort," Susan commented as they walked past.

"Oh, you just have to get to know him—then look out," Jess chuckled.

On his return to the little mountain town, Jess was struck by the similarities in clothing styles favored by these villagers and the Berkeleyites. Both favored natural fabrics in subdued earth tones, and hats were popular with both men and women. (In Berkeley berets had been the predominant choice for both sexes. Up here Australian bush hats and Stetsons were the choices for men; elegant straw hats with creative trimmings were favored by women.)

In Berkeley the retro tie-dyed look had added a dash of color. In Mount Shasta it was the ubiquitous cyclists who provided color on the streets, both in their dress and in the banners and ribbons that streamed from their bikes and trailers.

Cheryl and Kathy's clothing and fabric shop, From Ewe To You, was on a side street between a bookstore and another pottery shop. On this particular afternoon, the shop was bustling with customers, nearly all of them female, and the cacophony of voices was almost deafening. Several tables in the middle of the shop were piled high with fabrics, others with knitted vests and sweaters, while a multitude of hats in various styles sprouted from pegs mounted on the walls. Racks of dresses and skirts ran all around the shop's perimeter.

When Jess and Susan entered the shop, Cheryl and a woman wearing a forest-green felt hat with an eagle feather sticking out of it were talking over the counter. A couple of large, brand-new-looking earthenware bowls were sitting on the counter between the two women, and Cheryl was handing over a large bolt of dark brown cloth.

"You've got at least one more this size coming before I've got these bowls paid off, Ginny. And for goodness' sakes, take those beautiful place settings out of your window, or I'll end up owing you half my stock!"

They were both chuckling at this deft little compliment when Cheryl looked up and saw Jess and Susan. She beamed and held out her hand.

"Welcome back, stranger," she said. "I must say, you're looking a lot better than the first time I saw you."

Jess grasped her hand and held it. It was good to see her again, that round, rosy face, and those warm, inviting eyes. Over the din and confusion, Jess managed to introduce Susan. Then they exchanged introductions with Cheryl's neighbor, Ginny the potter, who in turn made way for a woman who introduced herself as "Nancy the candy lady," who purchased, with some cash and two boxes of caramel chews, a swatch of bright red dress material with white polka dots. While Jess and Susan stood watching, a never-ending stream of customers filed past the counter as Cheryl cut material and made change. (In the twenty minutes or so Jess and Susan lingered in the store, Cheryl collected, in addition to the bowls and the candy, six handmade candles and three freshly baked loaves of bread.) Finally, during one short break between customers, Cheryl arranged to meet them at the nearby coffee house after she closed up the shop in an hour or so.

Even before they entered the coffee house, Jess could hear the booming voice. Rufus Pitbottom, the cantankerous old rancher he'd met during his previous stay, was holding forth inside. Rufus was the center of attention at a small table—well, really, the center of attention of the whole coffee house. Stopping by for his regular afternoon coffee break, he had happened upon a table of tourists passing through from Seattle, and right now he was engaged in his favorite sport, known locally as "Rufus scares the hell out of 'em."

"Yessir, around here if a gal ain't pregnant by the time she's 15 she's considered a ole maid."

"Isn't . . . isn't that a trifle . . . young?" came the tremulous voice of one of Rufus's table mates, a stylish, 30-something woman in a light green-and-pink single unit outfit.

"Heck, we say if they can menstree-ate, they can pro-cree-ate." There was an audible gasp not only from the immediate table but from several others in the room. The half-dozen or so coffee house regulars were either stifling smiles or nodding along with everything he said.

"Up here we breed cattle, pigs and kids. I guess you could say we're into the nat'rul order of things. 'Feed her if she's a breeder,' is what we say up here. In the cities, women have got the idea that they oughter be educated, sometimes more than the menfolk, and workin' right alongside of 'em, even *above* 'em in some cases.

"Well, we jus' don't hold with that. What fer does a woman need ter learn to read 'n' write, if her man can? And workin' alongside the man at harvest time (if she ain't too pregnant) is allowed, even necessary, I'll grant you, but the rest of the time it's feedin' her family and breedin'."

Sometimes Rufus laid it on so thick that even the tourists caught on. Jess thought this might be one of those times, but so far the newcomers' faces registered only shock and disbelief. Evidently they thought that you traveled back a couple of centuries when you entered the mountain country.

"Well, I'm certainly glad *I'm* not one of your womenfolk," said a matronly, middle-aged woman at the table, getting up to leave.

"Now there's something we can sure agree on," Rufus called out behind her as she and her three companions headed for the door. The room was filled with laughter, from regulars and the remaining tourists alike. Jess and Susan sat down in the now-empty seats next to Rufus. Jess introduced the two of them.

Rufus fixed a broad, ingratiating smile on Susan. "Pleased to meet you. And don't mind me, ma'am, it's just a ole man's way of havin' a little fun."

"Well, you're one heck of an actor—at least I *hope* you were acting," Susan said. Jess could tell she had taken an instant liking to the grizzled old fellow.

"Why, thank you, ma'am," said Rufus, with a pleased look. "The way I look at it, I'm not only havin' a little fun, I'm also performin' a *service*. Those folks'll 'preciate Seattle more when they get back home, not havin' to deal with characters like me up there, and that'll *keep* them there, so we can enjoy our backward ways and pris-teen nat'rul beauties—both the female and mountain variety—without a lot of city folks moving here and tryin' to change things."

"Well, don't look at us, Rufus. We're not about to move up here, are we Jess?"

"Nope, not a chance."

"Oh, don't get me wrong. I don't mind a few folks movin' up here. Your friends the Shawntrees are fine people and I'm proud to know 'em and have 'em as neighbors. But you get too many of 'em movin' here and it spoils what they come here for, and for the rest of us, too. And then they try to tell us how to run things once they get settled in here. They want all the roads to be just as pris-teen as they were in the city, and they want a brand-new community building, and a new city hall, and I don't know what-all, and pretty soon us natives can't afford to live here, the taxes are so high. So I say let 'em think we're still livin' in the Dark Ages if it keeps them in their cute little domed towns."

Cheryl appeared in the doorway and waved. As Jess and Susan got up to leave, Susan patted Rufus on the head, leaned down and said softly, "You can growl all you want, you old bear, but you can't scare me." The eyes that looked up at Susan from under the bill of the old fishing cap were those of an adoring puppy.

The three of them squeezed into the front seat of the old truck, and rattled and bounced over roads lined with cracks and dotted with potholes. As they drove over the narrow old roads, Cheryl provided a running commentary on the farms and their crops.

"Over there, the two-story house with the faded green paint, that's the Baker place. Just startin' to harvest their potatoes—Yukon Gold variety, so rich in carbos most folks don't even bother to butter 'em. It'll be a few more months before we see any of their eggplants or crookneck squash at the market, though.

"And there's the Gentree farm, over on the left. Moved down here five years ago from Portland. Had their share of problems. Wife went back to Portland after the first year, moved back just in time to kick out the 20-year-old gal who'd been doing their house-cleaning. Anyway, they had good luck with white corn and snow peas this year.

"Over there's the Villagrossas. He's working on his second or third novel, forget which. She's one of the mainstays of the community theatre. Handy with a saw and hammer and a darn good actress, too. Versatile—does aristocratic types as well as sluts. Good crop of chard and spinach this year, from the looks of it."

Finally the big white house came into view. Cheryl said, "Don't mind William if he seems a little distracted. He's knee-deep in asparagus right now, and after that it'll be different kinds of greens and then some tomatoes and I don't know what-all. Things get a little crazy around harvest time."

Jess didn't say anything about it then, but he had an urge to pitch in around the farm again, between sightseeing trips with Susan. He had romantic notions of working up a good, honest sweat under God's blue skies for a few hours each day. The way he envisioned it, it would be a pleasant, *au naturel* version of his weekly workout in the gym.

When they stopped at the end of the driveway, near the barn, the harvest day was starting to wind down. There was still a hub of activity around the asparagus cleaning and sorting stations, which were located right next to the barn. As they pulled up in the truck, William drove by in the tractor, its hydraulic front lifts stacked high with trays of asparagus. As they watched, William unloaded the trays, whose bottoms were made of wire-mesh screens, on a sturdy table right next to a gleaming new porcelain basin about the size of a bathtub.

Jess recognized Tim Stillwater as one of the two young men placing the trays on top of the basin and hosing down the asparagus. His sister Rachel was at the next station, sorting and packing the stalks with a young man about her age.

Cheryl explained that the whole crew, including William, had spent the morning hours working their way down the rows cutting the tender asparagus stalks. Then, after a hearty farm workers' dinner, they had spent the afternoon on the cooler work of washing and packing.

William brought the last load of asparagus trays in from the field, dropping them on the table for the washing crew. Then, all bustle and energy, he hopped off the tractor, and in the space of a few minutes, gave Jess a big hug, welcomed Susan, and headed back out to the fields with a gunny sack draped over his shoulder to cut a few more bundles of swiss chard for tomorrow morning's market in Yreka.

"I reckon we'll still have time to throw back a couple bottles of our home-brewed ale, and maybe get a little somethin' to eat," he called back over his shoulder.

The three of them stood there in the lengthening shadow of the barn, chatting and idly watching the four young workers.

"These kids have been working around the farm since they were little tykes. For them, it's like tyin' their shoes," commented Cheryl. "Heck, Rachel or Tim, they could run this place if they had to. 'Course, they've got other interests. For Tim, it's baseball and horse-jumping. Not too much with the girls as yet, near as I can tell.

"Now Rachel, that's a different story. Boys are a kind of hobby with her, I guess. The latest one's standing right next to her," Cheryl chuckled, then added in a stage whisper. "Her flavor of the week. At her age, you know, she changes 'em like dresses—or costumes. The only things she's really stayed with over the years are her horses and her acting."

Jess watched absentmindedly as Rachel and her companion, carrying on a spirited conversation all the while, packed the asparagus into pyramid-shaped boxes. He thought of his conversation with her that night out at the stable. What a glorious life it must be—to be high-spirited and beautiful, to have your pick of boyfriends, and ride off whenever you wanted into these majestic mountains. She was in some ways the perfect expression of the region: wild and beautiful, with those long flowing tresses of dark hair and strong, sensuous, beautifully shaped legs bronzed by the sun.

Apart from admiring her obvious physical charms, Jess's appreciation of this free-spirited creature was similar to what he might have felt watching a deer in flight, or a soaring hawk.

And with this high-minded, lofty view of the young woman, Jess felt not the slightest twinge of jealousy or envy as Rachel walked off hand-in-hand with her young man when the day's work was done.

And when her lovely face, framed by dark curls, appeared to him as he was drifting off to sleep that night, he took this vision as a gift and nothing more.

CHAPTER X: REVELATIONS

*T*he next day was one of exploring. Early that morning, Jess and Susan hopped in the truck with Tim, who was taking a load of produce down to Redding. They got out of the truck just south of Dunsmuir, and, following Tim's directions, walked a short way along a paved road until they got to a dirt road, likely an old logging road, that led to the north side of the rugged Castle Crags.

The path was mostly in shade at the start, winding through a forest of incense cedars and pine. The novelty of being surrounded by tall trees, of breathing the crisp morning air filled with the muted scents of timber and pine needles, served to lift their spirits and push them along the path with seemingly little effort.

A creek ran roughly parallel to the road they were following. On the other side of the creek were the massive crags. There was still snow on their crests. The water from melting snow in the upper reaches of the crags had over the eons carved smooth streambeds out of the rough granite, and these creased the steep slopes all along their rough facade. Along each steep watercourse there were frequent waterfalls, and these had scooped out little green pools at their bases, so that each slender stream of water was laced with shimmering aqua-green beads from one end to the other.

In this mating of rock and water, it was the water, softer and infinitely more pliable, who had her way, always shaping the rock to meet her own ends. Splashing down the granite walls, sometimes taking great leaps, then pausing to rest in the pools below, she sculpted and polished as she made her way down the watery path.

Jess led Susan to a spot Tim had described. They crossed the creek at a point marked by two boulders, each having the shape and features of a human face—if you used a little imagination. Between these two boulders a tributary creek ran into the one they had been following. This tributary creek was one of the crags' spillways. Tim had described this one as a "stairway to heaven," which offered increasingly spectacular vistas as you climbed upward.

Tim had also told them of a local legend, going back to the time of the earliest white settlements in the region. As the legend had it, the two boulders were the petrified remains of two brothers, members of a tribe of giants who'd lived thousands of years ago in the crags. These brothers had constantly quarreled and fought with each other. Their father had put up with this for as long as he could; finally, in a violent rage, he had thrown them bodily out of the house. They went tumbling down the spillway, their bodies torn to pieces as they bounced down the rocky pathway. Only their severed heads made it all the way down to the bottom of the spillway, and there they rest today.

Tim had added, "If you climb high enough, you'll see their ancient home."

So they climbed along the small creek, which grew steeper with each step. As they climbed, the flowing water was gradually transformed from a relatively placid mountain stream into something rougher, rawer, more elemental. The forest and the undergrowth receded, and the two climbers' line of sight extended all the way to the very tops of the crags. Here, there were few boulders or rocks of any sort lining the bottom of the watercourse—only the rushing, foaming water passing over smooth, polished rock.

They did pass one large black boulder standing by itself in the middle of the watercourse. A thin film of rushing water covered it, managing through a kind of liquid alchemy to transform the rock into a huge black gem, glistening in the sun.

In this barren, majestic landscape, all was rock and water, water and rock. As they stood next to the rushing water, Jess felt he was as close as he'd ever been to the elemental forces of nature. The sound of water rushing over rock was the music of the eons.

As they climbed higher, they were rewarded with closeup views of the shimmering waterfalls. They appeared as silvery bands of sparkling water from afar, but up close one could see that they were a collection of cascading streamlets, and even these divided into thousands of shimmering droplets as one drew even closer—all of this somehow united in a beautiful cascading ballet of constant movement.

They were taking a rest while admiring a deep, dark-green pool at the bottom of one waterfall. Jess looked up and saw a massive, rectangular-shaped granite boulder perched on a ridge high above the waterfall. Its square corners had no counterpart in the roughly hewn crags above; it looked as if it had been dropped there from some other world. Or built by a race of giants. , ,

As Jess and Susan hiked down from the crags that afternoon, they spoke little. Jess was awed by the experience; he could not even begin to put it into words. He had entered a new world, one that had remained essentially unchanged for millions of years. He had penetrated to the very center of things, had seen nature stripped down to the very core of its being.

It was as if he had entered a cathedral with a tourist's anticipation of stained glass windows and vaulted ceilings and polished wood and instead come face-to-face with God himself.

* * *

Jess and Susan arrived at the farm late that afternoon, after walking part of the way and hitching a ride with a neighboring farmer returning from making deliveries in Dunsmuir. Right away they noticed that things were not quite as they should be. Tim, who had returned some hours ago, was maneuvering the tractor between the fields and the cleaning and sorting operations. The young man he had worked with yesterday was doing the cleaning by himself. There was no sign of William.

They stepped into the empty kitchen and headed into the living room, when they heard low moaning sounds—William's voice—coming from upstairs. The plaintive sounds were accompanied by Cheryl's voice, soft and murmuring.

Jess went partway up the stairs and called out, just loud enough for Cheryl to hear: "Cheryl, what is it? Is there anything we can do?"

There was a short pause, and then Cheryl's strained voice in a short, clipped response: "I'll be down in just a minute."

Jess and Susan exchanged worried, questioning looks. Cheryl came down after a few minutes, her face drawn. Forcing a tight little smile, she said, "Nothing too serious, but he's in a lot of pain right now. As he was hauling a load of asparagus, one of the trays started to slide off the lift, and when he stopped the tractor and went over to push it back into place, it toppled off. One corner landed on his right foot, crushed it pretty bad.

"Doc Burnham came right out and took a look at it, said the ankle and a couple of the toes were broken. William's supposed to stay off it for a couple of weeks. Then, with the doc's okay, he can hobble around on crutches for a couple more weeks 'til everything's healed."

CHAPTER XI: THE HARVEST

Cut-grab-drop. Cut-grab-drop. Cut-grab-drop. Cut-grab-drop. After nearly two hours, Jess had become absorbed in the rhythm of his work: Cut the asparagus stalks with the newly sharpened knife, just below the soil; grab the freed stalks in the middle with your other hand, being careful not to break off the tips; and drop them in the nylon sack supported by a shoulder strap and looped to your belt.

The rhythm was broken only when the 40-pound sack was full, and Jess half-dragged himself and the bag over to one of the trays, and, getting on his knees, carefully doled out the contents, again being careful not to break off the tips.

Susan had offered to help nurse William during the daytime, freeing Cheryl to tend to her shop. She would also help harvest some of the specialty items of produce, including chard, that Tim was to take to the markets in Mt. Shasta and Dunsmuir later in the week. Jess had started in the fields at 7, and it was now not quite 9, but sweat was already soaking through his shirt and pants.

Although there were five of them out in the asparagus fields, for Jess there was only the long knife, the tender green stalks of asparagus shooting up out of the soil, and the hot sun. Once, he heard Rachel's easy, lilting laugh, and her image flashed through his mind, but it was soon erased by the glint of the knife blade in the sun and the constant rhythm of the work.

On the second morning Jess woke up with with muscles stiff from stooping and reaching. As he went through the movements of the harvest, he felt as if he were trying to push an old, creaky, rusted-out piece of machinery down the rows. But the sweat that ran down his front and back after an hour or so seemed to lubricate the rusty joints, and after a couple of hours he was able to go through those same motions with a little more ease and fluidity.

The more youthful members of the crew seemed to have energy to burn. Rachel's favorite game, after dumping her load of asparagus at the end of a row, was to sneak up behind you and startle you by suddenly shouting, tickling you, or placing her hands in front of your eyes. Jess at first resisted this horseplay, but his thin veneer of grownup dignity soon yielded to the young woman's spirited sense of fun. After one of her surprise attacks, he snuck up behind her and roared, eliciting a scream of surprise and delight when she saw asparagus spears wedged in each of his nostrils. That, in turn, earned him a cold shower from the garden hose later that afternoon.

They ate their midday meal together at a round wooden table under the shade of a large oak behind the house. The lunch was high on carbohydrates—cream-style corn, potatoes, homemade bread slathered with butter and jam, and hefty slices of cherry pie. Susan and Jess did little talking. They mostly listened to a lot of high-energy teenage gossip about who was dating whom, who was likely to make the high school sports teams, who was doing what that summer.

Some of their talk struck Jess as unusual, compared to his own not-so-distant teenage years in Sacramento. For one thing, their conversation touched on people other than their peers. There was some rather malicious gossip about some of the farmers in the area. These young people, who considered themselves experts in the ways of husbandry, took perverse pleasure in recounting the foibles of greenhorn farmers newly arrived from "the domes."

But they also took at least a passing interest in the ebb and flow of events in their community. The hiring of a new clerk at the post office, the illness of the lady who sometimes helped Kathy and Cheryl at the shop, and the possible leasing of Rufus's ranch by a couple from the Bay Area, were all mentioned in passing, the oral equivalent of the short little paragraphs in Jonathan Brill's "Town And Country" column in *The Eagle*.

And there was a serious undercurrent running in and around the talk. During the course of this leisurely meal, Jess and Susan learned that both Tim and Rob, Rachel's boyfriend, were planning careers in farming. Tim had been told by his father that he could take over the management of the Stillwater operation if he was still interested in doing so when he turned 25. Rob, the youngest of three brothers, might either share the running of their farm or strike off on his own; at 21, he wasn't sure which.

On the subject of careers, Rachel revealed that she not only wanted to act in plays, she wanted to write them (perhaps inspired by the plaudits she'd received for "Real People"). She would do most of her scriptwriting in the winters, between acting jobs. Her plays would be "funny, clever, witty stuff about the way people really are."

"Well, there goes my reputation," Tim commented dryly.

Phil, Tim's friend, was a budding geologist. Someday he hoped to explore the inner core of Mount Shasta, which was still a smoldering volcano, as well as other active volcanoes around the world. He held the little group spellbound while he recounted, with an enthusiast's attention to detail, explorations of volcanoes with a recently developed two-person capsule capable of boring through lava rock and withstanding temperatures in the molten lava range.

"They've done laser probes that indicate the presence of vast caves near the mountain's base," Phil said in hushed tones. "There's been a local legend that there are people living inside the mountain—people from the lost continent of Lemuria who escaped some ancient, worldwide floods by holing up there, and just never came out. Now we'll find out if they really exist."

"Oh for God's sake, Phil, that's just a bunch of woo-woo fantasy stuff," scoffed Tim. "Nobody really believes any of that nonsense."

"Hey, you never know," Phil chirped. "We scientists try to keep an open mind . . . unlike some of you thick-headed farmer boys."

"Well," said Tim with a wry smile, "all I can say is, if they're down in there somewhere, they must have one heckuvan air conditioning bill."

Before they headed back to work, Jess couldn't resist bragging a little about his own career in deep space exploration. Within the next few years, he told them, he would be part of the Earth-based team monitoring a space mission to Proxima Centauri, the star nearest our own solar system. He alluded to the complex communications and tracking systems that would be needed for such a project, and dropped a few names, including that of Lionel J. Westover, former chair of the Astronomy Department at Berkeley, who was heading up Robo-Remote's Deep Space Exploration team.

But despite the dazzling technology and the awe-inspiring distances and the name-dropping, his listeners did not seem much interested. Phil's image of a small two-person capsule venturing to the center of Mount Shasta, *their* Mount Shasta, had stirred their imaginations—what mysteries *were* enclosed in that mountain? It was their natural curiosity about a familiar but mysterious object. These kids could speculate about the long-buried secrets of Mount Shasta the same way they wondered what Mr. Benson, the high school's straight-arrow principal, did on those weekend getaways to Portland. But who cared about a star twenty-five trillion miles away? That required an abstract kind of curiosity, the kind you had to work at, because you wanted to get an A in your high school science class, maybe, but the curiosity that came naturally and easily to these kids revolved around the universe that was right in their own backyard.

Tim's rather laconic comment was, "You'd better hope the government doesn't run out of money before your robots get there." He had a point. The U.S. government, which was funding the project, had had to slash its budget drastically in the last couple of decades due to the declining national economy.

* * *

Cheryl hadn't said anything to Jess or Susan or anyone else about the looming mortgage payments, the larger payments Mr. Griffiths and the bank had been patiently waiting for.

Old Mr. Griffiths had finally made it out to the farm, shortly after Jess had made his surprise appearance a couple of years ago. Tom Griffiths still had the ruddy look of a man who had plowed fields in the blazing sun year after year; he'd only been riding a desk, after all, for ten of his 68 years. He had cast an experienced and wary eye on the rows of asparagus seedlings; he knew, of course, about the Portuguese peppers and the other exotic plants that had been tried before, and William and Cheryl had braced themselves for the worst.

Mr. Griffiths had cleared his throat, and with a little half-smile playing across his thin lips, had said, "Well, I have no doubt that you folks believe in the viability of this asparagus crop, but I have to remind you that you've tried out new crops before that you thought were guaranteed money-makers . . . "

"Yessir, but I'm confident . . . "

"Oh yes, I know you are, William," Griffiths had said, gently cutting him off. "Of *course* you're confident. You *have* to be, because right now about all you've got is your confidence—'a smile and a shoeshine,' as my grandpa used to say." For an instant William had a dismal vision of Cheryl and himself back under the dome. He tried desperately to think of something to say that would persuade Mr. Griffiths to give them a little more time. . . .

But the banker was smiling broadly now, patting him on the arm, and what he was saying was so unexpected that at first neither one of them could quite take it all in. "But I'll tell you what. I'm gonna bet on you and Cheryl for the next couple of years, because I think you just might pull it off. I've been in this banking business long enough, hell I've *lived* long enough, to have a kind of sixth sense about whether someone's got the grit to pull something like this off.

"And we need folks like you up here, who are bustin' to try new things, maybe out of guts or desperation. In your case I suspect it's a little of both.

"So I'll tell you what, folks, the bottom line is, you've got to keep up with the interest, and come springtime in '49, we'll be expecting something regular on the principal. Fair enough?"

They were so ecstatic they had to restrain themselves from hugging the rugged old banker, but now here it was, two years later, and they had to deliver the goods. That was why William's injury, coming when it did, had been a serious blow. Cheryl had not wanted to burden Jess and Susan with these worries, but when they both volunteered to jump in and help fill the breach she had felt a sense of relief and gratitude.

When Jess came down early on what was to be his third day of asparagus harvesting, he found Cheryl looking out the kitchen window, her normally pink-cheeked face now chalk-white.

"Anything wrong?" he asked.

Cheryl didn't respond at first. She was, in fact, temporarily speechless. She didn't really want to believe what she was seeing, but she finally forced herself to say the word: "Frost." Soft and hesitant at first, not wanting to face the reality of it, what it meant.

Then, finally forcing the words out: "Frost. It'll kill the asparagus."

Within an hour the small crew was out in the fields, cutting furiously, slashing away as if their lives depended on it: Cheryl and Jess and Susan, as well as Rachel, Tim, Rob and Phil. (Ed had already headed for the Mt. Shasta farmers' market with yesterday's harvest of asparagus.) Every last spear of discolored, frostbitten asparagus had to be hacked off so that healthy new shoots could take their place. If the crew worked fast, only about one week's worth of crop would be lost—the new spears, shooting up at a rate of an inch and a half a day, would be ready for harvest in seven days.

Cheryl had taken a few moments when they were all gathered in the kitchen to tell them what she hadn't told them before: How much this season's harvest meant to her and William and the future of their farming operation, their own modest little dream.

With that for inspiration, Jess worked like a man possessed. All around him the others were hacking away at the limp little spears. HACK! HACK! HACK! Take that, you little bastards! HACK! HACK! HACK! The spears flew all over the ground around him. If he'd had the time, he would have gleefully ground them under his heel

After about two hours of this, Jess had to ease up. His energy was beginning to flag, and he paused and wiped the sweat off his face with his handkerchief. When he started cutting again, he settled into the slow, steady rhythm of the marathoner—this would, after all, be a task of several days' duration. At midday he gratefully joined the others under the oak tree. He and his fellow troopers, ravenous from the morning's carnage, dug into hamburgers and mashed potatoes and pies with all the gusto of a starving army, while Cheryl outlined the next few days' campaign.

"You guys are doin' great out there, just great," she said, her voice choking a little as she surveyed the circle of eager faces. "I figure about one more day of this all-out, and then four of us'll need to start putting the tomato plants in the ground." Cheryl and William had started the tomato seeds in big pots in January, storing them in the Stillwaters' two big greenhouses. It was a joint effort, and both families would share the proceeds. The idea was to transfer the plants outdoors in late April and start harvesting no later than early June, when the early tomatoes would fetch premium prices at the farmers' markets. The unexpected frost had thrown this project off by only a couple of days so far, and Cheryl was hoping that with a big push they could make up for lost time. And her motley crew seemed to be up for it—Rachel and Rob immediately volunteered for the tomato-planting crew, as did Susan.

The days that followed were long and intense and filled with hard physical labor, but this was eased by an atmosphere of festive camaraderie, as they teased and joked with one another in the fields and bantered back and forth over the heaping platters of food at midday. And, with their emergency task in the asparagus field almost completed, there were certainly reasons to celebrate.

Under Cheryl's direction, the work began to shift from the asparagus to the tomato fields, where row after row of small holes were dug to make way for the new plants with their still-pinkish-green fruit. One worker placed the plant in the ground and carefully tamped the earth down all around it, and then another would come up along behind and tie up the vines with strips of rags or pieces of string. Through this technique the vines would grow upward, making room for more plants in each row. Since there was now an almost-full moon over clear skies, this operation went on until well into the night. On the day the last of the spoiled asparagus was hacked off, Jess spent the evening tying up young tomato plants, amid the soft sounds of shovels working the earth.

Jess was impressed with the way Susan had plunged into this crisis. He was grateful, because he knew she was doing it essentially for his sake, because William and Cheryl were his friends. It was charming and endearing to watch this delicate, slender woman grapple gamely with shovel and trowel—and at the end of the day stumble through the kitchen door, her clothes and face and hair streaked with dirt.

That evening, walking back to the house, he made a decision: He would stay on a few more weeks, until William was up and working again. He was sure Susan would understand why he needed to stay on, why it was important for him to help see the Shawntrees through this crisis. He'd transmit a message to Robo-Remote tonight, before he went to bed, asking for a short leave of absence. He was sure Jessica could arrange it for him.

When the tomatoes were all in the ground, they had a few days of rest (except for Cheryl, who had to make up for lost time at the shop). William was still confined to his bed, and he and Jess passed some hours in idle conversation. William began by reminiscing about his life in Sacramento, thinking that might interest Jess, but Jess quickly shifted the conversation to other topics and seemed to be more interested in hearing about William's experiences since he and Cheryl had left Sacramento. Thinking about it later, the older man faulted himself for his insensitivity—the Sacramento debacle had not been that long ago, and talking about the city may have exposed wounds that were not yet healed.

But soon there was little time for idle talk. Fresh green life beckoned Jess and the others back to the fields, and the rhythm of the harvest began anew. Jess worked the fields in the mornings and took over what had been William's job in the afternoons—hauling the loaded asparagus trays from the field to the cleaning station. On the days when Tim took a load of asparagus and chard into Redding, Susan made a valiant effort to take his place in the fields.

Early one morning she and Jess emerged from the house together, he in his work clothes, she in city clothes. She was wearing a shimmering blue silk dress and a stylish white sunbonnet with a narrow brim. She was hopping a ride with Tim down to Redding. Later that same day, she would be catching a scheduled flight to the East Bay.

For the moment, with their different styles of dress, she and Jess made an odd couple. The contrast made Susan look all the more dazzling, a vision of shimmering blonde hair set against blue, her natural beauty enhanced by a newly acquired tan.

She had clambered onto the passenger's side of the truck. Tim was sitting patiently at the wheel with the motor running, staring forward.

"Safe trip," Jess whispered as he kissed her lightly on the cheek. "Thanks for being such a trooper." Then, half-apologetically, he added, "Some vacation, huh?"

Susan looked him full in the face and pulled him in for a long, lingering kiss. Then she let him go, leaving him totally speechless as the truck pulled away—and wishing very much that he was going back with her.

* * *

In the weeks that followed their labors shifted back from the asparagus field to the tomato crop, which was just on the verge of ripening. As Tim explained, even though the tomatoes were still pink, they had reached their full complement of sugar, and they needed to be picked soon, before they started cracking and while they were still firm and stackable.

So while Rachel and Rob stayed in the asparagus field in the mornings, Jess and Phil, and occasionally Tim, each toting five-gallon buckets, headed over to the tomato field. The old rags and strings they had tied around the tomato plants, by directing the vines upward, made for an easier harvest; you could pick the tomatoes with a minimum of stooping. Indeed, compared to the asparagus harvest, tomato-picking was a real pleasure, at times even a kind of sensual pleasure. Jess liked the feel of the firm little balls, the way their skins yielded ever-so-slightly to the pressure of his fingertips, allowing themselves to be plucked neatly from the vines.

In addition to the round, pinkish ace tomatoes, they also picked buckets of cherry tomatoes, and the slightly larger, oblong-shaped Roma tomatoes used to make tomato paste.

A few days after the beginning of the tomato harvest, with the yields dwindling in the asparagus field, they were joined part of the morning by Rob and Rachel. Jess had looked forward to this, having missed Rachel's laugh and her high-spirited playfulness.

But on this morning she was uncharacteristically subdued. He worked alongside her for awhile and tried to engage her in conversations about her horses, the theatre, dating, anything that came to mind, but nothing drew more than a few words in response.

At the midday meal she remained unusually quiet, as did Rob. Today most of the talking was done by studious-looking Phil, who had the beginnings of an erudite but rather wispy moustache. Although only 17, he was an engaging talker, because he was young and spoke of things that fired him with enthusiasm. He was largely inexperienced in life, and in his state of fresh-blooming optimism all things were possible.

Phil was going to study geology at Southern Oregon University in Ashland, after which, as he'd already announced, he was going to bore his way down through the center of most of the world's unexplored volcanoes. He thought he might take a few years off from volcano-exploring and do a little deep-sea exploration. The vehicles of exploration were quite similar, after all, and hopefully by that time, in a decade or so, a dual-media capsule could be developed capable of going to the bottom of the sea *and* continuing right down through the earth's crust to see what sort of rock the ocean's floor was composed of.

The young man envisioned a simple, pastoral home, a rustic

cabin near the base of Mount Shasta, where he could rest between adventures and examine his geologic findings. Perhaps he would lecture a bit, he wasn't quite sure.

There were echoes of Thoreau in this young man, who, at least at the outset, aimed for a simple life whose only real indulgences would be his elaborate explorations into the earth and sea. For the rest, he declared (a la the sage of Walden), "all you need is food, shelter, clothing, and good fellowship."

Rachel's friend Rob immediately picked up on that last word. "*Fellowship?*" he teased. " No female companionship? Why, I can't think of anything more romantic than a date in your cozy little capsule, heading down the middle of Mount Shasta," he said. "And then you can invite her over to your cabin to, uh, take a look at your lava samples." There was a sprinkling of good-natured laughter around the table which even Phil, blushing, joined in.

Rob looked over at Rachel for some sign of appreciation, but she stared blankly in front of her.

The next day, out in the fields, Jess was determined to cheer Rachel up, or at least elicit *some* sort of response from her. He proceeded very deliberately to pick the ripest, juiciest, most succulent tomato he could find. He snuck up behind her and tapped on her shoulder. When she turned around he reached up and carefully and thoroughly baptized her with the juicy globe.

She smiled as the red liquid ran in little streams down her face and said softly, "Just wait."

He didn't have to wait long. The next day, without warning, he felt pressure at the base of his neck, then both juice and pulp ran under his shirt and down his back while her hand finished the job, softly patting his back.

Jess reflexively reached into his bucket, feeling for a soft tomato. When his fingers had grasped one, he turned to face Rachel, who was looking up at him with a mischievous grin. Her eyes darted down to his hand. Realizing what he intended to do, she made no effort to resist. As the juice ran down her lovely face in tiny rivulets, she was oddly quiet, although her lips were parted ever so slightly as though she were on the verge of speaking. She moved in closer, her eyes questioning and inviting.

CHAPTER XII: PASSAGES

*J*ess had relived that moment with Rachel many, many times since his return to the East Bay. He could still feel the supple curve of her back, the soft pressure of her breasts. But what was really engraved in his memory was the way she had looked at him out of those bright green eyes.

In the days that followed his return from the Shasta region, Jess saw those eyes often, and they mingled with other images: with the luminous eyes of the old man on the hill, with the kaleidoscope of travelers on the old highway, the forbidding crags, with their cascading streamlets of water. The images would come crowding in, and he would have trouble focusing on the here and now, on his work; even Jessica sometimes faded into the background.

Only with Susan, when they held each other and made love and talked softly afterwards, was he at all sure of staying in the present, and even then he sometimes felt something tenuous and insubstantial in their relationship.

He was being pulled back up to the north country—yes, to that beautiful young woman with the glowing eyes—but it was more than that, although he could not have said precisely what it was about the land and the people of the Mount Shasta region that attracted him so strongly. Perhaps it was the basic honesty of these people who worked the land and lived in the shadow of its mountains and forests. He liked their directness, the feeling that in your dealings with them you were on solid ground. Certainly part of the attraction was the rugged beauty of the landscape, and the feeling that up there you were close to the wellsprings of life. And somehow it was all tied together—the rugged landscape, the harsh realities that stemmed from that environment, the basic honesty and directness of a people who had to deal with those realities, couldn't hide from them under a dome, couldn't erase them with the click of a button, nor manipulate them on a computer screen.

He hadn't realized he was drifting all those years in Sacramento and the East Bay until his feet had touched solid ground.

Susan, seeing the change in Jess, began asking those timid little questions that lovers do when they sense that things are not quite right. Jess was reluctant at first to share his restless thoughts, having a gut-wrenching premonition of where that would lead. But as the images kept crowding in on him, and the lure of the country up north became more and more irresistible, he finally blurted it out:

"I can't stay here, Susan. I want you and me to move up north."

Part of that was true and part of it, the second part, was what he *thought* he should say. He loved Susan, he loved her more than ever since they had rediscovered one another, but she was also part of a life he now wanted to leave behind. It was hard to imagine her living in the country up north.

Susan just stared at him, dumbfounded. Only a few weekends ago they had looked at a cute little bungalow just off Shattuck Avenue in a quiet tree-shaded enclave. She'd been going through it room by room since then, planning where their limited stock of furniture would go, what they'd need to buy, what color of carpeting would be best in the living room, the front bedroom. *That* was their future, as far as she was concerned, and now she'd been completely blindsided.

Choking back an impulse to scream, she managed to ask in a quiet, tightly controlled voice, "Jess, how would we make a living up there? I'm sure there aren't many banking jobs, and I *know* they don't have anything for Deep Space explorers."

"Well, we've got some savings, you know, and I'm sure the Shawntrees can use some help on the farm. They were struggling even before William got hurt."

"Jess, it was a wonderful, beautiful place to visit, and I'm glad we were able to help your friends while we were there, but I can't imagine *living* there." Actually, she could see Jess, with his brawny arms and muscular figure, carving out some sort of life there in the fields and the mountains, but she knew she wasn't fit for that kind of life. Susan liked the brisk, sometimes harried world of banking, the business lunches, the crisply pressed and well-tailored business suits, and the daily challenges of her very demanding job. Unlike Jess, she had no romantic notions about farming. Dirt was dirt, and gardening could be a nice weekend hobby, but it was no substitute for the challenges and satisfactions of running a modern office—dealing with the myriad personalities, keeping track of branch bank accounts on an hour-by-hour basis, putting out the fires, large and small, that constantly arose in an operation as sizeable as the Central Accounting Department at CalBank. She could not, even in her wildest dreams, see herself hoeing weeds and picking tomatoes on a farm in the Shasta country.

The solid underpinnings of her life were her job and her relationship with Jess. These were real and had meaning for her. The region up north was a beautiful but exotic place; it might as well have been Mars for all it meant to her.

They continued to talk, and, as Jess spoke of his dreams of building a new life up north, Susan was torn desperately in two directions. She wanted to be with Jess, but she didn't want to leave a successful career and move up into a kind of void. She could see herself clinging to Jess as her only real anchor up there, passing the time by washing dishes in the Shawntree kitchen and knitting sweaters in the Shawntree parlor while Jess went ahead and pursued *his* dream up there. She didn't see how she could share in that life as anything other than a junior partner.

They had a week of relatively calm discussions, with Jess's pastoral daydreams gently countered by Susan's practical objections. But one evening, when her nerves were frayed by a long, hard day at work, and after she'd heard the same, wearisome arguments too many times, Susan finally let go.

"All right, Jess, go, leave, go back to your precious little Eden! Forget about everything we've got here and what we've planned together, because when push comes to shove it's obvious that doesn't mean *shit* to you!"

"Susan, you know that's not . . . "

"No, Jess, I don't want to hear another word. I'm tired of discussing it. You go and do what you want, but I'm not . . . I *can't* go with you."

Susan skipped supper and went to bed early, crying herself to sleep, sad and lonely in the belief that she had lost something precious. Jess, seeing her distress, did his best to comfort her in the ensuing days. At one point he even reversed himself, promising he'd try to make a go of it in the East Bay after all. But they both knew this was just a gesture, one that sprung from love and tender feelings, but a gesture nevertheless.

After a few more tearful sessions they arrived at another period of relative calm. Jess, they agreed, would go up north and try living there for awhile, with Susan visiting as often as she could. More to avoid inflicting any further pain than from any real hope for their future, they left open the possibility that they would once again live together, either here or in the Shasta country.

So only a few months after they'd arrived back in the East Bay, Susan accompanied Jess to the bus terminal. Before the bus departed, Jess made most of the effort at small talk. Susan, having lost her family in Sacramento, and now, she was sure, her best friend and lover, was already withdrawing behind an emotional screen of anger and self-pity. She instinctively turned her cheek when he leaned over to kiss her goodbye.

"I love you," he whispered.

"I know you do, Jess," she replied, biting her lip to fight back the tears and to keep herself from saying, *but there's something you love more, isn't there?* On an impulse, as more tender feelings rose to the surface, she held out her hand and Jess grasped it eagerly and leaned in again to kiss her. This time she let him.

Jess, watching her from the window of the bus in the final moments before his departure, saw again the brave but frail slip of a woman just as he'd seen her when he first arrived. It was an image that haunted him all the way to Mt. Shasta.

CHAPTER XIII: SNAPSHOTS

*T*he market in Dunsmuir had barely opened, and already Ruby Stickner was calling out in her raspy voice to the stream of would-be customers passing by her stall. She had been the market's herb lady for as long as anyone could remember. It was a role that required a strong voice and an outgoing personality. Mrs. Stickner's voice had worn thin through years of overuse, but no one could ever accuse her of being a wallflower. In the other stalls, piles of bright yellow and green and red produce practically called out to the customers themselves, but a real sales effort was needed to move the dried-up bunches of grayish-green herbs, and old Mrs. Stickner, with her colorful bandana, full-length turquoise-colored pleated skirt, and white high-topped sneakers, was up to the challenge.

"You there! (to a gray-haired, wizened old man) You look like you need a little pick-me-up! Come on over and try my borage juice. It'll 'make ye glad and merrie,' as the old ones used to say.

"And (holding up a sprig with small, pointed leaves) don't forget to take a bit o' thyme for poor circulation." As the old man turned away, she called out mischievously toward his back, "Try some of my sage, old fellow, might even grow a few sprouts on that head of yours!"

Then, not missing a beat, she turned toward the next prospect: "You—yes, you!" (to a pretty young blonde-haired lass in a straw hat with fresh flowers wrapped around the band) Mrs. Stickner waved a bunch of delicate purple flowers. "Give him these in a tea mixed with honey, and he'll be yours until you find someone

153

better!"

The pretty young lady smiled and blushed but walked on.

"Tryin' to sell love potions to a young woman what has no need of 'em—now you're a smart one, aren't you?"

Rufus Pitbottom, wearing a pair of tattered overalls and a broad smile, had snuck up alongside the old woman. Lowering his voice to a conspiratorial whisper, he added with a wink, "*I'm* the one you arter be sellin' them love potions to!"

"What! Aidin' and abettin' a dirty ole man, they'd lock me up for sure! Better to sell you some o' my caraway seeds."

"Oh," said Rufus suspiciously. "And what would I be needin' them for?"

"Flatulence, you old fart! Aha, ha, ha, ha, ha!" Ruby doubled over with laughter at this *bon mot*.

When her mirth had subsided, she turned to the old man and whacked him on the back of the head. "Now get outta here and quit scarin' away legitimate customers, you ornery old cuss."

She was smiling as she said this and Rufus, taking his cue from that, said, "Now, now Ruby dear, don't get yer dander up. Can't a harmless ole man tease you a little bit? Ain't we known each other long enough to have a little fun?"

"Yeah . . . I reckon. Only I like to eat, too, and I ain't gonna have much on the table if I stand here all day jawin' with you."

"Well, you got a point there, old dame, I'll concede that. I'll get outta yer hair just as soon's you fill me in on the latest regardin' that niece of yours."

"She's about the same as she was last time we spoke. Not eatin', not goin' anywhere, layin' around the house all day. Lovesick as a bitch in heat."

"Ain't you got an herb you could give her for that?"

"Oh, there's lots of 'em, but she won't take 'em. You know how these young people are—she wants to lay around and moan and groan and suffer—all for the sake o' love."

"Well, I guess there's somethin' noble in that, but it seems like she just oughta go out and find herself another feller—this Jess guy has his eye on someone else, from what I hear."

"You're right for once, on both counts. I reckon she'll be all right after another week or so of moanin' and groanin', long as she don't come moonin' around here."

The young lady in question had been openly flirtatious with Jess a few times at the market, but that was nothing unusual. Young women flirted with him all the time, and Jess himself was blithely unaware that this had been anything more than a casual encounter.

While this one-sided romance was being discussed, Jess Renfree was just a few stalls down helping Jason Oglethorpe unload a truckload of watermelons and cantaloupes. Jess, who was living again on the Shawntree place and working on their farm, was also helping Ed Stillwater run the Dunsmuir market on Saturdays. In that role, he tried to be available wherever an extra hand was needed. The melon grower, who drove 40 miles from his farm just south of Yreka, was sometimes late to the market. His son had helped load the truck in the early morning, but, with school just started, he was no longer available to help unload, and Jess was pitching in.

"You're growin' 'em bigger and juicier every season," Jess said encouragingly as he helped pile the shiny green melons in a wide pyramid in front of Jason's stall.

"Bigger 'n' juicier 'n' *cheaper*," said the frazzled grower, sweat already streaming down his face and darkening the back of his shirt. Jason was a big, hulking man in his early forties. He wore big cowboy hats and spoke in a big, loud voice. It was a voice made for bellowing, for boasting, and for braying the age-old song of the toil and troubles of husbandry.

"I'm tellin' you, Jess, I'm not gonna drive all the way from

Yreka only to have these local guys undercut my prices every time. If I sell my stuff at the prices the Dunsmuir and Mt. Shasta folks are setting, why, hell, I'm practically working for free!"

Jess looked past the strapping figure of the farmer-cowboy to the overflowing bins of cantaloupe and watermelon. Jason had a habit of complaining in a loud and emphatic voice about some grievance, real or imagined, practically every market day, testing Jess's diplomatic skills to the limit. But the stuff he brought was first-rate, especially the succulent, juicy cantaloupes (eager customers were already starting to line up to make their purchases). Beneath the bluster, Jason was a hardworking, conscientious grower, and it was part of Jess's job to make sure he kept coming to the market.

"I'll bring it up at our monthly meeting, Jason. We agreed at the last one to boost melon prices, and it looks like they've gone up about five cents a pound."

"Well, that's just fine," Jason said sarcastically. "That'll just about pay for my gas, but it don't put bread on the table."

"I know, I know, and that's exactly what I'm gonna tell them. . . ."

"Well, see that you do, buddy. You got a nice little market here, but I can't just *give* my stuff away." With that he slapped Jess on the back and turned to the line of customers.

Jess unwound from this edgy encounter by taking a casual stroll through the market. He walked through the food vendors' stalls and savored the smell of the meat barbecuing on the big grills, the fat hissing and spitting as it dripped onto the coals. Mixed in with the smoky meat were the aromas of fried potatoes and onions and sausage and coffee from the breakfast diner, where folks sat at outdoor tables and downed greasy and abundant late-morning breakfasts.

A few kids and their parents browsed among the rocking horses and other wooden toys at one crafts booth. Strategically placed next door was the children's storytime booth, where a small circle of squirming children, seated in tiny little chairs, sat listening as a young teacher from the grammar school, Mr. Ficetti, read to them.

But The Joke Meister happened to be passing by at that moment, and the reading was abruptly interrupted. All the kids went running over to the colorfully decorated cardboard box that housed The Joke Meister. The Joke Meister was actually an extroverted young man named Artie Yee, a senior at the high school who had come up with the Joke Meister idea two summers ago as a part-time job. He had found the large cardboard box and cut a small hole near the top, to which he affixed a speaking tube. Then he had cut a softball-sized hole at the middle of the box. The way The Joke Meister worked was, when a coin or a paper bill or a tomato or a cookie or a sweet roll dropped through the hole into the canvas sack inside that caught all these offerings, Artie, aka The Joke Meister, would deliver a joke or riddle through the speaking tube. Many of these sprung from Artie's fertile brain right on the spot.

So there was a bit of scrambling while some of the kids ran from the storytime booth to find parents whom they could beg coins from. One of the kids, a red-haired girl who couldn't have been more than seven, already had a one-dollar piece clutched in her little paw as she strode from the booth to The Joke Meister. She carefully inserted it into the slot.

"Why do you need boxing gloves when you listen to my riddles?" asked The Joke Meister.

"I dunno," replied the girl, giggling through the gap in her front teeth as she said this and placing both her pudgy hands over her mouth in embarrassment.

"Because they always have a *punch* line."

This tickled the little girl. She giggled some more and, in the spirit of the joke, kicked The Joke Meister in the shins with her little pointed shoe.

"Yeow!" cried The Joke Meister. "I didn't say anything about kicking, did I?"

As if to correct her error, the little girl knotted her hand into a fist and delivered a solid WHACK! to the box. Then, apparently satisfied with the exchange, she strolled happily back to the story-time booth.

Another coin plopped into The Joke Meister's bag. This one was from an elderly man with a bulging string bag full of produce; he was making his regular weekly shopping trip through the market. A smiling, affable sort, it was his custom to drop a coin each week into The Joke Meister's slot.

"What goes up and never comes down?" came the query through the speaking tube.

The old man took off his baseball cap and scratched his grizzled dome.

"Be danged if I know," he said, a good-natured smile and a puzzled expression on his face.

"Your age!"

The man's eyes lit up in appreciation of the joke. "By God, you got that right," he said, dropping another coin in the slot and shuffling away.

Jess headed back toward the produce booths. On the way, he nodded to the two elderly sisters at their quilt booth. Jane and Sheila Bertoli both had such charmingly eager smiles on their faces; he wondered how they were able to keep up their enthusiasm hour after hour, week after week, when they might make no more than two sales on an average day. No doubt it was the trading that kept them going—you could get a lot of fruits and vegetables for one good-sized quilt.

On the outskirts of the produce section, he passed the Dartmoor booth, where young Sara Dartmoor, a sophomore at Mt. Shasta

High, was filling a customer's bag with peaches. She gave Jess a quick, friendly wave as she continued filling the bag. Sara was blond and had pretty, delicate features that reminded Jess of Susan, but her trim, muscular physique bespoke a vigorous life in the outdoors. Sara, her brother Tom, and two of their teenage friends trucked the produce in on Saturdays using bike trailers. For their efforts, their parents allowed them to keep half the proceeds from the Saturday morning market. This year, Sara's share of the proceeds would go toward next season's basketball and baseball uniforms, as well as a prom dress.

Just a few stalls down Rachel was staffing the Stillwater family booth.

"Hey lady killer!" she called out cheerfully as Jess approached her.

"Lady killer?"

"I was just talking to Rufus. According to him, Sally Jessup is pinin' away for you somethin' awful." Rachel, in her best theatrical style, fluttered her eyelids at him and uttered a loud sigh.

Jess was taken aback. "Sally *Jessup*!? Why, she's hardly out of diapers!" With a worried look, he asked, "She's not sayin' there was anything goin' on between us, is she?"

Rachel responded, with just the slightest bit of an edge to her voice, "The point, lover boy, isn't what she's sayin', it's what you two have or have not been *doin'*."

"Oh c'mon Rachel, if I was gonna fool around like that I'd at least look a little further than the high school playground, for god's sake!"

"Oh, that's right," Rachel said with a look of mock self-reproach, "I keep forgetting that half the girls around here are crazy about you. When you can pick and choose, I guess one more lovesick gal doesn't count for much."

This teasing could have gone on indefinitely. Jess, with his earnest and sometimes plodding manner, was a favorite target for the young woman's barbs. But they were distracted by a customer coming up to the booth. It was Mrs. Guntry with her brood of five. The oldest was no more than ten, and all were dressed in tattered, hand-me-down clothes. Mrs. Guntry, a short, squat woman in her forties, was dragging the youngest, Tommy, along by the shoulder of his thin brown windbreaker. She was in her usual state of disheveled irritation.

"One more word about goin' back to that goddamn storytime booth and you won't be able to sit down for a week. Now I mean it, dammit!" And with that she dragged the boy up to the stall.

As the other children cowered behind her, Mrs. Guntry grabbed a paper bag with her free hand and, deftly balancing it on top of a pile of yellow squash, began filling it with a variety of produce. All the while she kept a tight hold on the little boy's jacket, her grim expression melting into the semblance of a smile as she glanced over at Rachel and Jess.

"You'd think I was feedin' an army the way food disappears around the house," the woman said with a thin-lipped smile.

When she had finished making her selections, she finally let go of the boy and reached into the purse at her side. She fished around inside for awhile, finally pulling out a couple of wrinkled bills and thrusting them toward Rachel. Rachel knew that, as usual, she was a few dollars short but, as always, said nothing about that.

She just said, "Thanks Mrs. Guntry," and then, looking down at the children, said, "Do you kids want to help me get rid of those cantaloupes? They'll rot if you don't. Go ahead," she said encouragingly, "each of you take one." The children first looked to their mother, who nodded her approval, and then eagerly went over to the melons piled at the far end of the stall. Little Tommy was the last to reach up for one of the big, pink globes; its unexpected weight was too much for his small hands, and the ripe fruit fell to his feet, where it lay cracked and oozing juice and seeds.

"I mighta known, you little brat!" his mother yelled at him as she dragged him away from the stall. The child, who had started bawling the instant the melon hit the ground, was now letting out an ear-piercing wail that caused heads to turn up and down the length of the stalls.

"Shaddup, god dammit, shaddup!" yelled his angry, flustered mother, bending down to shake him roughly by the shoulders. By this time Rachel had rushed over with another cantaloupe.

"Here," she said, holding it out in front of the sobbing child, "this one's a little more his size."

"Nah," his mother said, brushing it aside. "Thanks, but you'd just be wasting another one." And with that she stood up and glared down at the child. The fact that a dozen shoppers had stopped to watch no doubt tempered her behavior, because she simply took the child's hand and strolled off, with the other four following along behind.

Rachel, with a sad, wistful look, had walked back slowly to the stall and replaced the cantaloupe. Sighing softly, she said, "Jess, do you know what I would really, really like, more than anything else?"

"What would that be—really, really?" Jess said, trying his best to sound cheerful.

"No, I mean *really*—seriously really. "

"Really, really, really, seriously really?"

Rachel grinned in spite of herself and gave Jess a playful poke in the ribs. "Stop making fun of me! But, really, what I would like is to fly over this whole town and bless everyone in it and make each and every one of them happy. Don't you think everyone deserves to be happy?"

"Well, . . . sure, I guess so."

"I know it sounds kinda dumb and hokey, but you can't help

but feel frustrated when you see those poor little Guntry kids every week and they're always dressed in the same old clothes she gets in the secondhand store. And she goes from one hard-luck guy to the next, never lasts more than a few months, and what with that and her drinking it just breaks your heart to think what those kids have to go through, when right across town they're kids with nice parents and a nice home and nice clothes. . . . It just makes me feel so helpless."

"That goes with having a big heart, Rachel. You've just got to accept that you can't help everyone your heart goes out to."

Jess could see that after venting her frustrations Rachel wasn't really listening to him. Sensitive and high-strung and idealistic, she sometimes withdrew into herself when faced with realities she didn't want to deal with. Jess hadn't been around Rachel all that much as yet, but he had already figured out one thing about her: With her upbringing on the family farm, that self-contained little oasis, she had developed somewhat unrealistic expectations about the world beyond it.

Jess reached up with both hands and gently turned her face toward him so that she was looking directly into his eyes.

"I know how you feel, Rachel. I may not have quite as big a heart as you, but I feel the same way sometimes. But you have something very few people have—and I'm not saying this just because I like you. You shine a light wherever you go."

Rachel gazed up at him with a questioning look.

Groping for words, he continued, "What I mean is . . . you have something in your spirit, in your aura, whatever you want to call it, that generates a feeling of happiness in people wherever you are. It's a rare gift. It's like having magical powers, even though you can't wave a wand and make everything better. . . ." Jess paused. He wasn't used to talking about things like this, and now he felt self-conscious and tongue-tied trying to capture the essence of this dazzlingly wonderful and mysterious woman.

"Anyway, all I'm trying to say is there's a sparkle about you that makes people feel better when they're around you."

He playfully tapped her on the tip of her nose, trying to think of something more to say but feeling awkward after his little speech.

Rachel came to his rescue. "You know, when I first met you, you kinda put me off with all that crap about testing and personality inventories. But I thought I saw something else peeking through. And, you know, I was right."

* * *

"Quiet, quiet, *quiet!*" Brett LaCrosse bellowed out the words as the sun began to set, drenching Mount Shasta in a luminous orange-red glow. The photographer was alternately checking his light meter and peering through the tripod-mounted camera at the mountain and the young woman in the foreground. There was an intense, maniacal look on his deeply tanned face as, hair flying, he jerked his head back and forth between the light meter and the camera.

"Brett, there's something I need to tell you . . . ," Jess said tentatively.

"And I need to tell you to *shut the fuck up* while I'm lining up this shot!"

Geez, the crap you had to put up with sometimes on these shots. . . . The fact is, Brett resented Jess's presence in the first place; just standing there, he was an annoying distraction. Brett, as an artist, had a special creative relationship with Mount Shasta, and when he was in the act of creating, blending his technical and creative powers with the awesome physical and spiritual power of the mountain, the last thing he needed was some *idiot* chattering away about . . . about God knows what.

In an ideal world, a world that respected true art, there would have been no Jess here, nor even, for that matter, Rachel. The fact that Rachel was posed between Brett's camera and the mountain was, admittedly, a concession to the realities of the marketplace. God knows you had to make those concessions if you wanted to make a living. The money, for a full-color calendar called "Natural Beauties Of The Northwest," had been too good to pass up.

"Okay, tilt your head just a little more to the left, dear, just a little itsy bit more—there! Hold it!"

Click! Click! Click! Brett had asked Rachel to tilt her head because the outline of her long, dark tresses had conformed almost exactly to the southern slope of the mountain, and by God he was not going to do anything that commercial, that *obvious.*

Next he had Rachel pose in profile against the mountain.

"Gimme just the hint of a smile, dear, something subtle, something Mona Lisa . . . . good . . . Hold it!"

Click! Click! Click!

Really, for a novice, Rachel Stillwater was a pretty good model. Well, she'd had acting experience—amateur stuff, but it showed. If only she hadn't brought along her stupid, distracting friend. Anyway, with the light fading—with the mountain bathed in beautiful, lush pastels—this was, oh God, a Van Gogh moment!

"Uh, Brett . . ."

"*Quiet*, goddamn it, *quiet*, or so help me . . ." Brett snarled the words through clenched teeth, his face quivering with barely suppressed fury.

"But Brett, you're . . ."

Summoning every ounce of self-control he had, Brett turned to Jess and said, in a tense, quavering voice, "Jess, I know you're trying to be helpful, but I've got about two minutes left at the very most to get a few more shots off before the colors fade. Okay? Now please, for the last time, *be quiet*!"

As Brett stepped back half a foot to get one last reading from the light meter, there was a crashing sound as tripod and camera toppled over on the tarp Brett had placed over the rocky ground. A short wire attached to a grommet at the edge of the tarp had gotten enmeshed in the laces of Brett's right shoe, a development that Jess had been trying to bring to the artist's attention.

Brett, speechless, stared in disbelief at the toppled camera and tripod. Jess, struggling mightily to suppress a smile, maintained a diplomatic silence. Rachel, who was undergoing a similar internal struggle, was afraid she'd burst out laughing if she tried to speak. So she quietly walked over to Jess and took him by the hand, and the two of them began the walk back into town.

Brett, left by himself, glanced forlornly from the mountain to the debacle at his feet. He was crushed; he had been on the verge of capturing a rare blending of light and color on the mountain. The opportunity for such a shot might not ever come again, he realized, sadly shaking his head. But despite his disappointment, there was already a feeling of sweet melancholy welling up inside him. Deep inside, he was glowing with the exalted martyrdom of the frustrated artist.

* * *

It was well into fall, and the first hints of cool weather were stirring in the breeze that wafted past the young man and the young woman. They were in no hurry as they walked down the path toward town. They stopped several times to look back toward the snow-speckled mountain. The first time, after looking back at the mountain, they turned to each other and laughed.

"Oh how the mighty have fallen," Jess managed to say before yielding to another fit of laughter. The two were laughing at the thought of Brett *the artiste* and his tangle of equipment; Rachel, her eyes watering, was laughing also from simple relief. She had known that doing the photo shoot with Brett was going to be an intense, nerve-wracking experience. When she'd expressed some of her doubts about the whole project to Jess, he'd gallantly volunteered to come along for moral support.

As the moon rose, they looked back again to see the mountain bathed in its soft light, and resumed their walk in a kind of reverent silence. They came to a spot, surrounded by thick undergrowth, where the trail leveled off before making its final descent to the paved road into town. They stopped once more, admiring the lights of the town, each quietly savoring the time alone together.

Jess broke the silence by turning to her and asking, "Still thinking about waving your magic wand over all this?"

Rachel's face darkened for a moment. "Oh Jess, I hope you're not making fun of me. I know you can't go around taking on all the world's troubles. But when you see something wrong in your own backyard, it's natural to want to do something about it. With the Guntry kids, though, it's hard to know *what* to do. Drop food baskets on their door every week? Buy them new clothes? Adopt them? I just feel so helpless and frustrated sometimes."

"Geez, it's a good thing you're not living in the East Bay. It'd tear your heart out to see the way some of those kids live, some of 'em not much older than the Guntry kids and living on food scraps and handouts and sleeping ten to a room."

"Oh Jess, I don't want to hear about it. Don't I have enough to fret about as it is? . . ." She bit her lip and looked down at the ground. "With all the bad things happening in the world, sometimes I just think I'm wasting my life. Especially with the theatre stuff. I get up there and wear pretty costumes and look pretty and have people admire me, and what good does all that do?"

"Well, for one thing, it must give people some enjoyment, or they wouldn't come, silly. And sure you're nice to look at, but being a good actress might have something to do with it, too, you know. And with all the bad things that *do* happen in the world, there's something to be said for giving people a few hours of pleasure, isn't there?"

"Well, I guess . . . " Rachel found herself being reluctantly persuaded.

Seizing the moment, Jess took her by her shoulders and, looking her full in the face, said, "You know, you're way too young and pretty to be going around all the time with gloomy thoughts like that. A beautiful young woman like you ought to be so filled with beautiful thoughts there isn't room for anything else."

Rachel had a playful smile on her face now. "Boy, listen to you! Sweeter'n a ripe peach in July. You start pourin' the honey around like that, no wonder you got half the gals in this town lovesick."

But I don't care about half the gals in town, Jess wanted to say as he slowly brought one hand up to her cheek and drew her in with the other. It had been awhile since he'd held her that time in the fields, but the small of her back seemed just as supple, her breasts just as softly yielding, her thighs just as wonderfully full and firm. And then he was lost in a tangle of dark curls and something warm and red and luscious.

CHAPTER XIV: CAPTAIN JACK'S STRONGHOLD

*T*he crowd gathered in the little coffee house that morning was the usual melange of ranchers, farmers and town folk. They were discussing the recent disaster in the East Bay. A crack had formed on the west, or bay side, of the dome. The crack ran 30 feet up from the dome's base, and had caused some minor flooding in the East Bay flatlands.

"They were darned lucky it turned out to be self-sealing," commented Cheryl Shawntree, taking a rare break from her shop. "At least there wasn't much impact on their air system." (After water from the bay had rushed in and filled the dome up to the top of the crack, the crack had been effectively sealed, posing no threat to the dome's air purification system.)

"Yeah, they were *lucky* all right," was the sarcastic comment from Bob Rawlings, a rancher from the Scott Valley, a little ways to the southeast of Yreka. He was a tall, thin, wiry guy sporting a brown Stetson and drooping moustaches that twitched when he was agitated. They were starting to twitch now. "If you call it 'lucky' to have your streets under water. Some of those folks are havin' to stay in makeshift shelters or with friends on higher ground. And you just mark my words—with the Sacramento thing a few years back, and now this, we're gonna see some of those dome people, the smart ones anyway, headin' up our way."

"Well now, that's all we need, ain't it?" Rufus Pitbottom was sitting in his customary spot at the counter, next to Rawlings.

"More city folk with their bright ideas, crowdin' the rest of us and drivin' up taxes, which are already higher'n a Mount Shasta fir."

"Oh, I predicted all of this years ago," said the editor of *The Mount Shasta Eagle* from his seat at the window. "Anyone could see these jerry-rigged domes wouldn't last—too many wheels within wheels, too many things to go haywire." As Jonathan Brill spoke, there was a shuffling of bodies around the room, as people positioned themselves for the usual give-and-take between the progressives at the window seats and the hardliners at the counter.

Jonathan added, "It's gonna be a real challenge to figure out how to accommodate the influx of people, given that we're startin' so late." This last remark was deliberately designed to get a rise out of those at the counter.

"Accommodate, hell," growled Bob Rawlings, taking the bait. "We start accommodatin' and accommodatin' and pretty soon *we'll* be cooped up in a goddamn dome."

"You got that right," Rufus chimed in.

"Bob, this county could easily double in population and you'd hardly know the difference," Jonathan responded, in his usual calm and condescending manner. "Oh, you might have some parcels cut up a bit, but I'll guarantee you that most of the folks comin' here are gonna want to live in town." He nodded toward the two people sitting across the table from him. "Not too many city folks are gonna be like Cheryl and Ed here and go in for farming."

"I got news for you, Mr. Editor, they're already comin' in, and I don't know about *workin'* the land, but *campin'* on it is more like it," said the rancher, with deep-throated anger in his voice. "In the last six months I've had to kick out about two dozen of 'em, most of 'em young. They've been settin' up camp in that grove of oaks near the main road. And I'll tell ya, that's just a down payment on what we're gonna have to deal with now that Oakland and Berkeley are partway under water."

Ed Stillwater, who'd been quietly sipping his coffee, finally spoke up. "I think you're all probably right: We're gonna see an influx of new people, and the question is, how do we deal with that? As Jonathan says, we need to start figurin' it out now, before they're right on our doorstep. Where're we gonna put more housing, more schools, more businesses?

"I know not everyone agrees with me, but the way I see it these folks are gonna have a lot to offer in the way of talents and skills, and they'll give this region a tremendous boost, a *tremendous* boost, if we can figure out how to integrate 'em into our community, and not treat them as if they were a bunch of mongrel dogs."

Bob Rawlings turned to face Ed and Jonathan from his seat at the counter. His face had turned beet red, but his voice was under control—just barely.

"With all due respect, Ed, I've got to tell you that folks just aren't gonna stand for havin' these nuts come up here and camp and piss and shit on their property. . . ."

"But Bob, I'm not talking about drifters, I'm talking about people with families, responsible . . ."

"Now just let me finish." Bob Rawlings had worked up a full head of steam and was not about to be sidetracked. "We've been up here, some of us, for generations, livin' off the land and takin' care of it, and those city folks went and fucked up their land, shot their valley all to hell . . ."

"But Bob, a lot of what you're talking about is due to global warming, and we all, all of us who drive anyway . . ."

" . . . shot their valley all to hell, you know, and shit, *they* got restrictions on people comin' into their precious domes—only so many per year—'population caps' is what they call it. . . ."

"Well, that's 'cause they've only got so much space . . . "

"Well, *we* only got so much space, Ed. So what I say is, they made their bed, now let 'em lie in it—and I ain't the only one who feels that way, neither."

"No, you ain't," Rufus agreed. "There's plenty of folks don't want a lot of outsiders comin' up here and messin' up Siskiyou the way they messed up the flatlands."

"What exactly do you have in mind?" Ed asked, addressing Bob Rawlings. "Hope you're not planning on taking the law into your own hands. I don't think folks would stand for that, either."

Bob Rawlings was losing patience, and the anger was back in his voice. "Ed, I'm gonna give you some friendly advice: This is a serious matter—real serious. We can sit around here today . . ." and he waved his hand to indicate the crowd gathered in the coffee house ". . . and discuss this whole thing in a nice, civilized way, and that's all well and good. But I'm tellin' you, Ed, there may come a time, not too far off, when you'd best just go quietly about your business and let us go about ours. People just aren't gonna stand for havin' their homes and their property invaded, and their way of life changed by outsiders."

Rawlings' aggressive style had put Ed on the defensive, and when he spoke again it was more in the form of a plea than an argument: "But I'm telling you, Bob, it doesn't have to be anything like an 'invasion.' You're just overdramatizin' everything. If we plan . . ."

"*Plan*—there, you said it. Let's just say, you got your plans and we got ours. Let's leave it at that, okay?" There was an edge in the rancher's voice that suggested any further argument would be futile.

After an awkward silence, the buzz of conversation resumed, gradually reaching its usual late-morning crescendo. For the rest of that morning, no one brought up the topic of the ruptured dome or its possible consequences.

* * *

The horses, loaded down as they were with food and camping

gear, proceeded at a slow trot over the rolling hills of the high desert country. It was the second day of their excursion, and Rachel and Jess were riding through the dry, sagebrush-covered country on the lower northern slopes of Mount Shasta, at an elevation of 5000 feet. The upper slopes of the mountain claimed as its lordly right the lion's share of rain and snow, leaving these lower slopes in its shadow thirsty and sparsely vegetated.

Rachel was riding Pilot, and Jess was on a mare named Alice, Pilot's stable mate. At the end of the day, they reached the Stewards' farm near the little town of Macdoel. The Stewards, who had a brood of five kids ranging from eight to 15 years old, seemed happy to have visitors. Although Jess and Rachel had arrived too late to join the Stewards in their evening meal, Jeb and Sara Steward insisted, after the horses were fed and watered and groomed, that the two of them sit down at the kitchen table and partake of what was left. And what was left was substantial: bowls heaped with cream-style corn, baked potatoes and green beans, all grown on the farm, of course, and all slathered, country-style, in butter, with a couple of turkey drumsticks thrown in for good measure. (It was November, and the Steward turkeys were in prime condition for the holiday slaughter.)

Macdoel was in a relatively temperate section of the high desert known as the Butte Valley, which was nestled in the Cascade mountain range. Irrigated by wells sunk deep in the rich sandy soil, the valley had been a little farming colony since the 1880s. With the general warming trend over the past 50 years, hardy crops like strawberries and potatoes had gradually given way to corn, melons, tomatoes and some green crops, although strawberries were still a popular winter crop.

The 80-acre Steward farm had been in Sara's family for over 150 years, and the land, formerly a lake bottom, was good growing soil, but after all the years of tillage it required a good deal of aerating and fertilizing.

Jeb and Sara were both products of that soil. They were lean and sinewy, and the long hours working the land had given them a physical vigor that was evident even in their conversation around the dinner table and in their lively, animated expressions.

Both were intrigued when they learned of Rachel and Jess's destination: Captain Jack's Stronghold, another two days' ride to the east. It was the site of ancient volcanic lava flows from Mount Shasta, and it was an altogether mysterious and romantic spot—perfect, Rachel had thought, for their first outing together.

From an intricate labyrinth of lava tunnels, a band of 60 Modoc Indians had held out against more than 1000 federal troops during the harsh winter of 1872-73. Rachel had come up with the inspired idea of camping in the middle of this natural fortress, in the very cave where the Modoc chief Kientpoos (or "Captain Jack," as the whites called him) had bivouacked.

Ever since she was a young girl, Rachel had felt empathy for the Indian tribes of the region, for their closeness to the land and the natural world, and for what seemed to her—looking back over a span of two centuries—their simple, joyful life. By taking Jess to this place where the Modocs had made their last stand she was sharing an important part of herself.

A feisty and warlike tribe, the Modocs under Captain Jack had been fighting for the right to remain in their traditional homeland, having just fled from a reservation they had been forced to share with a rival tribe. The Modocs were forced to evacuate the stronghold when their water supply, from nearby Tule Lake, was cut off by a line of troops positioned between the stronghold and the lake. The Indians were then captured in small bands as they fled.

"Mighty interestin' place, Captain Jack's Stronghold," commented Jeb Steward as Jess and Rachel topped off their repast with generous slices of chocolate cake. "Hard to believe those Indians could hold out as long as they did, outnumbered like they were. But once you see the place, you'll understand—the hands of man couldn't have built a better fortress."

"I figured it was time Jess had a look," Rachel said. "He's been so busy with the farm and the markets he hasn't had much time for sightseeing." She reached over and gave Jess's hand an affectionate squeeze. "I still remember when our 5th grade class went on a field trip to see it. Drove Ms. Rivera and the parents crazy once we got there. Some of the kids went and hid. Some of 'em they never did find. Had to flush 'em out by threatening to leave without 'em. The rest of us took turns being Modocs and Army troops."

Sara chuckled. "Yeah, it's a great place for kids. When our Tommy got back from a school trip there he spent a whole week building a 'stronghold' out of old boards and cardboard boxes and rocks. He was Captain Jack, of course, and by God he wasn't gonna let *nobody* turn him out of that stronghold. Claimed he had magic powers, like the Indians did, to stop the Army's bullets."

"Boy I'll tell you, when they hung Captain Jack and his sub-chiefs the white settlers cheered up and down the Siskiyous," said Jeb. "Can't blame 'em, in a way. Before the siege, those Modocs had been workin' a lot of mischief with the wagon trains that passed by Tule Lake.

"But it's funny how times change. Wasn't so long ago that the shoe was on the other foot, so to speak, and folks around here were *all* feelin' like a buncha Indians themselves, what with the fed'ral government taxin' 'em to death and tryin' to tell 'em what they could and couldn't do with their land. We *all* felt like we was under siege—until the national economy started to go bust and the government practically went broke itself."

"And it ain't much good for nothin' now, 'cept collectin' taxes and tryin' to stay afloat—and, oh, I almost forgot, keepin' the Chinese from invadin' us," Sara chuckled.

"Anyways, I reckon you two are in for a little adventure," Jeb
said. "You might want to keep your campfire burnin' all night—that
is, if you believe what some folks around here say. I've been hearin'
stories about Captain Jack ever since I was a boy, about how Captain Jack's ghost or spirit, whatever you want to call it, still patrols
the stronghold. And there're folks who say they've heard chanting
and war drums and I don't know what-all.

"Course, those same folks might have been *partakin'* of spirits
if it was one of them cold nights out there, so I don't put too much
credence in those stories," Jeb said with a chuckle.

"Well, *we* didn't bring any spirits with us. We'll just see if we
find any when we get there," Rachel said, dismissing the idea with
her own lighthearted laugh. She was thrilled with the idea of camping under the stars where the Modocs had made their last stand, and
she kissed Jess on the cheek and squeezed his hand in happy
anticipation of the shared adventure.

* * *

The day was crisp and clear as their two horses loped along the
shores of Tule Lake. The lake was filled with large flocks of waterfowl, mostly ducks, geese and coots. Occasional gatherings of big,
yellow-billed pelicans stood out among the smaller waterfowl. They
all seemed to be peacefully sharing the lake and enjoying the early
morning sun, although each tribe of birds was careful to keep a
respectful distance from the others.

In the early 20th century, long after the last Indians had been
driven off, the federal Bureau of Reclamation began draining part
of the lake to make way for more settlers, so that now Rachel and
Jess trotted past vast stretches of farmland where the waters of Tule
Lake had once been, waters that had once lapped the southern
reaches of Captain Jack's Stronghold.

They reached the small parking lot where tourists had once
stopped and had hiked the short distance to the stronghold. Weeds

grew out of cracks in the asphalt and sidewalk. There was a paved walkway leading up from the parking lot. At the spot where the walkway turned into a dirt path there was, from the days when this was a popular tourist attraction, an old display panel encased in glass; the glass was cracked. Behind it was a faded poster. The lettering on the poster had been bleached by the sun and was impossible to read, but there was a recognizable drawing of an Indian, presumably Captain Jack, next to that of an Army officer.

"That's probably General Canby," Rachel said. "He was shot by Captain Jack at a peace conference. Captain Jack was pressured to do it by his lieutenants, who figured, the way they were outnumbered, the only way they could possibly win was to kill their enemy's commanding officer. Didn't work, though. After five months, the Army finally forced the Modocs out by cutting off their water supply. Lined the troops up between the Indians and the lake, and that pretty much finished 'em."

They tied their horses to the display's posts, and unloaded their camping gear and provisions. Grabbing a couple of water bottles, they headed down the dirt path toward the stronghold to have a look around.

The path at first was bordered only by low-lying sagebrush. There was open country in all directions for miles. In the distance, mountains to the west and south converged on the snowy eminence of Mount Shasta. After they'd walked only a few hundred yards, reddish, rough-hewn lava rocks began to appear, strewn about here and there along the path. As they walked along, these rocks grew more numerous and imposing. They were entering the rocky defile that was the gateway to the labyrinth. Within a matter of seconds, they were plunging down from open country into shadowy, walled corridors whose rocky walls rose above their heads.

These corridors were the ancient pathways followed by streams of hot lava from an eruption near the base of Mount Shasta 30,000 years ago. The lava flows had cooled quickly on the outside, form-ing a tunnel as the still-liquid material in the center kept moving.

The walled corridor they were following wound its way in a semi-circle from east to west. At every turn there were natural lookout positions formed by gaps in the upper reaches of the wall, from which a defender would have been able to fire at will at enemy troops without exposing himself to return fire. Echoes from the ancient siege—war cries and the sounds of rifle fire—seemed to reverberate up and down the rocky passageway. At the end of the corridor, on a small knoll looking out over the surrounding plains, a small totem pole had been placed, and attached to it were colorful ribbons and offerings to the spirits of the long-dead warriors: coins, bird feathers, bunches of tule grass (during the Modoc fight, ropes woven from tule grass had been placed around the perimeter of the stronghold; the Modocs believed the rope's magical powers would prevent the enemy, and his bullets, from entering).

A short, open path through the sagebrush connected the portion of the stronghold they had just passed through to another lava passageway just to the west. They decided to change their plans and make their camp out here, between the two defiles, out in the open. The sun would soon be setting behind the long mountain ridge to the west. It promised to be a chilly night, but the prospect of camping in the old chief's cave was just a little too spooky. The ghost sightings Jeb Steward had mentioned had been easy to scoff at in his brightly lit kitchen, but now at dusk, in the heart of the old Indian fortress, they could not be so easily dismissed.

They decided, though, that in the spirit of the adventure they would build a campfire and cook their dinner in the sheltered opening of Captain Jack's cave, where he, his two wives and his daughter had huddled for warmth during that awful winter's siege. With a fire going, after all, it wouldn't seem so spooky.

They went back to the horses and rode them to the lake to give them a good drink and gather water for themselves. When they got back to the campsite with their gear, darkness had already settled in. They had gathered some dry twigs and brush along the way, and Jess hastily arranged some rocks to make a fire circle in front of the cave. One pot filled with polenta and another with beans were soon heating on a portable grill, and Rachel cut strips of green pepper to throw in. When everything was properly cooked, they threw it all into one pot, then spooned the simple but hearty meal onto their plates, and sat down before the fire.

A three-quarter moon had risen in the night sky, and the mouth of the cave and the surrounding lava outcroppings were bathed in an eerie mixture of silvery light and shadow.

"Wow," said Rachel, looking around as if she were taking it all in for the first time. "I think I'd go crazy if I were cooped up in this place for five months."

"Yeah, they must have really hated that reservation."

"Kind of funny, you know, that in trying to escape one trap, they ended up in another."

Jess looked thoughtful. He was gazing down at the fire. "Funny how that can happen, isn't it? I'd still be in the East Bay, probably, if it hadn't been for you, your mom and dad, and the Shawntrees. Would have gone from one trap right into another."

"Lucky you," she said, playfully kissing Jess on the cheek. "And lucky me."

Jess put his arm around her, gently brushing her hair to one side as he did so. He continued to look into the fire. "Yeah," he said dreamily, as if thinking out loud. "For most of my life I've been cut off and didn't know it." He looked up from the fire. "It's like . . . it's like if I'd lived in this cave all my life, never stepped out of it, and one day someone led me out and showed me the stars at night and the blue sky and the mountains. If you grew up with it, that's one thing. But to me it's still a wonderful, precious gift."

Jess smiled a quiet, inward smile. "I used to think of everybody up here as being kind of disconnected—you know, from everything going on in the world. But since I moved up here, I've come to realize it's the other way around. And the sad thing is, the people living in the domes are so used to it, they don't realize how cut off they are.

"You know, Rachel, when you think about it, it's really incredible that people down there choose to live the way they do, cooped up the way they are, closed off, not knowing from one day to the next if they'll be able to breathe or if they'll be treading water."

"Do you really think they *choose* to live that way?"

"Of course. It's not like they're forced to stay there. Look at the Shawntrees. They made a choice not to stay in the domes."

"That reminds me of something Dad said over dinner the other night. He's worried that a lot of folks from down there may start landing on our doorstep. Actually, he's not worried about that so much as the reaction from some of the hardliners who don't want a lot of newcomers moving in and taking over. I guess there's some talk of closing off the old highway for awhile."

"What!? Can they get away with that?"

"Dad seems to think so. He's talked to Sheriff Phillips, and the sheriff told Dad, confidentially, that he'd have to look the other way if he didn't want to start a civil war."

Jess thought of George Spanos, his former colleague at Robo-Remote. He'd received a transmission from George recently, out of the blue, saying that he was getting burnt out after six years in the PR department and was thinking about coming up to the Shasta region to scout around for "opportunities." He didn't mention the dome crack, but Jess had assumed that was a factor, too. He'd have to remember to get back to George when he returned.

And thinking of George made him think of Susan. Jess had

never been able to come right out and tell Susan that he had another relationship. The last time Susan had come up here, two years ago, he and Rachel had already started spending time together on a steady basis, but in an old-fashioned, friendly, chatty way. As he and Rachel grew closer, it had been easy to put off telling Susan. What, after all, was the need for that, with her 250 miles away? Why cause her unnecessary pain? And besides, maybe she'd found someone else after all this time. And, not to put too fine a point on it, but he and Rachel were still just friends, had not yet . . .

Well, there were all sort of reasons for putting it off, and now it didn't seem to matter anymore.

"So," Rachel was saying, "I guess there's gonna be a big meeting at the Grange Hall to decide what to do. Dad thinks it's a foregone conclusion."

Jess continued to stare at the fire. Out here in the far reaches of Siskiyou County, far from the East Bay, nestled in this ancient fortress, George and Susan and even the growing signs of trouble closer to home all seemed a long way off. Here at the lava beds there were echoes of human strife from long ago, but it was safely distant, buried by the passage of centuries; tonight their world was one of stars, and mountains, and miles of sagebrush-covered landscape.

When they had finished their simple meal, they scrambled up the path in the moonlight to the spot where they had laid their tarp and their sleeping bags. Their horses were tied to a nearby juniper tree.

This was the first cloudless night of their trip, and it was lovely to stretch out on their sleeping bags under the star-speckled sky.

He turned to look at Rachel. She was looking at him with a little smile on her face, her eyes glimmering, reflecting the night sky. They kissed softly, and Jess reached up to caress her cheek and stroke her hair. He had been anticipating this moment since they'd left the Strawberry Valley, how he would gently stroke her hair, just as he was doing now, and gaze long and lovingly into her eyes, eyes that now sparkled with starlight. For the first time in his life, beautiful strings of words . . . *word pearls* . . . came effortlessly into his head . . . *a universe reflected in her eyes . . . pools with no bottom . . . an endless universe beyond those eyes . . .*

His musings were interrupted when Rachel, harboring more down-to-earth thoughts, let out a little yelp and pulled him toward her. She gave him a fleeting kiss before unbuttoning his shirt and nuzzling against his chest. Then she worked her way upward with her tongue and lips, finally licking one ear slowly and tenderly before pulling his face in against hers and burying her eager tongue in his mouth.

Jess's poetic impulses vanished under this assault. With her eager assistance, he slowly removed Rachel's shirt and pulled down her jeans. After he had fumbled with the zipper on her sleeping bag, they eased inside and nestled together in the warmth, he not minding the cool air on his back as he pressed against her firm and yielding flesh, feeling the incredible power of her loins as he reached out greedily for every soft and sensuous part of her.

And when it was over and they lay quietly side by side in their sleeping bags, Jess looked from his sleeping lover to the twinkling array of stars above and waited for the words to come again. But there were no words to express the feelings that overwhelmed him now as he lay next to Rachel under the stars—the two of them surrounded by a vast and powerful universe. With a profound sense of comfort and peace, Jess drifted off to sleep.

It was in that realm somewhere between sleeping and waking that Jess first saw the lonely figure of Captain Jack silhouetted in the moonlight. The chief was standing not far from where Jess lay and was facing toward the westward ridge.

Jess's first thought was that something was terribly wrong,

because the Indian chief shouldn't be standing there like that, exposing himself to enemy fire. Jess wanted to call out, tell him to get down, for God's sake. He started to cry out, but the cry stuck in his throat. Blinking his eyes, still heavy-lidded from slumber, he realized that he *wasn't* dreaming, that there really *was* someone standing on a rise in the distance. As Jess awakened, the ethereal figure metamorphosed into a real, living human being—yet there was still something otherworldly about this figure standing stark and solitary at this isolated outpost.

Jess propped himself up, and as he did so he thought he heard the sound of murmuring voices. Yet there was no sign of anyone other than the one ghostly figure. Jess tried to whisper something to Rachel, but he couldn't get the words out. He finally woke her by pressing the back of his hand against her cheek. When her eyes fluttered open, he put his finger to his lips, gesturing in the direction of the silhouetted figure.

Rachel gasped when she saw it. She looked back at Jess with fear and wonder in her eyes. Jess, trying to appear calm though his heart was racing, shrugged his shoulders and again put his finger to his lips.

Should he go and investigate . . . or wait—and wait for what?

Jess couldn't bear the tension of waiting and doing nothing; and he was intensely curious about this apparition. Rachel watched, wide-eyed, as he slowly and quietly pulled himself out of the sleeping bag. Then, hunkered down below sagebrush level, he crept around in a semi-circle until he reached an outcropping of rock about 40 feet behind the figure. Although it was still in silhouette, he could see that it was a man, and that he had shoulder-length hair and was wearing a heavy padded jacket, jeans and hiking boots. Up this close, Jess sensed that there was something familiar about him.

The figure turned to look south, toward the other lava corridors. Now, seeing him in profile, Jess was sure he was familiar, but he couldn't quite place him.

A male voice rose up from out of the corridor. "Hey man, any sign of Little Ed and Scratchy? I was thinkin' now that it's almost morning, we might get a glimpse of 'em."

"Yeah, that's what I was hopin' too, but so far no luck."

That voice! Could it possibly be . . . ?

Jess saw a thatch of brown curly hair rising up out of the ground from the nearby corridor. Then a round, pudgy face; Jess could almost make out Chester's blue eyes in the growing light—yes, it was Chester, Chester from the streets of Berkeley!

And so that *was* John, by God! He thought he'd recognized the voice as soon as he spoke.

"What the heck are you guys doin' way up *here*?"

Chester nearly tumbled back down the rock-lined path when he heard Jess's voice. John, frozen in disbelief, stared at the figure that had emerged from behind the rocks.

Jess, who'd recovered from his own initial shock, walked right up to John and, gripping him by the shoulders, said, with real feeling, "Man, it's good to see you!" Then, turning toward Chester, who was standing there, open-mouthed, he said, "Aren't you guys a long ways from home?"

Chester was the first to regain his tongue. "Well, as they say, home is where the heart is, and, in our case, it's also wherever we happen to be." Looking around him with apparent satisfaction, he added, "This'll do for now. Good view of Mount Shasta, good deal on the rent, and no cops in sight."

"Yeah, not bad at all," chimed in John, who was beginning to recover his voice.

Rachel came up beside Jess. "Jeez, we thought you were the ghost of the old Indian chief," she said with obvious relief.

John smiled and said, "Well, you never know. Sometimes I feel like one of those old Indians."

Jess, clearing his throat, provided the introductions: "Rachel, this is John and Chester. They're a coupla refugees from the streets of Berkeley. I can't wait to find out how they ended up here. Guys, this is Rachel. She grew up around here, just on the other side of the mountain.

"So, guys, how *did* you end up here? Especially you, John. Last time I saw you, you were talking about taking 'The Big Walk,' and then you just vanished."

Rachel looked puzzled. "What's 'The Big Walk'?"

"That's when you just up and walk out of the dome with no oxygen," Jess explained. "It's, uh, a simple way of committing suicide."

"Suicide?! Why would he want to do that?"

The conversation had quickly lurched in a direction Jess hadn't intended, and he wasn't sure John could handle Rachel's directness. Deflecting the question, Jess said, awkwardly, "Well, when I met him John was kinda at loose ends."

"Still am," John said in his usual slow drawl. He didn't seem to mind being put in the spotlight, even if it had a rather morbid tinge to it.

"Hell, your ends get so loose in a place like Berkeley, pretty soon you don't know which way is up," the ever-voluble Chester contributed. "Drag your ass around a city all day where nobody wants you, scroungin' for food, scroungin' for a place to sleep—hell, I thought more'n once about takin' The Big Walk myself. . . . And would have, too, if it wasn't for her."

Adele, who was emerging from the lava corridor, smiled at the compliment and yawned. She was still the same beanpole-shaped waif that Jess remembered; but in the growing light he noticed for the first time her bright green eyes, which had gained added luster from her newly acquired tan. This wilted city flower was beginning to bloom in the mountain air, it seemed.

"If you want to know how we ended up here, you'd better get comfortable, 'cause it's kind of a long story," John said.

"I'll bet it is," Jess said. He and Rachel, their expressions eager and attentive, took seats on the bare ground. Chester and Adele sat down opposite them. John, with his back to the long mountain ridge to the west, remained standing.

"So one day I just decided the heck with it, I'm gonna follow Mr. Hemingway's example and find a way out, take The Big Walk.

"So I said goodbye to Chester and Adele here, gave 'em my pocketknife, my toothpaste, and my entire stake, which was about three bucks. When we hugged, especially with Adele here cryin' " (and at this point there were, in fact, tears in the young woman's eyes) "it brought home to me what I was about to do, that there were people who actually cared about me, might even miss me. And that made me hesitate a little." Here John himself brushed a tear from his eye. Chester was still dry-eyed and smiling complacently, as if he were watching a familiar old movie that had a happy ending.

"So I almost decided not to do it. But it didn't take long for that to wear off. The void, the boredom of that whole life, it just wears you down." John paused to gather his thoughts. Adele had stopped crying. Jess and Rachel were still hanging on every word.

"I got to the East Side escape module and waited until the gate-keeper opened the doors to let a truck through. I had gone over to the other side of the truck from where the gatekeeper was, like I was gonna talk to the driver, and when the module doors opened I just ran alongside the truck until I was outside.

"I didn't run for very long. In fact, I was coughing so bad after a few seconds I could barely walk. The air and the heat get to you real fast. I just sort of stumbled along the road there, thinkin', 'So this is it, pretty soon all the lights are gonna go out and that's gonna be it.' . . ." John, as he relived those moments, had grown pale.

"And then . . . ?" Jess prompted.

"For goodness' sake, give him a chance!" Rachel said in a stage whisper.

John took a deep breath and continued. "And then this guy just stopped his car and motioned for me to get in. He didn't open the door or anything, and by then I'm so out of it I can barely see him or his car, let alone open the door, so I just kept stumbling along.

"The next thing I remember is my legs crumpling up and me hitting the ground, and as I'm on my side, feeling like my lungs have collapsed, this guy has got his arms around me and he's lifting me up and easing me over to the car and—boom!—I'm in the car and layin' across both seats and then I completely blacked out. The next thing I know, when I come to, we're about 200 miles out of Berkeley, headed north.

"The guy was pretty cool. He just looked over and said, 'You looked like you needed a ride.' And me, I don't know what to say. I'm thinkin', 'Is this my guardian angel, or what?' 'Cause I never had nobody look out for me before—'ceptin' maybe Chester and Adele here, sometimes—and now all of a sudden, when I'm at the end of my rope, this guy shows up, kinda like magic. Maybe it's one of those religious deals, you know?

"So I figured, well, maybe I hit the jackpot for once in my life. I'm gonna fasten my seatbelt and see how far this magic ride goes.

"Well, it went all the way to Portland. The guy even fed me, got me a room one night when we stopped in Medford. I kept one eye open all that night, but he was cool—no tricks up his sleeve.

"And then when we get to Portland—poof!—he just disappears. We stopped at a gas station, and I went in to use the restroom. When I got out, he and the car had disappeared."

"Did you get his name or anything?" Rachel asked.

"Just a first name—Jonathan, like mine. Said he was in the recycling business, traveled a lot, but he wasn't really very talkative. Mostly asked a lot of questions about me, like why I was walkin' outside the dome. I dunno, maybe he got bored listenin' to my life story, was why he vanished. Who knows? . . . "

John stopped again, seemingly lost in his own thoughts. The sun had just risen over the mountains, bathing him in its fresh morning light. Jess saw that, like Adele, John looked a lot healthier. His dome pallor had been replaced by a ruddy tan.

But there was a more profound change, too. As John stood there—square-jawed, broad-shouldered—with the mountains in the background, his appearance, his whole presence, was dramatically different from what it had been on the streets of Berkeley. The main difference, Jess realized, was that now he *had* a presence, whereas before, on the streets, he had seemed like a lifeless lump of clay, a leaf in the wind.

"So anyway," John said, coming out of his reverie, "I ran into Chester and Adele almost as soon as I hit Portland. They were about as surprised to see me as you were, Jess. I think they were even a little bit glad to see me. They'd split just as soon as the dome cracked and, when they got to Portland, hooked up with a guy from the East Bay named Little Ed. He'd been there about six months and knew the ropes—where the free feeds were, the squatter houses, stuff like that. But he was gettin' ready to split, didn't want to deal with the city thing anymore. . . . "

"Cops ran your ass around up there the same way they did in Berkeley," Chester said. "Me and Adele figured we'd better clear out with Ed before we get put in another work camp, or worse. Scratchy wandered into town about that time, too. He'd gotten fed up with what was goin' down in the East Bay, just like us."

John continued: "So Little Ed was gettin' ready to clear out, and the rest of us figured, what the heck, couldn't be any worse someplace else, but this time, let's head for the wide open spaces. We all kinda grabbed onto that idea. Got us motivated. I think we all felt we could make a fresh start out in the wilds somewhere. Get away from the cops and the rules and all the shit that goes on in the domes.

"But there's the problem of a stake. If you're gonna be out in the middle of nowhere, with no panhandlin', then you gotta have some ready cash for grub and so forth. We pooled our cash—there were five of us—and we got maybe 50 bucks total, which ain't gonna last us more than a day or two out there.

"But we got one big asset in terms of puttin' together a stake, and that's Little Ed. Ed is what I'd call a street actor. He's a good-looking guy, a little weathered from the streets, but basically good-looking—a little on the short side, but, you know, got that movie-star sleek black hair, square jaw, and all that. And he's smooth, *real* smooth. Guy can walk into a place and be just about anyone he decides he wants to be.

"And somehow in all those years on the street he's managed to acquire a few costumes. He's got one good suit, and he's got one of those uni-sex outfits, and he's got what he calls his mountain climber's outfit kind of a gortex jumpsuit, actually, and some hiking pants with lots of pockets he wears underneath the gortex, and some fancy climbing boots.

"So the idea is, Little Ed can blend into just about any high-class situation you can think of, anyplace where there's money around, basically.

"So, as to getting our stake, first he goes into Portland Outfitters with his orange gortex suit and his boots and goes into his mountain-climbing act. After about ten minutes of bullshitting he has established himself as Mr. Mountain Climber. He's swappin' stories with the store help and the customers about climbin' K-2 and K-9 and K this and K that, and after a coupla hours he is walkin' out of the store with a coupla portable GPS units, complete with videophone hookups, *and* tents *and* cookware *and* the latest in thermal sleeping bags. He's even got someone to drive him and all his gear to the classiest hotel in Portland, the Heathman, where he is supposedly staying. Portland Outfitters had become the official sponsor of his next climb. He was gonna plant some official flag with the Portland Outfitters' logo on the top of Mount Everest, as I recall.

"But we still need cash, so the next thing we do is open an account at Portland National under Little Ed's name. Now, this is when Scratchy enters the picture. You saw him at that squat we had in Berkeley. Granted, Scratchy ain't much to look at, but he can *talk*—or chant, depending on his mood. Once he gets going, the guy can do these incredible New Age riffs, you know, on the One Great Spirit and the spiritual connectedness of each and every blessed living thing, and so forth and so on.

"So Little Ed, in his suit, and Scratchy, looking like he just came down from the mountaintop, set out to make the rounds of the publishing houses. There's a bunch of 'em in Portland. I won't bore you with a lot of detail, but this is basically a sales job, a numbers game, as Little Ed would say, and it took 'em two days and six publishing houses before they hit the jackpot: Which was a contract to deliver a minimum 300-page manuscript with the working title *Channeled Truths Of The Eternal Universe by the Blessed Brother Scratchy*, and—the important part—a $2000 advance wired to the account of Mr. Ed Brickwell, Literary Agent, at Portland National Bank. We've got our stake!

"Funny thing is, Scratchy was so impressed with his performance at all those publishing places he says he's going to go ahead and write the damn book.

"Next day the five of us were on the bus headed out of Portland. Got down to Ashland, then hitched over to Klamath Falls. Even that town was too big for us—any town that had cops was too big, far as we were concerned—so we bought some food and hitched and walked down this way. Along the way, we heard about Tule Lake and the lava beds and Captain Jack's Stronghold, and it sounded like it might be a good place to hole up for awhile. Figured we could pick up groceries every once in awhile in the little town near the lake.

"Only thing is, we didn't reckon on the local vigilante squad when we were makin' all these plans. Got up one mornin' bright and early. We were camped near the main road, next to a little stream. We were somewheres near the border, just barely on the California side. Had just gotten our stuff packed up and on our backs when we see these trucks pullin' over, maybe 500 feet from our camp. We waited just long enough to see these guys gettin' out of the trucks with rifles. Obviously this is no welcoming committee, so we hightailed it just as fast as we could in the opposite direction from the road. Heard a few shots—maybe warning shots, maybe not.

"Me, Chester and Adele ran just as fast as we could, and by the time we felt safe enough to stop and look around, behind a bunch of trees, Ed and Scratchy were nowhere to be seen.

"So we headed down here, traveled nights mostly, just to be on the safe side. Managed to stock up on food in the town of Tulelake before we got down here.

"Just been here two days, but it's a cool place, man. Out in the middle of nowhere, where nobody's going to bother us. You could see how those Indians could hole up here as long as they did and fight off a whole army." Sweeping his arm from west to east, John added, "You can see anybody comin' for miles. Heck, if we had a few guns, we could fight off a whole army, too."

Adele, who had been huddled, shivering, next to Chester, during this long discourse, piped up: "How 'bout we get a fire goin'? I'm freezin'." The idea drew nods from the others.

"How about breakfast down at our campsite?" Rachel suggested, then added, as an afterthought, "Funny you didn't see our fire last night."

"Probably still sleepin'," Chester said as they descended down the trail toward the cave. "We're still on a travel-by-night schedule. Looks like you two were tucked away out of sight pretty good anyway."

John and Adele showed up a few minutes later with some bacon, eggs and bread, and, combined with the host camp's oatmeal and coffee, the five made a hearty breakfast.

They lingered by the fire afterwards, sipping their coffee. The three former street people from the East Bay were silent for the most part, quietly enjoying the warming sun and their new surroundings. They had embraced this new life in the wilds with the fervor of recent immigrants, especially the romantic associations with the brave Modocs. After all, in the domes hadn't they themselves been under siege?

Rachel finally broke the silence. "So what are you gonna do now?" she asked.

"Just sit and wait and see what happens," Chester replied. "We're expectin' Ed and Scratchy to show up anytime now. We were thinkin' about puttin' in a few calls on the GPS videophone to our buddies in the East Bay and let 'em know where we are. What with the dome crack and all, who knows, some of 'em might want to join us."

"You guys better be careful, especially if more people join you," Rachel warned. "There's farms practically a stone's throw from here, you know, and it won't take long before people know you're here. Those guys who ran you out of your camp aren't just an isolated thing—it looks like there's gonna be more of that as time goes on. People up here, some people, anyway, are scared there's gonna be more and more people comin' up here from the cities, and they're preparin' to . . . well, I'm not sure exactly what they're gonna do, and I don't think they do either . . . but just be careful, that's all."

"Don't worry." John's voice was relaxed and confident. "As I was sayin', you could fight off a whole army here, if you had to. 'Course," he added, looking significantly at Chester and Adele, "you'd need a few weapons, just to keep 'em at bay."

When he spoke again, looking back at Rachel, there was a hardness in his voice that hadn't been there before. "I guess it's just that, as Chester said, we've had our asses chased all over Berkeley, and then Portland, and we're not gonna let it happen here. We're tired of all that shit. 'Sides, we're not botherin' no one, anyway, so they got no call to mess with us." Chester and Adele nodded in agreement, although not with quite the same conviction.

From his perch on a rise just above the cave, Jess could gaze out over the sagebrush plains to the lake that looked like a shimmering mirage in the distance. Yep, he thought, not a bad place to hole up at all, and it sure as hell beats living out on the streets. But Rachel's right, even out here you might not be left alone, you might be looked on as a threat.

He and Rachel gathered up their cooking gear and their sleeping bags and saddled up their horses. Before they left, as they said goodbye, they made a solemn vow to tell no one about the refugees' whereabouts. Rachel promised they'd come back and check on them after awhile and see how they were doing.

As they were heading back in the direction of the lake, Jess thought of the 19th century poet and writer Joaquin Miller, whose work he'd encountered while browsing in the Shawntrees' library. Miller, himself a refugee from Oregon, had written extensively about the region after it was first settled. He had even lived for a time with the Shasta Indian tribe on the other side of the mountain, and he had grandly proposed, two hundred years ago, that the several tribes of the region be given their own lands, to establish a self-governed Indian republic, at the base of Mount Shasta. That idea had gone nowhere, of course; it carried little weight in a region where the desirable land went to those who, with greater numbers and superior weapons, had claimed it by force.

CHAPTER XV: STEMMING THE TIDE

*T*he refugees traveled by car, truck, bus, plane, or by hitch-hiking. Some were pulling trailerloads of furniture and other worldly possessions, while others had simply packed a few suitcases and headed for the door. And as they traveled, in their attempts at small talk, their seeming lack of concern about what awaited them, and in their determinedly cheerful expressions, they tried to keep up the fiction that all was well. To outward appearances, this was, like the Oklahoma Land Rush, just another one of those migrations in the great American tradition of seeking a better life in new surroundings.

But it was more like the flight from the Oklahoma Dust Bowl of the 1930s. The refugees heading up the old highway through the mountains were, despite their brave facades, desperately scared and angry. They had packed up and left the domes of the East Bay, Modesto, Stockton, and Redding because they no longer felt secure there, no longer felt sure from one day to the next that their homes would be safe from flooding and the air would be breathable.

To be sure, most of their neighbors were staying put for the time being, but for this first wave of refugees, the breaching of the East Bay dome had been the final straw. They were not about to stay in the East Bay, or Modesto, or Stockton, or Redding, and wait for the next disaster.

Although most of them would not have expressed it this way, they were refugees from the losing side of a war. This war was coming to an end after a long, drawn-out siege, and these refugees were participants in the first stages of capitulation. It had been a war against Nature, and the outcome was never really in doubt. The society from which they were now fleeing had always acted as if it had been the victor, taking its spoils as it pleased from the Earth and treating Nature in all its life forms like a vanquished foe. It was a war in which the "victors" had finally been forced to retreat to the domes—the glorified prison camps of their own making—and they had found them precarious shelters at best.

As this first big wave of refugees inched forward on the old highway, they barely noticed the glorious mountain scenery all around them. They were understandably preoccupied. Their eyes searched the road ahead for the roadblock they knew they'd eventually encounter. When Mount Shasta finally made its imposing debut on the far horizon, it looked, to their eyes, like a sentry, a harbinger of the hurdles they would have to overcome in the weeks and months ahead. And wasn't it also taunting them, reminding them with its massive size and imposing presence which side had triumphed, which side would always triumph?

* * *

The southern roadblock was set up at Castella, just a few miles south of Dunsmuir. This location had been chosen because it was south of any exit the newcomers might take and because there was an underpass here, making it relatively easy for motorists to be sent back the way they came. The roadblock at the county's northern boundary had been set up just north of Yreka, near the Oregon border.

The ranchers and farmers and townsfolk who formed the volunteer corps at the roadblocks were far from unified on how the flow of refugees should be stanched. The generally accepted rule was that only those who could prove they had a residence in the county or legitimate business there (such as the delivery of merchandise) would be allowed to exit the highway. But any rule is subject to an infinite number of interpretations, and exactly what approach was taken at the roadblocks depended on who was on the crew at any given time.

Through trial and error, the roadblock crews had found that forcing each and every refugee to turn back was not a wise policy, since it led to constant shouting matches and fistfights and potentially even more violent confrontations. So the vast majority of travelers were allowed to continue on their way, with the understanding that they would stay on the freeway all the way to the Oregon border.

Although most of the crew members brought firearms with them, these were viewed primarily as props to deter resistance. The arrangement negotiated between the lawful authorities and the vigilantes provided that there be at least two deputy sheriffs positioned at each roadblock at all times, as a deterrent to any outbreak of violence.

On one Sunday morning, three weeks after the roadblocks had been established, the crew at Castella consisted of four volunteers: Rufus Pitbottom, retired rancher; Otis Fallon, a clerk at the Mt. Shasta post office; Jason Oglethorpe, farmer from south of Yreka; and Ruby Stickner, herb seller.

Rufus, Jason, and Ruby are already known to the reader. Not so with Mr. Fallon. Otis, not being an habitue of the coffee house, nor the farmers market, nor much of any public place other than the grocery store (where he was inclined to select his purchases without any unnecessary socializing and make a quick exit), was not very well known to his fellow townsfolk, either. A short, bald-headed, wiry little fellow, he had unexpectedly shown up at the Grange Hall for the fateful meeting on the refugee problem. All but lost in the crowd of ranchers and farmers that stood at the back of the hall, he had finally shouldered his way to the podium halfway through the meeting and delivered a rousing speech (which he had spent several days composing and rehearsing). He likened the pristine beauty of

Mount Shasta to the strength and purity and "natural integrity" of the region's native population, and he warned that these qualities would be diluted by the invading hordes from the domes. (Fallon himself had moved to the area from Redding ten years before.) He concluded, to thunderous applause: "To protect our children, our way of life, and our precious natural resources, we must take action to stop this invasion!" On the strength of that speech, he was elected to the Save Our Precious Siskiyous (SOPS) organizing committee.

Ruby Stickner had joined the roadblock crew to, in her own words, "add a woman's touch and keep the menfolk from scarin' the bejesus out of people."

So that morning, just before 11, when a car bearing a very nervous-looking young couple pulled up to the roadblock and stopped, Ruby was the first to approach them and offer a few sprigs of delicate blue borage.

"Now, dear," she said as she handed the small bouquet to the young woman at the wheel, "pluck the petals off one by one, brew them in a tea, or just chew them slowly, and ye'll be better prepared for the trials ahead."

This was hardly what the couple had expected. They were too dumbfounded to say anything, but the young lady managed a weak smile and a soft "thank you" as she took the flowers.

Jason Oglethorpe appeared at the window next to Ruby. When he stooped down to speak to the couple, his big, flushed face, topped by the ever-present cowboy hat, seemed to fill the entire window—indeed, blocked out the scenery beyond it—just as his booming voice seemed to fill every last nook and cranny of the car's interior.

"Howdy folks! I guess you all know we're not allowin' any stopovers *or* stay-overs between here and the Oregon border. We'd like you to seriously think about turning around, but if you do proceed there's one gas station at Weed where you can stop if you need to, but I should tell you that the station is being monitored to make sure you get back on the highway."

This last statement was pure fiction—the vigilante group had barely enough volunteers to staff the two roadblocks around the clock. The next statement Jason would make was also untrue, or, to put it more diplomatically, was one of Otis's imaginative contributions to the vigilante effort.

"Otis here is putting a tiny microchip somewheres on the underside of your vehicle. I can't say where, of course. This will enable us to monitor your whereabouts *at all times* while you're in Siskiyou County."

Jason managed to work his mouth into a tight little smile. It was a kind of half-apology for the decidedly unfriendly act of putting, or pretending to put, a monitoring device on the car. "Basically, folks, as long as you stay on the highway and keep movin', everything'll be fine." After Otis had reached under the car and done his little bit of playacting, Jason slapped the car's roof and allowed the thoroughly intimidated couple to go on their way.

Next came a rickety, antique truck bearing an elderly couple of about the same vintage. Between them sat a little dark-haired girl who looked no older than eight or nine. Ruby was about to offer them her flowered herbs and start her spiel when she heard Rufus's booming voice behind her.

"Heck, Ruby, these folks don't need none of your smelly ol' flowers—don't you recognize the Hadwallers, Elmer and Gladys?"

"Why, Rufus Pitbottom, you ol' shit-slingin' skallawag!" came the good-natured greeting from the man behind the wheel.

"How's the missus?" asked Gladys Hadwaller.

"Tol'erble, tol'erble," Rufus replied. "All this agitatin' and talk of an 'invasion' ain't good for her digestion." He made a sour face. "We been gettin' by on milk toast an' oatmeal, an' right now I'm so tired of that grub I can't stand it. But other'n that, we're fine."

Turning his attention to the little girl, his face brightened again. "Say, who's this little bright-eyed beauty?"

"That's Alice, our granddaughter," Gladys responded. "She's Burt and Gwen's. We're bringin' her up here for a little respite from the East Bay troubles. That's where her parents settled, you know."

The line of cars behind the Hadwallers had continued to grow during this friendly conversation. It was now backed up so far that it wound out of sight around a curve that was at least a quarter-mile south of the roadblock.

Rufus put his arm around the herb lady. "You remember Ruby Stickner, don'tcha, folks? Her brother Leroy farmed just south of my place. He died 'bout five years ago. I'm sure you'd remember him if you saw a photo. Big fella, big round bald head, always smilin'?

"At any rate, his kidneys failed. Took the big guy six months to die, even at that. But the old gal here's still alive and kickin'—mostly kickin', if you ask me," he added with a wink.

" 'Course we remember Ruby," Elmer said. "For gosh sakes, we bought sumpin' off her—think it was horehound, wasn't it Ruby?—last time we was at the market."

Otis and Jason, having watched this exchange with mounting impatience, had finally walked back to the next car. After the warning to keep moving had been delivered and the imaginary microchip had been placed on that vehicle, Otis motioned the driver to go around the Hadwallers' rig. He then approached the pickup with an exasperated look on his face.

"What seems to be the problem here, Rufus?"

"No problem a-tall, Otis. These here are the Hadwallers and their granddaughter Alice. Just ketchin' up with 'em. Been so busy with all this agitatin' and roadblockin' the past few weeks I've lost track o' half my neighbors."

"So they're from here?" Otis asked suspiciously.

"Are they *from* here? Heck, they been here about as long as Mount Shasta, I reckon," Rufus said indignantly.

"Well, you know the rules, Rufus. We'll need to see some valid id with a local address."

"Oh jeez, Otis, don't start with that. I've known 'em all my life. That ought to give you some idee how long they've been in these parts."

Jason had walked over. Mindful of the ever-growing line of vehicles, he said, "Let it go, Otis. We'll make an exception this time if Rufus'll vouch for 'em."

Otis set his jaw and glared at Jason. "That's not what we agreed to when we started planning these roadblocks. Everyone who gets off the freeway is supposed to have a valid id with local address, or we detain them until they can produce one—those are the rules."

Jason, glancing back at the line, said in a tired but firm voice, "I said let it go, Otis. Look at all these people. We can't get too bogged down with every little situation, when . . ."

But Otis wasn't about to give way easily. "Well, even if these two live here, I'll just bet that little girl doesn't," he said obstinately, folding his arms and glaring at the little desperado.

"I said, let it *go!*" Jason fairly shouted the last word as he turned his back and walked toward the truck and trailer that was next in line. Otis, grimacing and shrugging his shoulders, followed a few steps behind.

The two elderly people in the pickup breathed audible sighs of relief.

"Sorry about all that fuss," Rufus said reassuringly, patting Gladys on the shoulder. "Some of these guys get a little carried away." He looked wistfully at the seemingly endless line of vehicles. "Me, I'll be glad when all this fussin' is over. Sometimes I think maybe we oughter just let 'em move in and make the best of it. Guess I'm getting too old for all this agitatin'."

"These are tryin' times, that's for sure," Gladys said in her soft, kind voice. There was the sound of grinding gears as her husband attempted to get the truck in first gear. "We'll just have to have you and Clara over before long, so we can show off our little grand-daughter here and have a real visit."

Rufus, easily restored to his good-humored self, beamed on his old friends. "That'd be real nice. I'll look forward to it. Maybe you can fix me some real food, too," he added hopefully as they pulled away.

The Hadwallers waved and drove off. Fortunately for them, what with all the talk and the bickering among the vigilantes, no one had thought to look under some blankets in the back of the pickup, where two adults lay. While the men were arguing, however, Ruby Stickner had heard someone cough and had seen the blankets move ever so slightly. She had decided to say nothing.

* * *

The smuggling of friends, relatives and even strangers into the region during this troubled period was a common practice during the first few months of the roadblocks. The vigilante committee soon learned of the practice—new faces always stood out in the small towns of the region, after all—and they began making more thorough searches of incoming vehicles. Jason Oglethorpe, Otis Fallon, and Bob Rawlings, another one of the hardliners, even went so far as to round up four or five of the illicit immigrants and forcibly escort them to the Oregon border, where they were pointed northward and left to fend for themselves. The point was to send a message to "legal" residents that the importing or harboring of "illegals" would not be tolerated. But the committee members, including even its hardliners, were not prepared at this time to take the more radical step of meting out punishment to those residents who did so. It was more politically expedient to go after the refugees.

Along those lines, the committee had received reliable reports that a group of especially undesirable refugees had made a temporary camp at Captain Jack's Stronghold. These were reportedly former street people from all over the Pacific Northwest. Estimates of the total number of undesirables assembled at Captain Jack's ranged from 50 to as high as 100. Clearly, this situation would require immediate action by the committee, and quite possibly a show of force.

All along the old highway you could see abandoned cars and trucks; these were a byproduct of the vigilante effort. Their desperate occupants had hoped to find refuge in the Siskiyou region. Instead, finding a roadblock and believing that their vehicles had been electronically bugged, they abandoned them and sought shelter on foot. During the months that the roadblocks were in effect, countless escapees from the cities—bedraggled, half-starved, their clothing torn by manzanita and bramble bushes—showed up at the doors of local farmhouses. Most were taken in, as Jess had been some years before, with few questions asked.

* * *

The new arrivees at Captain Jack's Stronghold were stretched out on the level ground above the lava corridors. Some simply lazed in the warm sun, staring at the hazy mountains in the distance, while others sat laughing and chatting in small groups.

They had come up here from the domed towns of California's great Central Valley, as well as the East Bay, and had flocked from as far north as Seattle. Like John and Chester and Adele, they had no roots anywhere, and it had been easy to leave the streets and the cops and the squatters' houses when word reached them of a free-wheeling camp in the mountains—a "New People's Republic," as John had grandiloquently dubbed it, of footloose kids just like themselves.

Those coming from the south had generally followed the route through the Butte Valley taken by Rachel and Jess, while those from up north retraced the route followed by John and Little Ed and the others, and crossed the Oregon border on the lightly traveled road that runs south of Klamath Falls.

Once they arrived, they found Captain Jack's a free and easy paradise compared to life in the domes. Here there were no scowl-ing older folks, no cops, no work camps—only blue sky and fresh air and wide open spaces, and the easy camaraderie of their com-panions from the streets.

Talk of a possible confrontation with some of the locals cast a small cloud on the horizon, but on a warm sunny day such as this it seemed a distant speck. There was a festive, celebratory air about the camp. Finding this little island of freedom, after the harsh life in the domes, was certainly worth celebrating, as was the simple joy of being young and free in this starkly beautiful setting.

They were certainly a colorful group. Both men and women wore bandanas in bright colors—blues and reds and yellows. Some, in acknowledgment of their surroundings, had converted these to headbands, with an occasional feather added. The retro look was still popular; tie-dyed shirts and blouses were much in evidence. Coarse-beaded necklaces and large, pendulous earrings were worn by both sexes. Some of the men and women were bare-chested.

The apparel, as well as the lack of it, contributed to the feeling that this was a kind of tribal gathering. It was certainly true that, as they talked and shared their stories of their gritty lives under the domes, something, some unifying spirit, was transforming this spontaneous coming together of young people into an extended family. They had had many of the same experiences; they had, to a large extent, a common past, and there was a growing feeling that they would share a common fate in the days ahead.

Rachel and Jess had returned, as promised, having arrived that very day on horseback. They were surprised at the size of the gathering as they wound their way around the little circles of people, trying to catch sight of a familiar face. When they made inquiries about John and Chester and Adele, they were directed to "Captain Jack's cave," the very spot they had breakfasted together a few months ago.

The old Indian chief's cave had been turned into the camp's headquarters. When they arrived, Adele was talking in urgent tones to someone on a GPS videophone unit. A collection of about 20 rifles, half of them sleek-looking laser models, lay in a neat pile just inside the cave. John and another man, who was handsome and dark-haired and had a muscular, stocky build, were crouched next to a smoldering campfire. They were speaking in low tones. John occasionally snapped a small twig from a pile near his feet and threw it in the fire. A slender, haggard-looking fellow dressed in tattered clothing, whom Jess immediately recognized as Scratchy, sat on the other side of the fire, muttering to himself.

If the gathering outside could be loosely described as a tribe, these were undoubtedly the elders. Their average age had to be at least 25. Scratchy had to be at least 30.

Rachel and Jess had been standing on the rise above the cave, watching this interesting scene for several minutes before anyone noticed them. When John and his companion finally looked up, John gave a yelp of surprise and pleasure and jumped up to greet them.

"Jess! And, uh . . . . "

"Rachel, the farm girl from the other side of the hill," she said, coming to his rescue.

"Yeah, yeah . . . Rachel. Great to see both of you."

"You've got quite a crowd here since the last time we saw you," Rachel said.

"Yeah, we put the word out on the streets, and it spread fast. After that East Bay thing, a lotta folks were ready to split." He gestured toward the dark-haired man: "This here's Little Ed."

"Aha!" Jess cried. "The Man Of Many Roles. We've heard about your latest exploits."

But the Man Of Many Roles was surprisingly taciturn, meeting their gaze with a silent, crafty look; he seemed to be sizing them up before deciding if he wanted to extend a hand or say even a polite word of greeting.

"I told 'em all about our little adventure gettin' down here," John said encouragingly, trying to elicit a response from his companion. Little Ed simply nodded.

Almost as an afterthought, John gestured toward the older man and said, "An' this here's Scratchy, our author-in-residence."

Scratchy looked up, blinking as if he'd just been awakened. Although he made brief eye contact with Jess and Rachel, he seemed oblivious to his surroundings. He turned his gaze back to the fire and resumed his mutterings.

"What's with the guns?" Jess asked.

"Oh, it's just a little contingency thing," John replied with what sounded like forced casualness. "Just in case the locals won't leave us in peace. As we put the word out, we're also askin' those who can to beg, steal or borrow a weapon. Most of 'em kinda shy away from that stuff, of course.

"We don't want to have to use 'em, but we also don't mind if folks around here find out we have 'em, either," he added pointedly.

Adele clicked off the GPS unit. She acknowledged Jess and Rachel with a quick nod, then turned to John. "I couldn't get any visual from those guys near the border, but I think they got ambushed at the same place we did. We're gonna have to put out a warning for anybody taking that route in the future, 'cause it's definitely being watched. These guys were able to keep 'em at a distance by returning fire. Think they may have wounded one of 'em—no casualties on their side, though. I told 'em the approximate mileage from our location. Traveling by night they figured they could get here in two to three days."

"Oh man!" This was the first utterance from Little Ed. "The first battle!"

"Well, more like a skirmish," John said uneasily. As if to himself, he added, "I was hoping it wouldn't come to this."

"Well I say it's time to get the troops ready," Little Ed said. "The locals aren't gonna appreciate gettin' fired at, whether anyone was hit or not."

Before John could respond, Scratchy stood up. His voice had grown louder, and was rising up in an insistent chant: "Light and dark, light and dark, color and life, hatred and strife!" He repeated this refrain over and over at a faster and faster tempo, his voice louder and louder until he was fairly shrieking the words.

Then, suddenly, he stopped, his face growing calm. With a peaceful, serene look softening his craggy face, he raised his eyes heavenward and said in a hushed voice: "Give us the courage and unity of the Spartans at Thermopylae. Give us a leader with the eloquence of Demosthenes and the wisdom of Solomon."

Little Ed, who was obviously used to these performances, gave Scratchy a withering look. "Scratchy, look, we already got the book contract, so give it a rest, okay?" To the others, he explained, "Guy had a lot of that shit crammed into him at the Big U, and now he's gotta inflict it on the rest of us. You gotta nip it in the bud or he'll go on like that for hours. And gettin' that book contract's just made him worse. He doesn't mean no harm, though. All that education and a lotta drugs has just made him a little dingy."

But Scratchy either didn't hear these remarks or was ignoring them. He began again, this time in a normal speaking voice: "I see a tribe of many colors and shapes led by the Wise and Brave One. I see the dark ones spilling out of a huge cauldron, crawling over the sides out of the black scum . . ."

"He majored in political science, as you can probably tell . . ."

" . . . slithering over the ground toward the camp where color and life are spread on God's open ground. I see the dark forces oooooooozing over rock and earth, blackening everything they touch . . . " Then his voice rose again in an eerie singsong: "Light and dark, light and dark, color and life, hatred and strife!"

"Okay, Scratchy, enough already! That was really beautiful—really e-voc-a-*tive*—now shut the fuck up!" Little Ed said this at an ear-piercing volume to get the poet-scholar's attention. He was successful, judging from the resulting silence and Scratchy's crestfallen look.

Seeing this, Little Ed said in a gentler voice, "Look buddy, you're wasting all that stuff on us. Write it all down, man, share it with posterity."

At this suggestion, Scratchy's face took on a happy, animated expression, as he pulled out a tattered notebook and began scribbling furiously, contentedly muttering to himself all the while.

"The guy's got a point, though," Ed resumed, turning to John. "We gotta get that bunch of ragamuffins out there organized into some kinda fighting unit, or, stronghold or no stronghold, those vigilantes'll mow us down."

The little group was silent as they pondered Ed's words. Rachel and Jess found themselves silently groping for ideas, too.

"Have you thought about a strategic retreat, if it comes to that?" Jess asked.

"Nah," John responded immediately. "With the size of this group, they'd find us wherever we went."

"But what if you split up into small groups?" Rachel suggested. "It'd be easier to stay with sympathetic families that way. There are lots of them around here, believe me, who don't like what the vigilantes are doing."

This notion was considered in silence for a few moments. Finally, Little Ed said, "I think we all feel the same way about this. We been kicked around, treated like dirt for so long, we're at the point where we got two choices: Blow our brains out or quit runnin' and fight.

"Now, if it does come to a fight and we see we're losin', *then* your idea of scatterin' in small groups would make a lot of sense. But I see no point in retreatin', either en masse or in small groups, before we've even had a fight. Hell, we been retreatin' all our lives."

"A-men," said John emphatically. Adele nodded in agreement.

"So, as I was sayin'," Ed continued, "before we get these vigilantes on our doorstep, we've gotta get the troops organized into some kinda fighting unit. How're we gonna do that with that scraggly bunch out there?"

There was silence again as they pondered the question.

"Okay everyone, now listen to me." All eyes turned to look at the slender little slip of a woman who had spoken. Adele went on to say, in a firm, commanding voice: "I want everyone in the camp, including you guys, to find a medium-sized rock and bring it to the open area in half an hour. Put the word out."

A half hour later the entire camp, about 100 strong, were standing in a circle, each one holding a rock in front of them. A huge pile of dried sagebrush lay in the center of the circle. The sun was just beginning to set behind the hills to the west. Chester, who had been on a food-buying expedition with six others, had gotten back just in time to join the circle. He stood solemnly by Adele's side.

"Okay, everyone lay down your rock and join hands," Adele said in the same clear and firm voice. There was some chattering around the circle as this was done. Once the circle was formed, however, the group was quiet again, with all eyes turned expectantly to Adele.

She had garbed herself in a hooded white robe, trimmed with purple. Closing her eyes, she began humming a beautiful, lilting melody. It was not anything familiar, but was more like a jazz improvisation, never repeating itself—a beautiful, ethereal melody culled from somewhere deep within her. The message in those clear, radiant notes was joyful and uplifting. She was soon joined by other voices, male and female, some chanting, some humming, all of them weaving themselves into a harmonious whole as they grew in number and volume. It was too unpolished and discordant to be called a heavenly chorus, but it had the essense of all such choruses: the joining of souls through music.

As the united voices reached a crescendo, the group, taking its lead from Adele, raised their joined hands in unison toward the sky, where the first stars were making their appearance.

At a nod from Adele, Chester broke from the circle and struck a match to the tinder in the center. The voices died down as the assemblage watched the flames leap toward the darkening sky. As the flames soared higher Adele's voice rose over the gentle droning of the circle.

"Oh Spirit that joins us all, unite us in aims and deeds as you have united our voices. We pray that our path in the days ahead will be as one with yours—for that is what gives us strength and courage. Rather than seeking to defeat our enemies, we would ask that you bring them enlightenment. But if that is not possible, then we ask for courage in meeting them on the battlefield."

With that she again led the circle in raising their hands toward the night sky. The spontaneous chorus resumed, but in quieter and more reverential tones. The circle of uplifted faces was lit by the flickering light of the bonfire. Jess, his hand linked with Rachel's, gazed across at these upturned faces set against the now-glittering sky. Once again he felt both awed and comforted, just as he had on the night he and Rachel had slept on this very spot. Once again he had the sense that he had connected with something vast and powerful; now, more than ever, he felt that he was somehow part of it.

And when they arrived home a few days later, Jess sent a strange and urgent message to the East Bay.

CHAPTER XVI: INTERLUDE

*S*ix years have passed since Jess's arrival in the Shasta country, and it has been that long since we last visited the dining room at the Stillwater farmhouse. On this particular evening it is, if anything, more awash in life and color than ever. Twelve people are seated around the long dining room table, and the room is filled with their chatter and their laughter, rising above the cheerful clatter of the silverware.

The tapestry that hung on the dining room wall opposite the painting of a farmhouse is no longer there. It has been replaced by an original oil painting by 14-year-old Lucy Stillwater. The painting fills a large portion of the wall. It is a highly stylized portrait of a female figure with large black eyes and sharply defined black eyebrows and black hair. A large white robe, its folds arranged in bold, geometric patterns, frames her face and covers her figure entirely. It is a powerful painting, and those who look on it for the first time often find themselves mesmerized by the woman with the large eyes and the billowing robe. Tonight as its quiet, wistful creator sits just below her work, you might wonder what other marvels lurk beneath her placid surface.

There are three new faces at the table: Felicia Ramirez, her husband Salvador, and their son Arturo. Although they are new, they have the same healthy, vibrant glow as the others around the table. This was not the case only a few weeks ago when the Ramirez family first showed up at the Shawntree farm, walking down that same gravel path that Jess once staggered down. They were in better condition than Jess had been, and they were in

213

good spirits, but their faces were haggard and drawn and their clothing torn and dirty. They had walked nearly 15 miles through open country.

Jess was the only person on the farm that day. He was just on his way from the barn to the main house, having oiled and attached the furrower to the tractor in preparation for spring planting, when he saw the bedraggled strangers.

"Got any room for an outlaw family?" Salvador Ramirez had asked as Jess approached them. The short, dark-haired man was surprisingly jaunty, considering the circumstances.

Jess had responded in kind. "Well, I dunno. We might be able to bed you down on a couple of bales of hay if you're willing to work the fields."

"Best offer we've had all day," Salvador said, and this time he was only half-joking. So was Jess, for that matter. With the asparagus harvest starting, it wouldn't hurt to have a few extra hands on the farm.

Salvador and Felicia had owned a small e-commerce prescription drug business in the East Bay. Their son was just finishing his first year at Berkeley when the dome cracked. Their home was a modest bungalow on the flatlands near the bay and one of the first to be inundated by the floodwaters.

Felcia had two brothers and a sister who had died in Sacramento, and she was not about to wait and see what new tragedies this latest disaster might bring. So they quickly packed some clothing and a few personal items and headed for their climate-controlled van parked near the East Side escape module.

The Ramirezes were never quite sure why they stopped on the old highway and headed across the fields and the open country looking for a safe haven. The Ramirezes were flatlanders, unless you wanted to count a time long, long ago, when some of Felicia's ancestors had lived in the Sierra Madre range of Mexico, in the

town of Victoria de Durango. Salvador's family had lived for generations in the farming country around Salinas, while Felicia's fore-
bears had been mostly townsfolk, who in the new country continued a tradition of running little mom and pop stores and restaurants
in the towns that dotted the Sacramento Valley.

So they could not have told you why they stopped here, in the
Shasta region, when they could have continued on to Portland or
Seattle. They were tired of dome life, to be sure, but it was more
than that. As with Jess and the Shawntrees and the Stillwaters,
something beckoned to them in this mountain region. Perhaps, like
Jess, they would find out what it was once they had been here
awhile.

And just like Jess a half dozen years before, they soon found
themselves caught up in the rhythm of farm life. After a few weeks
breathing fresh mountain air and helping with the myriad chores in
the fields and in the house, the Ramirezes were restored to their
natural health and vigor—if anything, more so than before. Arturo,
in particular, took to this new life immediately, finding it a welcome
change from his studies. He and Tim Stillwater, who was only a
few years older, established an immediate bond. Both were strong
and athletic and quiet-spoken, and each had a dry, understated sense
of humor.

Tim put Arturo to work on an ambitious project that Tim hoped
would introduce the first citrus crop to the Siskiyous. Although
temperatures had warmed dramatically, the winters here at a 3000-
plus elevation were still too cold, and the fluctuations in temperatures too unpredictable, for oranges. So he was building five huge,
barn-like greenhouses, each half a football field long, to protect the
trees. There would also be enough space left over to shelter early
crops of tomatoes and cucumbers and other warm-weather crops.

So in the afternoons Arturo helped Tim with the greenhouses
and in the mornings helped Jess and William and the rest of their

crew with the asparagus harvest. He was a strikingly handsome young man, with an athletic build; clean, chiseled features; and dark, wavy hair. He moved with a natural athletic grace, whether he was hoisting boards for the greenhouses or stooping to cut tender asparagus stalks, and it was certainly no coincidence that quiet little Lucy Stillwater, who had shown only moderate interest in the greenhouse project before, began to monitor its progress on an almost daily basis, stopping by on her way to school and on the weekends, and sometimes bringing them something fresh-baked from the kitchen. And on this evening, on those rare occasions when Arturo speaks or is spoken to, Lucy cocks her head ever so slightly and listens just a bit more attentively.

Jess is sitting across from Rachel. He prefers to see her from this vantage point, to watch her sparkle and shine in company. With a lover's tender eyes, he savors every move and gesture: the jaunty angle of her face as she laughs; the way her eyes, in that same moment, flash their appreciation; the supple curve of her elbow, resting on the table; the sensuous toss of her head as she brushes her hair back over her shoulder.

Jess, at 30, is still the same handsome, sturdily built fellow he was when he first showed up at the Shawntree farm. His face is tanned and healthy-looking, and age has only just begun to etch a few creases and lines across it.

He takes understandable pride in having achieved a modest success for the once-struggling Shawntree farm. The asparagus crop now covers another three acres, and has proven to be, after all the years of experimenting, the cash crop William had hoped for. In only a few more years, barring unexpected setbacks, the mortgage should be paid off. The abundance of this year's chard and tomato crop is also testimony to the farm's increasing prosperity. In two months, by early June, Jess will have a hectic time of it, what with supervising harvest crews and helping Ed run the farmers' markets in Dunsmuir and Mt. Shasta.

Jess, with the elasticity of youth, has successfully made the transition from high-tech worker to William's righthand man. He has in fact proven to be a very steady hand, keeping the small operation running smoothly while William, rejuvenated by the farm's hard-won success, seems to leap from one experiment to another, trying new soil additives in one field, and an exotic new crop in another.

Jess is beginning to feel a little cramped in his second-fiddle role. He has, more than once, suggested to William that they extend their season by doubling their greenhouse capacity, but William—gently but firmly—said this should wait until the mortagage is paid off, even though William himself always seems to find the funds for his outlandish experiments.

Jess is, in truth, just a bit envious of Tim, seven years his junior but already beginning to take over the day-to-day operations of the Stillwater farm. Ed, at 60, has decided to devote most of his energies to the half dozen farmers' markets in the region, and Kathy, while helping out with the rest of the family during harvest season, is spending most of her daytime hours at From Ewe To Ewe. The increased responsibilities mean longer hours for the Stillwater youth, but they have also allowed him to put his distinctive stamp on the operation by trying out new ideas.

Jess, bursting with energy and ideas of his own and a vague longing for new challenges and adventures, is like a spring freshet surging with new snowmelt, ready to run off in a hundred new directions.

And what of Rachel herself, with her sparkling green eyes and shimmering black hair and lovely face? She is a young woman now in her mid-20s. She had, at 19, a healthy, sturdy build; and now, at 25, that sculpted, sturdy look has evolved into something softer and rounder, as if Raphael had taken over from Michelangelo. The energy and sparkle are still there, but there have been subtle changes as she grows older.

Rachel, as Jess once said in so many words, is the kind of person who glows with an abundance of life-energy. She is the kind of person others are drawn to like chilled winter travelers to a warm hearth. It seems natural to lean on her and confide in her. But listening to others and drawing them out are social arts that have to be learned and refined, and as she learns them she is outgrowing the youthful tendency to talk only of herself. Her conversation still sparkles, but now the sparks are often used to light other fires.

She has chosen to stay on the family farm despite an opportunity several years ago to act in Ashland, that world-renowned mecca of the theatre arts. This farm girl from Mt. Shasta came to the attention of the acclaimed director Nigel Johnson via Rachel's former high school drama teacher, who'd taken a position as Johnson's assistant. She managed to wangle an audition for her star pupil, and the esteemed director was impressed with the young woman's onstage poise and graceful beauty. He offered her an apprenticeship position on the spot.

It was a pivotal juncture in her life. On one of their first encounters, Jess had compared the spirited young woman to a soaring hawk or a deer in flight. But she had matured into something more like a beautiful, majestic oak, whose soaring strength depends on its deep roots. She had been sorely tempted by the Ashland offer, but as she thought about it she came to realize that only a part of herself would be nurtured by the experience, that too much of herself would be left behind in the home and the community and the mountains she had grown up in.

So while she did not become a star of the Ashland stage, she has in the ensuing years become a mainstay of the community theatre, not only as an actress but often as producer and director. As a sidelight, she sells custom-made costumes out of her home and through Cheryl's and her mother's shop. What with working full-time at the farm during harvest season and part-time the rest of the year—and stealing an hour or two here and there to spend with the handsome young man seated across from her—she rarely has an idle moment.

Just now she is quietly pensive as the conversation flows around her. She is haunted by an image, something that she saw earlier in the day that keeps reappearing in her mind's eye.

As she was passing by her brother Ted's room that morning, she noticed that he was hunched over his drawing board in the far corner of the room. Her curiosity was piqued as she watched him sketching diligently away, apparently oblivious to anything outside the boundaries of the little sheet of paper.

And you never knew what might appear on that sheet. His very first efforts, during his *Space Blasters* period, were some truly outlandish space vehicles (one was cleverly modeled on a coffee percolator, another on the flower vase that sat on their hallway table).

Inspired by Phil's stories of volcanic exploration, Ted had also done some highly imaginative drawings of a mythic colony living in the interior of Mount Shasta, a race of god-like creatures who lorded it over an inferior race of gnome-like dwarfs.

Rachel, proud of her brother's artistic talent, had always taken a keen interest in his work.

"Hey Ted, whatcha workin' on?" Rachel called out as she entered the room.

Ted, now a gangly 17-year-old, still with his trademark thatch of brown hair, deftly turned over the sheet and protectively crossed his arms over it.

"Wouldn't you like to know?" he said with an impish grin.

Thoughts of hideous gnomes or more lurid scenes immediately crossed Rachel's mind.

"I've seen naked women before, you know," Rachel teased.

" 'Snot a naked woman," Ted said, blushing.

"Then why won't you let me *see* it? I promise I won't tell anyone," she said coaxingly. Her curiosity was thoroughly aroused now.

Ted slowly turned the paper over, revealing not gnomes or naked women or spaceships, but . . . a house, a fairly plain but cozy-looking two-story frame house. This was a complete surprise, and Rachel was momentarily speechless. Like his other work, it was skillfully and meticulously executed, and Rachel found herself absorbed in the simple scene before her.

The house was two stories high. A small portico sheltered the front door. There were two large windows on either side. On the second story three smaller, gabled windows peered out beneath a steep roof. A chimney poked out to one side of the roof's peak. The artist had adorned the house with an abundance of foliage, including a spreading oak on one side. Tall rose bushes and creeping ivy worked their way up the front walls.

"Do you like it?" Ted asked anxiously, looking directly up at his older sister.

"Oh yes, it's lovely," Rachel said softly, still looking intently at the drawing. "Why didn't you want to show it to me?"

Ted, groping for an answer, said, "Because it's . . . it's not finished yet."

Rachel, puzzled by his awkward response, decided not to pry further. All artists, after all, even those who happen to be your brother, have secret places where no one else should trespass. Ted took up the pen again with an obvious desire to avoid further discussion, and Rachel quietly left the room.

Now, ten hours later, she was still thinking of the drawing. Her first reaction to it, in Ted's room, had been one of delight and pleasure. The simple dwelling, softened by natural adornments, was closer to her dream house than even she could imagine. But when she thought of the days ahead, and a planned trip back to the lava beds, with all that portended, the house became a kind of taunt, an elusive, unattainable dream that dissolved whenever she tried to draw closer to it. Why, it seemed to ask, were they casting their lot with a scraggly band of refugees from the domes? What did their fate matter to Rachel or Jess?

They were leaving this Friday, in three days, having exchanged messages with the encampment to the effect that a major vigilante assault was imminent. This was no secret; it was being openly discussed at all the public gathering places in town.

Looking across the table at Jess, Rachel wondered if he was having any of the same doubts, but she could see no sign of any. His face bore the same peaceful, serene expression it usually did when he was listening to others talk. He had repeatedly expressed his determination to provide what help he could to John, Chester, Adele and the others. Although she was not able to learn any details, Rachel knew that he had made some sort of special arrangements for the encampment's defense. When she had pressed him for details, he had dismissed the whole thing with a shrug and a few enigmatic words. "Wait'll we get there—I don't want to spoil the surprise, and, believe me, there'll be a lot of surprised people, including me, if we pull this off."

So they were leaving in a few days for the encampment, and an almost certain confrontation with the vigilantes. Like Jess, her heart went out to the ragged, rootless refugees who'd found a temporary home at the lava beds, and who were about to make their improbable stand out there on the fringes of the wilderness. Why would anyone begrudge them a few acres of barren ground anyway? Were the vigilantes truly convinced that if the refugees were left there unmolested, they and more like them would eventually overrun Siskiyou County? What had gotten into these men, most of whom she knew to be decent, sensible people? They reminded her of a bunch of dogs, who, through the same sort of insanity that operates on a human mob, could quickly be transformed into a crazy, destructive pack of wild animals.

Rachel was drawn from her reverie by the sound of Jess's voice. He was straining to sound casual. ". . . so I hope you can spare us for a few days. We don't plan to be gone long, and we figured with the Ramirezes here you'd have the early harvest pretty well covered."

Kathy, who sensed what lay beneath Jess's placid demeanor, said only, "Be careful." Ed cast a searching look at his daughter and at Jess, but said nothing.

Rachel, trying to avoid her father's gaze, abruptly asked Tim when the greenhouses would be finished. As it turned out, the last sheet of translucent plastic covering had been installed that very day, and only a few more finishing touches remained. As she had hoped, her normally taciturn brother, and even quiet Arturo, spoke enthusiastically about the project and what it would mean for next season's harvest. This, in turn, drew in veteran farmers Ed and William (who now looked on himself as an old hand in the business) to share war stories about weather-induced crop failures of past years.

Little by little, as the conversation jumped from one topic to another, the pall that had hung over the table after Jess's announcement dissipated. But the troubled thoughts that had entered Rachel's mind were not so easily dismissed. And when she drifted off to sleep that night, she had a dream about the house. In the dream, she was wandering through its ruined interior in a kind of daze, trying to salvage a few precious items from its charred remains.

CHAPTER XVII: ARMAGEDDON

A crew had spontaneously formed around the old van, and bags and boxes of groceries were being carried by willing hands to the camp's commissary. Bernie, the van's owner, was briskly sliding boxes back toward the workers; he grunted with each shove, and occasionally stopped to brush the sweat off his face with the back of his hand.

Like Chester, Bernie had a thick crop of curly brown hair. He also sported a rather wispy, drooping moustache and wire-rimmed glasses, which seemed fitting adornments for a young man who was stoop-shouldered and whose face was sallow and puffy. He was from Portland and something of an intellectual, having just completed his junior year in philosophy at Lewis and Clark College.

But there was more to Bernie Forquet than a study-hall pallor and wire-rimmed spectacles might suggest. Somehow, he had arrived here by commandeering his vehicle past the Oregon border to this isolated spot at a time when even those on foot were having difficulty getting through. Although Bernie was vague on details, he had found his way using a convoluted route on obscure back roads. He apparently used the same mysterious itinerary for the twice-weekly grocery runs to Klamath Falls, sometimes picking up a few new refugees at a prearranged rendezvous. That these refugees often arrived in a frazzled state at the lava beds was taken as evidence of Bernie's ingenuity in carving out a route where few had gone before, especially those with low-riding vans.

Bernie was also the major provider of armaments for the encampment. The unorthodox strategy developed by John and the others for the defense of the encampment involved a very broad concept of "armaments," but some of these were conventional—so Bernie picked up the occasional rifle in town. Each purchase was made in limited quantities so as not to arouse suspicion. Whenever possible, he took the further precaution of having one of the new refugees make the purchase. This stratagem was aided by a gradual shift in the type of refugees coming to the camp. While street people continued to predominate, there now was an occasional journalist or teacher or lawyer. These tended to be single and relatively young, and among the more rakishly adventurous members of their professions—and their respectable appearance made them better prospects for the purchase of weapons. Even so, some of these balked at purchasing weapons in their own name, and a few decided to pass on the van ride altogether when they learned that the Rainbow Gathering they thought they were joining was taking on aspects of an armed encampment.

After the last of the food was unloaded, Bernie ambled over to the camp's headquarters. When he got to the little rise above the cave, everyone except Adele was seated around the fire circle in front of the mouth of the cave. It was May, and there was no need for a fire other than for cooking; the small circle of stones had become a gathering spot from force of habit. A grim-faced Adele was standing just in front of the cave, talking over the GPS unit. Behind her, in the small cave, was a small mountain of rifles and ammunition boxes. As Bernie descended, Little Ed was speaking.

" . . . Jess is right. We gotta launch our assault right off the bat. Don't even give 'em time to think before we knock 'em off balance, shake 'em up. That way they'll be wondering what we're gonna do next. It'll put 'em on the defensive right from the start."

There were silent nods all around the circle. The group was

composed of Little Ed, Jess, Rachel, John and Chester. Scratchy, as usual, was off in a corner muttering to himself. Little Ed cast a wary look in his direction from time to time. With Scratchy, there was always the chance that a loud and vocal inspiration might strike at any time.

None of them had noticed Bernie yet.

John said, "The main thing is to knock 'em off balance right from the start. Above all, keep 'em from making a direct attack on the encampment, at least buy some time."

"Buy time for what?" asked Chester, looking up at Bernie and acknowledging him with a nod.

"There—you put your *finger* on it," Little Ed said, hammering out each word. "The first assault is useless if we don't follow it up right away—boom!—with something big."

"I dunno Ed." John had a pensive, worried look. "Maybe they'll be willing to talk after that first offensive. Might be worth a try. But I want to hold off on a second assault. Unless you've got some bright idea I'm not aware of, any second assault is bound to involve exposing a lot of our people to enemy fire. And we lose the advantage of our strong defensive position here."

"But I'm tellin' you, if you give them the time and the opportunity to mount an attack, then you've lost."

"But Ed, we can't just throw people out there to get picked off one by one. Let's face it, we're not the U.S. Army. Those are not a bunch of superbly trained, combat-ready troops lying around in the sun out there. The fact is, we've got one great razzle-dazzle play to lead off with, and that's it for now. If you've got an idea that doesn't involve mass suicide, let's hear it, but . . ."

Little Ed, who had no such idea at the moment but who believed in taking the offensive at all times, cut in: "Let me remind you that the last bunch that tried to hole up here had their water cut off and had to make a run for it. A defensive strategy works if you've got all the time and all the supplies in the world, which they didn't and which we don't either."

"Ed, I didn't say we should just 'hole up here'. . . ."

Sensing that this debate was likely to go on for some time, Bernie, who'd been shuffling from one foot to another, finally interrupted: "Sorry to cut in, everybody, but I got just a brief report. I doubled up on the groceries, as you suggested, but no go on the rifles. The passengers from Eugene never showed up at the truck stop, and I wasn't gonna risk it myself. I'm startin' to get snide remarks at the market about 'feedin' a buncha hippies' already, so I figured I didn't need to raise suspicions any more than I have already."

"Didja get the other stuff?" John asked anxiously.

"The fireworks? Oh yeah, it's gettin' close to the Fourth, so no prob. I told 'em it was for the Lions Club shindig. I didn't say which Lions Club and they didn't ask, fortunately. Got enough of 'em to light up Mount Shasta."

"Good job, Bernie. That's too bad about the rifles, but we're doin' okay in that department as it is," John said, glancing over at the stockpile in the cave. "Now go get a little rest. We're all gonna need it."

Bernie backed away while snapping off a mock salute. "Right, sir, thank you, sir, assault at dawn, sir. I'll alert the troops."

"Hey, you never know," John called out as Bernie disappeared over the rise.

There was a short, sharp click as Adele turned off the GPS unit. "Better put the camp on alert, guys," she said, making an effort to keep her voice steady. "There's some kind of vigilante caravan forming in Yreka. Could be our welcoming committee."

* * *

It was a Sunday, and the sound of hammering and sawing resounded in the woods and fields of the Stillwater farm. In the old melon field, just north of the barn, Tim and Arturo were putting up the framework for a two-story house that would have two wide windows on the first floor and three smaller, gabled ones up above. With the harvest season now in full swing, the two young men were stealing a few early morning hours for this project in the hope of surprising Jess and Rachel on their return.

If the gods were smiling on any mortals that day it was certainly on these two handsome young men, as they cheerfully went about building the new home. The foundation had been poured just the day before, and now they applied themselves to the more pleasant task of building the framework. As they did so they bantered and talked lightheartedly, their words floating like dandelion seeds in the warm spring air.

"This time of year they come out in their little shorts, and their little tops, and it's all you can do to walk through campus without drowning in your own drool, man," Arturo said, laughing at his little joke. "You should see them, Tim. The women in Berkeley are beautiful.

"But they are also *muy loco*. I think maybe they spend too much time thinking, you know? You listen to them in the coffee places talking among themselves, and they are always analyzing every-thing—like, you know, what so-and-so meant when he said 'hello' or 'how are you?'" Here Arturo adopted a soft, mock-feminine voice: " 'I mean, was he being *sarcastic*? Was this his idea of a *joke*? What kind of *message* was he trying to send?'

"They drive each other nuts with that kind of stuff, and then when you're with them, *you* wonder what they're thinking. You're afraid to even say 'hello.' You're like two spies sitting across the table from each other, each using a different code. Here, it seems, like with Rachel, you can talk to them the way you would another guy—it all seems so simple and direct."

Tim shrugged. "I don't know much about the women in your

parts, but, yeah, here it's pretty direct. If you like someone, you just pretty much tell them. If she feels the same way, she won't be shy about telling you either—most of the time, anyway—and you just go on from there."

"Ah, now that's the way to do it—simple and direct! This is something I am going to try out at the first opportunity," Arturo said with an eager gleam in his eye. Then, trading on their budding friendship, he asked the question that for some time he had been burning to ask: "And so how is it you have no one special, amigo?"

Tim didn't seem to mind the question. "Oh, there was someone up until a few months ago," he said casually. "We met at the Yreka market. She was one of my best customers. She always took a lot of time selecting her purchases. Made sure, right off the bat, I knew they were for Mom and Pop and the brothers and sisters back home. She had a really sexy way of fondling and squeezing everything. What with one thing and another, we had a lot of time to talk, and things just kind of clicked.

"It was one of those long-distance romances, though, which was okay at first, 'cause it kinda leaves you wanting more, you know? But after awhile it got to be kind of a pain. She didn't have a car, and she and her folks live along the Klamath River just north of Yreka, and it's kinda hard to justify drivin' the truck an hour each way for a visit.

"Then, when harvest time rolled around, that was the true test. Was I interested enough in Yvonne to work ten or twelve hours, then drive up to see her? Unfortunately, the answer was no. That romance just didn't pass the harvest test."

"Too bad," Arturo laughed, "but at least you'll have something to console yourself with. Harvest time means shorts and halter tops here, too, right?"

"Right you are, and spoken like a true romantic," Tim shot back, driving a nail home. "I can see I'm going to have to take you on a little window-shopping trip in town before long."

Over on the neighboring farm, in the Shawntree parlor, Cheryl was spending part of her day off in the usual way, spinning yarn, while Felicia, a steaming cup of coffee at her side, was using some of the yarn to knit a bright red woman's beret for the store. Felicia had a pensive, brooding look as she bent over her work. From time to time there would be a pause in the clicking of the needles, as her troubled thoughts rose to the surface.

"It'll all blow over in a year or so," Cheryl was saying reassuringly. "I know you and Sal and Arturo feel trapped right now, and you're wondering if you made the right decision, but just be patient and you'll see. Little by little you'll be able to go into town, maybe help at the shop every once in awhile. Pretty soon you'll just blend right in, like anyone else.

"Oh, some of the diehards may make a little trouble—the ones who aren't happy unless they're shootin' off their mouth and makin' someone miserable. But even a lot of the guys who are out on those roadblocks now, they'll come around once they see that you folks are nice, decent people who aren't gonna make any trouble."

"I hope you're right," Felicia said uneasily. "Sal is okay as long as he can keep busy helping with the harvest, but come fall and winter I don't know. . . . He's not a man who can sit idle for very long."

Seeing the worried look on her friend's face, Cheryl quickly interjected, "But Arturo . . ."

This little bit of prompting had the desired effect. Felicia, her face brightening again, said, "Oh yes, the new life agrees with him. He is a strong boy, very active, and the physical life here agrees with him. When he was at the university, it was all mental. Here he can have both. He will find a way to pursue his studies, even if we have to enroll him in an e-university. And I am so glad that he is able to help with building the house."

"Yes, that will be a wonderful surprise."

"I know it is selfish of me, but the building of the house makes me think all the more of Arturo's future, and whether in this new place, among strangers, so many of them unfriendly, he can even begin to build a life for himself, and find someone to share that life."

"Arturo? Felicia, a fine, good-looking young man like that? His problem is going to be keeping the young ladies at bay. They will find *him*, believe me, and then you'll have something to worry about.

"Speaking of being selfish, I wish we could keep him right here on the farm, he's been such a good worker. . . . But you'll see. Things will settle down after awhile; you'll be just another family in the community."

They were silent for some time, while the clicking of the knitting needles, the whirring of the spinning wheel, and the intermittent sounds of hammering in the distance filled the room.

Finally Felicia gave voice to her thoughts. "For myself, I do not worry. I have always found something to do with my hands and my head. Even in prison, in a solitary cell, I would find something to occupy me. But my husband and my son are not that way, they cannot stay confined here for long. My husband must go out in the world and make his mark, maybe start a new business, and my son must go out and make his mark, too, in some way. Otherwise, they will both go crazy.

"All men are a little crazy, Cheryl. It comes from always wanting what they don't have. And once they do get what they want, they find something else to want that they don't have." Felicia sighed. "It has to be this way, I guess. It is this crazy wanting, always wanting, that keeps them going. Otherwise they'd go completely crazy."

* * *

The 20 men had hiked in from the road under cover of darkness, to a position approximately 500 yards from the encampment. They had hunted, and they had fought with their fists, but they had never done anything like this before. It had not been easy to recruit men for this mission, and those who had enlisted had hidden their nervousness as best they could, behind a bantering, jocular repartee in the parking lot in Yreka. There, in the space of a few hours, this ad hoc vigilante army had received its one and only training session. This had consisted of a discourse by Rufus Pitbottom on how to properly load, aim and fire a rifle; and even at that, a good part of his talk was taken up with anecdotes drawn from his hunting experiences. Next came a half-hour pep talk by Bob Rawlings; its major theme was "preserving the Siskiyou way of life" in the face of the refugee invasion.

"If we don't draw the line right now, we'll have every panhandler, every street punk from Seattle to San Francisco camped out on our doorstep," he told his attentive audience. "By God, they'll turn this whole region into one big leftwing hippie campground if we let 'em!"

Thus inspired, the troops had driven in a truck-and-van caravan to a dirt road that veered off the main highway near the lava beds and parked near a grove of junipers. Now, having hiked in to a position a short distance from the lava beds, they listened quietly as Rawlings, drawing on his experience as a former Coast Guard lieutenant, spoke in the precise, stilted language of the military commander.

"Okay, we will attempt a peaceful evacuation of the site first. We will use rifles and rocket-propelled grenades only if necessary to persuade them to evacuate. Remember that our primary objective is to dislodge the occupants, but the secondary objective is to minimize casualties on both sides. For that reason, we will make a direct, hand-to-hand attack only if the first two approaches fail. Men, listen carefully at all times for my orders. . . . Any questions?"

Except for a couple of nervous coughs and the clearing of throats, the group was silent.

"Okay, check weapons. All rifles should be in the safety position until I give orders to attack and fire.

"Matt, load the grenade launcher and put it in firing position." A chubby young man wearing a black cowboy hat, sweat trickling down his face, unfolded the launcher's three pairs of metal legs so that the shiny steel barrel was raised to a position one foot off the ground and roughly parallel with it. Matt Slocum then clicked open a small panel at the base of the barrel. Reaching into a gunny sack at his side, he pulled out a long, baton-shaped grenade and shoved it up the bottom of the barrel until it clicked into position.

"Okay, prepare to position shield." At this command, eight of the men positioned themselves around five interlocking titanium sheets, each of them three feet high and eight feet wide, stacked on top of each other.

* * *

Bernie, out of breath, rushed down into the headquarters camp.

"They're here!" he shouted. "We just spotted ten vehicles parked behind the juniper grove off the road."

Only Scratchy was sitting up with his eyes wide open. The rest looked up from their sleeping bags, blinking awake.

"Well, at least their little surprise party isn't as big as we thought it might be," Little Ed said in a groggy voice. He had already propped himself up on one arm, and was calmly surveying the others.

Jess and a newcomer to the camp appeared at the rise above the cave. The newcomer's features were barely visible against the night sky, but it was George Spanos, Jess's former colleague from Robo-Remote.

"We saw Bernie running over and wondered what was up," Jess called down.

"Is everything ready?" John asked.

"Well . . . almost," Jess said hesitantly. "We were just about to do a test run."

"No time," John said crisply. "They're here."

"Oh my God," George said. He and Jess disappeared behind the rise.

By this time Adele had emerged from her sleeping bag. Stepping over to the fire circle, she held out her hands. One by one, the others—John, Chester, Little Ed, Rachel—stumbled out of their sleeping bags and, with Scratchy, joined hands around the fire circle. No one spoke as they looked up at the night sky. For a few moments, while united in spirit, each was alone with his or her thoughts.

* * *

"Okay, erect the shield."

As the crew scrambled to lock the pre-fitted titanium sections together, Bob Rawlings cleared his throat and brought the bullhorn up to his mouth. As he was about to speak, Rufus sidled up and spoke in an anxious whisper.

"Okay now, okay now, say it kinda friendly-like, Bob—you know, like we're *invitin'* them to come out of them ditches and join us."

"Yeah, Rufus, and I'll ask them what kinda topping they want on their pizzas, too," Rawlings deadpanned. He said this gruffly, out of the corner of his mouth, his moustache twitching erratically.

Suddenly his voice boomed out across the plain.

"Attention campers!" There was a short pause and then his voice boomed out again. "Attention campers!" Another, shorter pause. "You are in an unauthorized campsite. You must vacate it immediately." Another pause. "I will repeat: You are camped illegally, and you must vacate the campsite immediately.

"If you comply peacefully with this order, you will be transported across the border in the next 24 hours. If you do not comply peacefully with this order, force will be used until there is full compliance. It is therefore in your interest to cooperate at this time."

The shield was now in place. Rawlings peered over it toward the encampment, then turned to Rufus. The vigilante commander had a lopsided smile on his face.

"Well, how was that? Think I offended anybody?" he asked sarcastically.

"Well, it coulda been a *little* friendlier. See, my idea is that we kinda invite 'em over to join us . . . "

Rawlings cut him off. "Okay Matt, take the launcher off safety and place in firing position."

"Check." With trembling hands, Matt shoved the barrel forward so that its end peeped through a small hole in the shield. A constantly changing number flashed on a small digital screen attached to the launcher's base. This was the projected distance the grenade would travel. Matt slowly raised the barrel until the screen said "413," a distance, in meters, that was just short of the nearest trenches. Next to him lay a neat pile of grenades.

"Rifles in firing position." The men got up on their knees and, resting their rifles on the shield, aimed them toward the nearest trenches.

Rawlings had picked up a battery-powered, high-wattage spotlight and was cradling it on one knee. He would use it at the first sign of movement on the other side.

"Awfully quiet," Matt muttered uneasily, peering over the shield. "You don't suppose *they're* plannin' some kind of attack, do you?"

"Nah," Rawlings growled. "They probably figure they can hole up forever in those bunkers, just like the Indians did. If they do, they're in for a little surprise."

Rufus sidled up again. "Bob," he whispered, "whyn't you give it one more try? Maybe they didn't hear you real good that first time. Mighta been asleep."

Rawlings, grudglingly acceding to the request, put down the spotlight and picked up the bullhorn.

"Attention campers!" The voice boomed out once again. Then there was silence. Rawlings, rendered speechless by the sight in front of him, let the bullhorn fall to the ground. The rest of the men stared, slack-jawed, up at the sky. It was suddenly ablaze with a dazzling array of fireworks that soared and swirled and burst into cascading showers of light. Powerful spotlights similar to the one that lay at Rawlings' feet cast constantly moving, blazing paths of light toward the heavens.

A scratchy recording of the "Marseillaise," the French national anthem and fighting song, blared forth from the lava beds. Above the music a voice was chanting the same phrase over and over: "Light and dark, light and dark, color and life, hatred and strife!"

Then the music faded and the chanting stopped. The spotlights swept from the fading fireworks to the open field in front of the lava beds, where the refugees had gathered in a large circle. They were holding hands, and from them arose an otherworldly chorus of voices. The voices rapidly rose to a crescendo and stayed there for what seemed an interminable period, then just as quickly softened to a whispered chorus.

All this was just a prelude to the main event. As the eerie, haunting chorus of voices continued in hushed tones, the circle slowly opened to reveal three slender, stick-like figures emerging from the center. They marched three abreast, and the one in the middle proudly carried a white flag with the letters "RR" emblazoned in red. All three carried rifles. Their metal bodies gleamed in the unnatural light from the spotlights.

These unlikely soldiers were discards from the Robo-Remote scrap heap. The one in the center was, in fact, none other than Rob. George and Jess, who had remained in the trenches, felt something akin to parental pride as they watched the pennant-bearing robot march bravely toward the enemy lines.

"Present arms, hut-hut-hut!" called out Jess, who had been peering out over the edge of the trench. All around him, the refugees were trooping back from the field, their youthful faces reflecting the triumphant joy of a conquering army.

Out on the battlefield, the three robots stopped abruptly, each dropping down on one jointed knee and raising their rifles to the firing position. At the same time, the spotlights were pointed at the vigilantes' shield, and 20 cowboy hats simultaneously dropped out of sight behind it. Only one very large barrel protruded from behind the shield.

"Ping! Ping! Ping!" Bullets, fired from a position not more than 50 yards away, began ricocheting off the shield. In his hurried efforts to rehabilitate the robots, George had not had time to program them to identify and aim at designated targets, so the positioning of the rifles had to be done manually by him and Jess. The big shield made a fairly easy target, but hitting any single vigilante, especially one who was moving, would be an iffy proposition at best.

"Well, this is a heckuva fix," Rufus muttered from behind the shield. "How're we gonna fight against a buncha skinny tinmen?"

"Aw, relax, Rufus," Bob Rawlings replied, ducking his head back down when a "ping!" got a little too close. His moustache, which had begun twitching violently when the fireworks started, had slowed to an occasional spasmodic twinge. He was now coolly assessing the situation.

"Whaddaya mean, 'relax'?"

"Well, think about it, Rufus. I don't see the skinny little

bastards carryin' any cartridges for reloading. So they gotta head back for 'em." Raising his voice and addressing all the men, Rawlings said, "Okay, men, when those guys head back to reload, we follow 'em in, bring the shield right up to their goddamn trenches, and then, by God, we let 'em have it!"

Sure enough, the sound of ricocheting bullets ceased after awhile. The first light of dawn was beginning to glow on the eastward horizon. Carefully peeping out over their shield, the vigilantes saw the retreating forms of the three robots. But no sooner had they begun inching their shield forward than the strains of "The William Tell Overture" began blaring forth from the loudspeaker, and six more stick-figured forms emerged from the trenches, each carrying a rifle. George had not wanted to attempt the intricate task of reloading the rifles by remote control, so he was sending his robots—nine in all—out in waves.

The "pings!" soon redoubled in frequency, and once again the cowboy hats sank behind the shield.

So the vigilantes were being kept at bay, at least for the time being. There was a kind of beautiful symmetry in this, in these rejects from the Robo-Remote scrap heap doing battle for refugees from the human scrap heap of the cities.

While Jess had been the instigator of this strategy, others had provided their own creative trimmings. Bernie had found the old loudspeaker and stereo and records in a secondhand store in town. Although Bernie had procured the fireworks, they had been John's idea. And Scratchy, as we've seen, made his own unique contribution.

The essence of the encampment's strategy was to dazzle the vigilantes, to catch them off guard with this spectacle. The opening assault was not conceived as a military undertaking so much as it was a theatrical event, designed to not only dazzle but intimidate its captive audience. Along these lines the second wave of robots was to be the psychological *coup de grace,* suggesting that there could be endless waves of robots, while their human allies remained comfortably ensconced in their camp. In theory, the stage would then be set for the surrender or retreat of their opponents.

But the encampment's clever strategists had not reckoned on Bob Rawlings, who, despite his nervous twinges, was not easily intimidated. After a period of observation and reflection, he had come around to the view that, by God, those skinny little things oughta go down just as easily, if not easier, than something made of flesh and blood. So, looking around to make sure the others were watching, he raised himself up and, resting his rifle on the shield, coolly aimed it at the nearest robot.

"POW! Ping!" The sounds came in rapid succession as the robot tottered backward.

Encouraged by Rawlings' example, several other vigilantes took aim at the same robot, with similar results.

"Okay, okay, everybody fire at once this time!" Rawlings yelled over the ricocheting "pings!" Twenty rifles were raised and aimed at the same robot. At Rawlings' "Ready, aim, fire!" a deafening "BOOM!" resounded from the shield, and the robot toppled onto its back.

The robot's titanium body was just as impervious to bullets as the vigilantes' shield, and George soon had the robot back on its feet and firing away. But the momentum of the battle had shifted to the vigilantes' side, at least for the moment, and Rawlings was quick to seize the opportunity.

"Okay Matt, fire away!" he yelled, and there was another "BOOM!" as the grenade was launched, followed by an eruption of dirt and rock directly in front of the trenches. In the command post, Jess and George and Rachel and the others ducked under a heavy shower of debris. That was followed by another explosion, and yet another, in quick succession, leaving them choking and gasping for breath amid clouds of dust. In the confusion George and Jess had stopped working their consoles, and the six robots stood motionless on the field. The vigilantes had begun inching their shield forward again.

"Reactivate the robots, goddamn it, get 'em moving!" Jess yelled over the deafening roar of yet another grenade explosion. As the debris pummeled them, he managed to aim and fire one of the robot's rifles, but there was no report. It was time to send in the next wave of robots.

"Retreat! Send in fresh wave!" he yelled over his shoulder, but there was no response. He looked back and saw that George was in a sitting position, slumped against the trench's rear wall. There was an ugly gash on his forehead where he had apparently been struck by a rock.

Jess dashed over and grabbed George's console. Alternating between the two consoles, he managed to turn the robots around and start them moving toward the trench.

Although they were standing no more than two feet apart, Little Ed was yelling at Bernie: "Go back there and make sure all rifles have been issued! Tell everyone to prepare for an assault!"

"The enemy's or ours?" Bernie asked cryptically, looking at John for directions.

"I dunno, I dunno, just tell 'em to get ready," John said dazedly, mumbling the words. Then, starting to pull himself together, he said, in a firmer voice, "Tell 'em to get ready and we'll issue orders in a few minutes."

"John, we gotta do somethin' and we gotta do it fast!" Little Ed yelled. Gesturing in the vigilantes' direction, he added, in a mocking tone, "*In a few minutes*, they'll be close enough to jump in the trenches."

"Pa-diiiiiing!" As if to reinforce Little Ed's point, a bullet ricocheted off one of the rocks directly above.

"I know, I know, Ed, but I can't see sending our people out there to get shot at, mowed down. I just can't do it." John had a sad and weary look on his face. He surveyed the trench in both directions as if looking for a way out of their increasingly desperate situation.

"*I'll* send 'em out, then—hell, I'll *lead* 'em out." Ed fairly shrieked the words, the veins sticking out on his neck "Anything's better'n waitin' for them to jump in and mow us down right here!"

"Aw shaddup, both of you. *I'm* goin' out!" It was Rachel, looking calm and serene, standing with her hands on her hips at the rim of the trench. Her dark hair was streaming out from under a big white cowboy hat. She had also donned her riding boots. She disappeared behind the rim for a moment and then emerged in a flying leap, landing on top of Rob the robot's shoulders.

"Giddyup!" she yelled, waving her right hand above her as if twirling an imaginary lasso. "This cowgirl's ready to ride!"

Jess, at first speechless, managed to blurt out, "Rachel, are you *nuts* ?"

"Yeah," she said, looking down at him, "nuts enough to know that this is the only way to get 'em to stop pounding us and maybe listen to reason." Then, seeing the frantic look on Jess's face, she added, in a softer voice, "They won't fire on me, they wouldn't dare." There was a look of fiery determination in her eyes, and her whole being exuded a rapturous, contagious energy. Jess felt it enveloping him; almost as if he were a robot himself, he began to fumble with the controls.

When the first of the six retreating robots appeared at the foot of the steep, narrow path that ran down into the trenches, Rachel bent down and kissed Jess on the forehead. "Don't worry dear," she whispered in his ear, "I'll have them eating out of my hand. You'll see."

Jess's heart gave a leap as he pressed the button that activated

Rachel's robot. Rob jerked forward, causing Rachel to lurch in the opposite direction, but she quickly righted herself by grabbing onto the robot's head and wrapping her bluejean-clad legs more tightly around his torso.

"Keep your hands off his face," Jess yelled out, thinking of the clear plastic orb that served as the robot's sensory receptor. Fumbling at the controls, he sent the other two robots with their reloaded rifles out behind her.

The vigilantes were now not more than 100 yards from the trenches. From their new vantage point, they could make out that there was another wave of robots emerging from the trenches and that there was something different about them. There was . . . something . . . on top of the lead robot. It was a person . . . a woman . . . a woman wearing a cowboy hat. And she was yelling something.

What Rachel was yelling alternated between a yodel and a cowboy yelp. She was drawing on all her acting skills now, playing the role of robot-riding cowgirl, high-tech Annie Oakley, for all it was worth. Waving her hand high above her, digging her heels into Rob's titanium torso, and shaking her black tresses with each lusty yell, she personified, she *was* the spirit of the raw and untamed West. It was the performance of her life. By the time she got within 50 yards of the enemy position, she had upstaged the fireworks, the music, the chorus, and the robots in commanding the slack-jawed attention of the vigilantes. "Stop your damn foolishness and get a load of *this!*" was the message in each robust yell, each vigorous toss of her head.

Jess, meanwhile, was trying to stay cool and calm as this impromptu performance unfolded. Not wanting to place Rachel too close to the enemy camp, he brought all three robots to a halt 40 yards from the enemy position. As a defensive measure, he put the two flanking robots down in the firing position.

Without missing a beat, Rachel reached down and grabbed the rifle out of Rob's hand. With a toss of her head and a few more cowboy yelps, she began firing at the shield. Her cries of "Yip! Yip! Yip!" were answered by the "Ping! Ping! Ping!" of the shield.

Most of the men were too dumbfounded to even think of returning her fire. When one young vigilante slowly raised his rifle, Rufus dashed over and slammed the barrel into the ground.

"Bejesus! Can't you see who that is?" he hissed, glaring at the young offender.

The "Ping! Ping! Ping!" continued, as Rachel made seemingly random shots up and down the length of the shield. Like ducks in a shooting gallery, the cowboy hats bobbed up and down. As a hat appeared, Rachel playfully shot in its direction, always being careful to aim well below the top of the shield. The other two robots had now commenced firing also. Compared to Rachel's well-aimed bullets, the vigilantes were in much greater danger from these remote-controlled shots, which sometimes glanced over the shield.

After a final "Yip! Yip! Yipee!" Rachel leapt off the robot and threw the rifle on the ground. She doffed her cowboy hat, giving her head a shake and letting her hair fall down below her shoulders. Hat in hand, she gave a little bow, then gazed up at the men with her sparkling green eyes, eyes that burned with her love of life and her courage, eyes that made her radiant beauty all the more dazzling. Having doffed her hat and with it the role of high-tech cowgirl, she was now once again the young woman whom many of them had known from her earliest years, having watched her grow into a beautiful young woman—a remarkable young woman, to be sure, but also one of them.

Rachel was indeed the one person from the encampment who could best convey to these scared and angry men the urgent message that there were real human beings in the camp, people not so very different from them, whom they had no real quarrel with. If anyone had a chance to work out a peaceful solution to this confrontation before there was loss of life, it was Rachel.

She walked slowly toward the vigilantes, and when she was still about ten strides from them, she stopped. All 20 men were peering over the shield, staring at her in expectant silence. Clearing her throat and forcing herself to smile, she said in an ever-so-slightly quavering voice, "Now that I have your attention, guys . . ."

Before she could finish the sentence she gave a short, muted cry and toppled forward. Simultaneously there was the dull sound of a bullet hitting the shield. At the instant her face hit the ground, a thin trickle of blood began to run down her chin in the direction of the white cowboy hat she still clutched in her hand. She gave a low, barely audible groan and closed her eyes.

In the dawning light, Jess had seen a flash of light as one of the vigilantes placed his hands on the top of the shield. From that distance, he had no way of knowing it was from a wristwatch. Without thinking, he had hastily swiveled one of the robots to fire in the vigilante's direction. The shot had been poorly aimed and had struck Rachel in the back, passing all the way through her body.

Rufus was the first one over the shield. He looked down at the fallen young woman and passed the back of his hand across his eyes, looking away for just an instant. Then, looking up toward the trenches, he cupped his hands to his mouth and yelled at the top of his lungs, "Git a stretcher over here double quick! And some bandages, lots of 'em!"

Before the words were out of Rufus's mouth Jess, panting for breath, arrived at the scene. He dropped down to his knees at Rachel's side, grabbing her wrist and frantically feeling for a pulse. It was so weak he wasn't sure, in his confused state of mind, if it was there at all.

"Okay buddy, let's see what we can do about this wound." It was Bernie's calm voice. He was on his knees next to Jess, and he was clutching a large plastic bag. Rachel gave another low moan. In intense pain, she was trying to scrunch herself up into a fetal position. Near the middle of her exposed back there was a dark and growing red stain showing through her denim blouse.

Bernie gently lifted the blouse from under her bluejeans and exposed her bare back. Blood slowly pulsed from a small hole. He grabbed a roll of gauze bandages from the bag and, wrapping a long section of it around one hand and breaking it off, used it to wipe away most of the blood. He then tore off another long section and, grabbing a bottle of disinfectant from the bag, hastily poured it over the gauze and cleaned the wound as best he could.

"Jess, there's a box of cotton balls in there somewhere. Grab three or four of 'em and stuff 'em in the wound!"

When Jess had done so, Bernie crisscrossed several strips of gauze over the wound and taped them down. Then, leaving Rachel on her side, they unbuttoned her blouse in the front and exposed the exit wound, which was just below her right breast. They treated this wound in the same manner as the first. Putting bandages and disinfectant on a mortal wound seemed laughably futile, but it was all the two men could do.

By the time they were finished, a makeshift stretcher had been prepared. Two blankets from the camp had been folded on top of one section of the vigilantes' shield. Six people, a mixed group of vigilantes and refugees, carefully lifted the stricken woman onto the stretcher and began a slow trek toward Bernie's van, which was parked in the old tourist parking lot just north of the camp.

The stretcher bearers—Bob Rawlings, Rufus, Matt Slocum, Jess, Bernie, and George (who himself had a bandage wrapped around his head)—were silent as they carried the stretcher to the van. There was only the sound of boots crunching the rocky soil. It never occured to the three vigilantes that there was anything odd about this sudden transformation of roles. They were simply following the age-old maxim of the mountains that you came to the aid of a neighbor in distress. This, of course, was not just any neighbor, but Rachel Stillwater, beautiful child of the Siskiyous, and their actions were graced with a touch of chivalry.

Jess, too numb yet to feel guilt or even grief, looked down on the pale, lifeless face of his beloved, searching in vain for some sign of life. It was soon thereafter, riding with her in the back of Bernie's van, that the pain engulfed him like a tidal wave, the all-encompassing, gut-wrenching pain that came with the first realization of what had happened. It was pain compounded by guilt, by what might have been had he aimed just a few feet one way or the other. He sought relief by searching her face again for something, the flutter of an eyelid perhaps, or a slight movement of the lips, but there was nothing. It did not help when he looked away, out the rear window, at the solemn caravan behind them.

One by one, as they drew closer to the farm, the other vehicles dropped out. The day was clear and bright. They had turned off the main highway now, and the open fields were wearing their brightest greens, sprinkled with an Impressionist riot of the first wildflowers of the season—the scarlet larkspurs, red Indian paintbrush, yellow star tulips, golden fawn lillies, and blue myrtles—a dazzling sample from nature's palette.

Had he been driving with Rachel alongside him, Jess would have rejoiced in this display of nature's spring finery. As it was, the joyful scene outside, bursting with new life, served only to mock the tragic one inside the van, and Jess silently cursed the whole world of nature with its surfeit of joy and life.

He snapped out of his dismal reverie at the sound of the wheels on gravel. Mechanically, he joined Ed Stillwater and Bernie and Tim in carrying the long stretcher into Rachel's bedroom. They carefully half-lifted and half-slid her onto the bed, her head falling listlessly onto the pillow and lolling over on its side toward the wall. Kathy, Lucy, Ted, and William and Cheryl, who'd rushed over from next door, were tearful and solemn witnesses to the awful scene.

The family's doctor, Dr. Gayle Burnham, had driven in from town. In the hallway outside the bedroom she questioned Jess about what had happened. She was a thin, rather nervous, prematurely graying woman in her forties. She peppered Jess with questions, often interrupting his response with another question. She seemed restless and clearly anxious to get on with the examination.

Dr. Burnham, who had come to the Mount Shasta region twenty years ago, fresh out of a Portland medical school, retained some of the city person's ways—her demeanor was sharp and crisp and she talked much faster than the natives. She also had the slender person's tendency toward edginess. But all this was balanced by a natural warmth that had eventually won over her small-town and rural clientele.

When Dr. Burnham emerged from the bedroom after her half-hour examination, she grimaced for an instant in anticipation of what lay ahead. Wanting to choose her words carefully, she bought a little time by sipping from the coffee cup that was offered her. Finally, she cleared her throat and said, "Well, all the life signs are there, but they're very weak. Weak pulse, weak but steady heartbeat, very shallow breathing. No evidence of major internal injuries, which is something—actually, something of a miracle, considering what's happened to her. The bullet passed through the right lung, which isn't life-threatening, as long as there isn't an inordinate amount of fluid from the lung filling the chest cavity. Too much of that fluid can compress the lungs and prevent her from breathing properly."

At this point, had she been dealing with one of the families in town, especially one that had arrived in the last few years from Seattle or Portland or the East Bay, Dr. Burnham would have immediately called an ambulance and packed Rachel off to the hospital. But these farm families, even the city-bred ones, tended to be stubborn and backward when it came to medical attention. Setting broken bones was okay, and you could prescribe natural painkillers and herbal remedies, but even the suggestion of x-rays or surgery brought on all sorts of ranting about the need to let things take their natural course. The last time Dr. Burnham had wanted to take a Stillwater to the hospital, twelve years ago when Rachel had been in a horrible bicycle accident, she had been told by the patient herself that she'd sooner have a gun put to her head. If it wasn't for the folks in town, Dr. Burnham, for all her love of the Mount Shasta region, would have given up long ago and moved to one of the domes.

She took a deep breath, and, putting the best light on the situation, said, "She's a strong, healthy girl, so she just might pull through. But be sure you clean the wounds and change her bandages twice a day. After a day or two, try to get some liquids—herbal tea and thin soup—down her."

Dr. Burnham already had her hand on the door when she stopped herself and turned around. "When she does start to come around, keep her quiet for awhile. Keep the conversation to a minimum."

"That'll be the hard part," Ed said, smiling for the first time that day. "Thanks for coming out, Doc." The suggestion that his daughter might recover had, as the doctor intended, helped to lift Ed's spirits, and kindled similar feelings in the rest of those gathered at the door to see the doctor out.

CHAPTER XVIII: LIFE'S EBB AND FLOW

*T*he visitors came and went throughout each of the next few days. Sometimes there would be several trucks and even a few bicycles parked outside the house. The visitors would troop in, one by one, gaze sadly at the quiet, lifeless figure on the bed, and leave as somberly as they entered.

Most of them were people whose lives she had touched—all sorts of them, of all ages. The drama teacher, Miss Widener, came down from Ashland, and there were the actors and technical people from the community theatre group. Ruby Stickner stopped by with a fragrant yellow-and-purple bouquet "that'll have her up and dancin' and flirtin' and kissin' in no time." Mrs. Guntry and her little brood, for whom Rachel had knitted sweaters and wool caps the previous Christmas, stopped by to pay their respects.

Rufus Pitbottom showed up one morning at the front door, dressed in his only suit, a red string tie, and what looked like a brand-new white Stetson (in fact it *was* new, purchased for the occasion at considerable expense). He was clutching, with both hands, a green vase with a dozen white roses.

Kathy opened the door. Squinting and shuffling his feet from uncharacteristic shyness, Rufus held up the flowers. "From me and the missus, Mrs. Stillwater. Clary woulda come, but she's feelin' poorly. Cain't remember if it's her rheumatism or in-dee-gestion this time, but she woulda come if it weren't for one or the other of 'em." He and Kathy, who was well aware of his wife's perpetual hypochondria, exchanged knowing smiles.

"Won't you come in?" Kathy asked as she took the flowers. Her voice was cheerful, but, in this third day after her daughter had come home, she was almost as ashen-faced as Rachel. Sleepless nights were etched across her face in fatigue lines; her eyes were bleary and sunken.

Rufus doffed his hat and twisted it about in his hands. "Thanks, ma'am, but I know you've got enough to fret about without me takin' up your time. Me and the missus just wanted you folks to know we're thinkin' about you and hopin' fer the best for that little gal o' yours. She's a rare one, and it would tear my heart out if anythin' happened to her."

Kathy, touched by the old man's heartfelt words, said, "Are you sure you won't come in, Mr. Pitbottom?"

"No ma'am, no ma'am. I thank you, but I think it's best if I be on my way." As he said this Rufus was taking short little steps backward toward his truck. "Ever'body from here to the Oregon border is prayin' for her recovery, ma'am," he said in an increasingly louder voice. "Some of 'em, not necessarily yours truly, have a good deal o' clout with the Lord above, so you can rest assured that . . . whoa-ah!"

Rufus had fallen backwards, landing flat on his back. He had tripped over an unseen stone that lay on his path to the truck. Fortunately, he was unhurt. Kathy, preoccupied with her own thoughts, had not even noticed the obstacle. She rushed over to Rufus and, grabbing his right hand with both of hers, hoisted him up.

Rufus dusted himself off and picked up his new hat. A crooked smile was already working its way across his face.

"Well, well, well," he said, "another fallen angel rises from the dust. You tell that young 'un of yours that if Rufus, with his creaky old bones, can get back up, by God . . ."

He finished the sentence with a wink and headed for his truck.

* * *

While time seemed to stand still in the dark, shuttered bedroom at the end of the hall, the wheels of life began to churn again outside it, haltingly at first, but slowly regaining their daily rhythm. The last cucumber and squash and watermelon seeds were dropped into the welcoming earth. Tim and Arturo made the first of many journeys down to Redding to pick up orange tree seedlings. Kathy and Cheryl returned to their work in town. Lucy and Ted went back to school. William and Ed and Salvador and Felicia went back to their tasks on and off the farms.

Only Jess remained in the darkened room, keeping a constant vigil at Rachel's bedside. To all outward appearances, he never seemed to give up hope, even though more than a week had passed with no signs of life other than the barely perceptible rising and falling of her chest. It was Jess who carefully changed the bandages. Every few hours he would force a trickle of water between her lips. Once, as he did so, kissing her cheek and running his hand through her hair after he had withdrawn the cup, he thought he saw her eyelashes flicker as if she were trying to open her eyes and look up at him. It was on such meager crumbs as this that he managed to keep his hopes alive.

One evening, as usual, he drifted off to sleep in his chair. As he did, the image of Amos, the black man on the hill, loomed before him, and he was uttering that word—"travelin'"—that had weaved itself into Jess's life since the Sacramento disaster, had become a watchword for his new life up here.

He saw Rachel before him, lovely and vibrant once again. His heart was bursting with joy at the sight. But though he tried to hold onto it, the vision faded. Then he saw her back at the lava beds, standing alone, almost in the same place that Captain Jack, or rather John, had been standing on that first night. Her lovely face was clearly visible, framed by the night sky as she looked out across the plains toward Mount Shasta.

And in the dream he saw himself approaching her, putting his arms around her waist from behind, and saying softly, "Where were you, Rachel? I thought I'd never find you."

"I've been right here all along, silly," she replied, her voice at once puzzled and a little cross. "Did you think I was going to leave you?"

Jess awoke and opened his eyes and looked at Rachel. He wanted to believe that she had really spoken, but he could tell from her lifeless face, so stark and pale compared to the vibrant vision in the dream, that nothing had changed. The cruel dream had raised his hopes and then dashed them to pieces. He buried his face in his hands and wept for the first time since the awful accident.

The first rays of light were already peeking around the drapes later that morning as Jess drowsed fitfully in the chair. Half awake, he heard the soft tread of someone entering the room.

"Mornin', son." It was a deep male voice. In Jess's drowsy state and with his eyes still shut, the voice conjured up vague images of mournful, black-clad figures.

Jess wanted to stay wrapped in the protective cloak of sleep, but he forced himself to open his eyes and see Ed standing over the bed. Yielding to the inevitable, he stretched out his arms and legs and yawned.

"Whyn't you join me and Kathy in the kitchen for a little bite to eat, son? Kathy's got somethin' whipped up by now, I expect." Ed's voice was determinedly cheerful. When Jess didn't answer, he put his hand on Jess's shoulder and said coaxingly, "C'mon son, you've gotta eat every once in awhile."

Jess followed the older man down the shadowy hallway into the brightly lit kitchen, which was filled with the inviting smells of fresh coffee and potatoes frying in the pan. Kathy called out a greeting.

Tim was already out in the fields, and Ted and Lucy had just left for school, so it was just the three of them sharing a breakfast of home-fried potatoes and eggs and toast. After some casual small talk about the harvest and the weather, Ed abruptly brought the conversation around to what was on his and Kathy's minds.

"It's been nine days that she's lain on that bed without showing any sign of life, Jess," he said slowly and deliberately.

"Yeah," Jess responded in a flat tone. He knew where this was heading, and it brought the agonies of the night rushing back with redoubled force. His first impulse was to get up and run out of the house, run up to the forests and the mountains where he could scream and cry all he wanted and not have to listen to what was coming next.

"Jess," Ed was saying in a gentle voice, "I know you're still hoping that something will happen, that . . . that she'll recover somehow." He stopped, blinking his eyes and looking away for a few moments. "But that may not be realistic. We have to prepare ourselves for the other . . . possibility. Not many people, even someone as healthy as Rachel, are going to survive what she's been through."

Kathy's eyes were welling with tears now. Jess stared at the kitchen floor. Ed continued, speaking slowly and having to struggle to get the words out. "We have to prepare ourselves to let go, Jess. It's not easy, but there is one blessing. It looks . . . it looks . . . " Ed coughed. He swallowed and tried again. "If she does leave us, it looks as if she'll go peacefully." He stopped abruptly, and looked away. Kathy, biting her lips, forced herself to meet Jess's gaze. Her brave smile was too much like her daughter's, and Jess had to get up and leave the room.

Jess could barely see where he was going as he staggered back down the hall and into the bedroom. He couldn't bear to look at the figure on the bed, lying there as still as death, and he was too wrung out, too numb from the endless days of grief to cry. He had reached a state where there was no sadness, no feeling at all. He felt as though he had fallen into an awful black void.

He had been sitting in the chair for awhile, staring alternately at the drawn shades and at his beloved Rachel, the hours slipping by unnoticed in the darkened room, when he had a thought that cast a ray of light into the gloom.

He had been thinking about a conversation he and Rachel had had some time ago about death and dying. In the course of that conversation, Rachel had made an unusual request. Jess at first had thought she was joking, but she made it clear she was quite serious, and had even extracted a solemn promise from Jess to honor her request if the time ever came. He hadn't thought about it since then; it had been a subject easily dismissed as too premature and too grim to dwell on.

Now her words came back to him vividly, as if she'd just spoken them the day before. Had she had a premonition of her early demise? It was ironic how that conversation, and the resulting vow—the conversation that had seemed so grim and the vow that had seemed so unnecessary at the time—now served to lift up his spirits. For it gave him one last, sacred task to perform for the woman he loved.

* * *

Late that night, long after everyone else had gone to bed, Jess emerged from the house carrying the enshrouded figure of his beloved. Only her face was visible; the rest was carefully wrapped in blankets. Jess slowly walked with his burden down the gravel path and out to the road. He crossed the road and walked silent and unnoticed past the crumbling farmhouse with the chipping paint where the elderly retired couple lived. Behind their acreage was the beginning of the trail that led up the forested slopes of the Eddy mountain range.

The sky was clear, and it was easy to find the trail in the light of a half moon. It was one he had hiked a number of times, including once before with Rachel. He thought of how on that hike he had carried her over a stream swollen with melted snow. He had staggered under her weight, both of them laughing at his awkward gallantry. Now, with her frame wasted away, she seemed hardly a burden at all.

He stopped once to rest, by the same stream he had carried her over before. He forced himself to drink a little water and eat a few bites of the sandwich he had stuffed in his pocket. More from habit than anything else, he forced a trickle of water from his canteen between Rachel's lips. Then, on an impulse, he sprinkled a few drops of water from the stream on her face, thinking of this as a kind of farewell from the mountain streams she had known since her childhood.

He sat for awhile longer listening to the stream's gentle music. The rushing water spoke of something ageless, eternal, its soothing message coming from a place where death was a part of the unending cycle of life.

A breeze stirred the boughs overhead. Drawing comfort from the stream's timeless message, he breathed deeply of the cool mountain air.

When he rose again, cradling Rachel in his arms, his soul was at peace for the first time since the accident.

If he regretted anything now, it was that he was making this trip with Rachel in the nighttime, when the birds and other wildlife were invisible and the colors of the wildflowers were muted. He could have looked on the bountiful life and vibrant colors of the season without sadness now, would even have gotten pleasure from sharing them with her one last time.

But they were approaching the timber line now, and the trees and other vegetation were growing sparse. He did catch sight of two deer, a doe and her fawn, standing stock still and watching from a safe distance. They bounded off, down the slope and into a thicker part of the forest, as he reached the last few stands of trees on the upper slopes.

Above him, lit by moonlight, were the bare, rocky slopes. As he slowly proceeded upward, on this last stretch up the mountain, he felt an awesome sadness, a sadness that seemed to pervade every tree and rock, from the forests below down to the very core of the mountain whose slopes he climbed. Perhaps, if he only had ears for it, he would have heard the old mountain's mournful farewell to the young woman who had once played in its shadows.

Finally, he reached his destination: the mountaintop that commanded views of the entire Strawberry Valley. To the east, the first glow of dawn was just beginning to light up the snowy pinnacle of Mount Shasta.

Jess carefully laid Rachel down on a bare flat spot near two scruffy, stunted pine trees. He gently drew the blanket folds away so that her face was fully exposed. Then he drew two sage sticks from his coat pocket and placed one near her head and one at her feet. He lit them and watched the wispy threads of smoke drift upward.

He lay down next to her and watched the last stars fade from the gradually lightening sky. His soul and his body were completely at rest now. He had the sense of being in a wonderful, peaceful, timeless state of existence; he felt he could lay here next to Rachel forever.

He gazed on his lover's face for a long while, until the strain of his long upward trek gradually caught up with him, and he drifted off to sleep.

The visions of the previous night began to repeat themselves. He saw Amos, his face now angry and threatening, saying the famil-

iar word over and over, each time more insistently. A terrible emptiness gripped Jess, and the horrible word, as it was repeated, echoed
menacingly in the dark void that enveloped him. Then once again
he saw Rachel at the lava beds, looking out over the moonlit plains.
This time she was wearing a white robe which, like her blankets,
covered everything but her face. She raised her arms, and, as he
watched, horrified, she slowly rose upward, the robe billowing out
all around her.

"No! No! No!" Jess heard himself cry.

"Jess, Jess." He heard her soft voice, speaking his name.

His own desperate cries and the sound of his name being
spoken in that familiar voice woke him up. He opened his eyes and
for an instant felt another glimmer of hope. But her face was just as
it had been before he'd fallen asleep. In the dawning light it was, if
anything, more pallid than the day before.

Jess closed his eyes again. He was very tired now, and he
desperately wanted to escape from the dawning of this new day, so
he welcomed the blackness that began to envelop him.

"Jess, Jess, where are you?" came that same soft voice out of
the darkness as he started to drift off to sleep again. "Jess, Jess . . . "
Trying to escape the tormenting, insistent voice, he rolled over on
his side.

"Jess, Jess . . . ," it persisted. Was he going mad? Was he going
to hear that voice for the rest of his life, every time he closed his
eyes? He thrashed back and forth from one side to the other, trying
to drive it out, but it came again and again and again.

He stopped moving, and, lying there in the temporary stillness,
he thought calmly to himself: This is what it's like to go crazy. I *am*
going crazy. I can't endure hearing that voice another minute, let
alone for the rest of my life. Maybe it would be better, right now,
to throw myself on the rocks below.

The more he thought about it, the more sensible it seemed. It would be such an easy way to end his agonies. On the side opposite the one he had climbed, there was a sharp dropoff only about 50 yards away. It beckoned to him, almost seductively, perhaps in the same way the walk outside the dome had once beckoned to John. You just had to take a deep breath and . . . walk over the edge. . . . He got up and slowly rose to his feet.

"Jess, Jess, where are you?" On hearing the voice again, his first impulse was to run toward the cliff without looking back. But something more powerful held him back, caused Jess to stop in his tracks and look back toward the figure lying under the pines. When he did, he saw a pair of eyes looking back at him.

"Jess, Jess," she said weakly, her voice puzzled and anxious. "I've been calling and calling you. Where are you going?"

Jess stared in disbelief, without speaking or moving. It took a few seconds for him to realize that this time he really wasn't dreaming. Rachel continued to move her lips, but he was having a hard time seeing her through the tears, and he could barely hear her over what sounded like the singing of angels and the pealing of bells, all of them mixed together—and if he had had ears to hear it, the deep, joyful rumbling of the venerable old mountain itself.

Kathy was home alone when Rachel, leaning on Jess for support, came haltingly down the walkway. After being carried most of the way down the mountain, Rachel insisted on walking these last few steps. Kathy, who was rarely at a loss for words, shrieked with joy and surprise when she saw the two of them from the kitchen window, and it was only after a great many tears and hugs that she recovered any speech at all—and even this consisted only of "oh my God" repeated over and over and over.

And then, in the hours and days that followed, the Stillwater house shook to its foundations with laughter and the loud, excited talk that comes from happiness and relief. Lucy and Ted were immediately summoned from school, and Tim and William from the fields and Ed and Sal from the Dunsmuir farmers' market. Cheryl and Felicia, who had been helping in the shop, drove in from town. Within a matter of hours the news of Rachel's return and miraculous recovery spread throughout the region. In the next few days many of the same visitors who had come and gone before with mournful expressions joined in the ongoing celebration at the Stillwater house.

No one was much surprised when Rufus, wearing his new hat and string tie, showed up again at the front door, but it was a bit of a shock to see Bob Rawlings at his side, also wearing his Sunday best.

Rawlings was holding a vase of roses this time and, after a little prodding from Rufus, he addressed Kathy: "We . . . that is, me and Rufus and the other guys, was awful glad to hear about your daughter, ma'am. She's a brave little gal. Got too much spunk to just take off and leave us, and thank God for that." With this little hurried speech, practiced in the truck all the way over, he handed her the vase of flowers.

Kathy, deeply touched, made sure both of them got back out to Rufus's truck safely.

And then, a few days later, the evening they celebrated the miracle of Rachel's return, didn't the little dining room fairly spill over with laughter and love and good spirits—and, yes, even a few more tears? People, even those as warm and outgoing as the Stillwaters, don't usually express their love in plain words, but on this occasion it was present in the abundance of good, wholesome food; in Ed's eyes as they misted over every time he looked over at his daughter; Lucy shyly clearing away Rachel's empty plates and pouring her water; Tim putting his arm around her as they talked.

The dishes were finally cleared away and Ted's drawings of the new house, which now included extensive drawings of the interior, were spread out on the table. Everyone present, except Rachel and

Jess, seemed to be familiar with all the details of the house, and they eagerly gave the couple a room-by-room tour. Felicia, who had no prospect of a home of her own any time in the near future, enthused over the cupboard space in the kitchen as if it *were* her own; Tim pointed out the large workbench in the garage, complete with table saw and fancy woodworking vice; and Kathy spoke grandly of the upstairs corner bedroom with the huge picture windows that would offer panoramic views of Mount Shasta and neighboring Shastina.

Then, with a little prompting from Kathy, Lucy brought out her contribution (to the accompaniment of appreciative oohs and ahs): a large oil painting showing Rachel astride her horse. The young artist had employed vivid hues—Rachel was clad in a bright red shirt, with a liquid blue sky in the background—and had used big, bold brushstrokes, a technique that captured the vibrant energy of her subject. Henceforth this portrait would hang next to Lucy's painting of the mysterious white-robed woman on the dining room wall (the one that Jess couldn't bear to look at for many years to come).

But the best gift of all, of course, was seated at the place of honor, her green eyes sparkling like a dew-kissed meadow in the early spring. Looking at her from across the table, Jess was reminded of the little mountain stream and its timeless message.

In the weeks that followed, long after life on the farms returned to their normal rhythms, Jess still heard echoes from the night he'd spent on the mountain with Rachel. They came to him when he lay next to her just before falling asleep, or sometimes just on awakening, when he turned to look at her: heard again the heavenly music that had filled his soul when he saw those bright green eyes looking at him once again.

And there were echoes of a different sort that lasted long after the adventures just recounted. Many of those same scraggly refugees who had camped at the lava beds stayed on in Siskiyou

County. A few of them, it's true, never really left the streets, never put down roots, drifting from one locale to another, always with their hands out. But those who stayed in the region eventually found themselves caught up in its life and work. The miracle of each succeeding generation embraced even these former street urchins, as they began the slow, grudging march toward respectability that begins with work and starting new families.

John, for a time, went to work on the Shawntree farm. Chester and Adele, more suited to town life, readily found employment there, Chester at the front counter of The Fancy Hat Emporium and Adele as an apprentice potter to Genevieve Kerkhoven, the woman whose always busily spinning wheel graced the front window of her shop.

Little Ed, in time, became a mainstay of the community theatre, selling sports equipment on the side. Scratchy lived off the proceeds of his bestselling book, and a sequel: *Channeled Gourmet Recipes From The Late, Great Chefs.*

And as the refugees went on to start their own families, they would tell their children the story of how they came to be here, of the great battle at the lava beds, and of the young woman whose courageous actions and brush with death brought a halt to the hostilities, paving the way for a time of reflection and healing.

EPILOGUE

*T*he last two students, Jason Renfree and his friend Jeffrey Ramirez, appeared at the bend in the trail. Talking and laughing as they went, they straggled over to the shady spot, under the two junipers on the slope of the mountain just above the trail, where their classmates were already seated. Up where they were, high up on Black Butte, they had a clear view of the old highway and the broad, forested plain that stretched between Black Butte and the towering slopes of Mount Shasta.

"Thought we were going to have send out the rescue squad," Mr. Thomas said as the two boys perched themselves on a large rock. Though in his forties, the teacher was still youthful looking, with his trim build and smooth, tanned face, which was often smiling. He was smiling now as he delivered this gentle remonstrance to the two boys. He found it hard to be stern with them, despite their dawdling on this occasion and their constant habit of chattering in class—they were likable, high-spirited kids, eager students who were always asking questions—and, besides, their dawdling had actually helped him collect his thoughts.

He took a deep breath. The task of explaining the Old Society to his students seemed to get more and more difficult each year. He had studied this period thoroughly in his college days, but its practices seemed increasingly bizarre to him. There were times when he felt as if he were talking about some ancient culture, governed by a totally different set of values from the present one.

For this fifth grade class, he had adopted a kind of show-and-

265

tell approach. He pointed to the ribbon of highway below, where you could see tiny figures walking and pedaling bicycles. "Now class, can everyone see the old highway down there? That old highway used to have trucks on it from all over the country. It's hard to believe now, but they brought us oranges from Florida, tomatoes from Mexico, shoes from Asia, coffee from South America. . . ." He paused, waiting for the inevitable question, the one that came every year. This year it came from Jason Renfree, whose hand had shot up.

"Yes Jason?"

"Mr. Thomas, how come they brought all that stuff from all over, when we can make it all right here?"

It was the anticipation of this question that always caused Mr. Thomas to pause and reflect, because it was not an easy question to answer, not for these kids who lived in a region where everything sold in the stores was made or grown right here. Mr. Thomas started with the easy part of the answer: Cheap fuel prices were one of the reasons it had been possible to transport goods over long distances and sell them for less than what it cost to make them and sell them right here.

Then he pointed to the two big yellow arches to the north, right next to the old highway. "Those big arches over there, class, are the other part of the answer to Jason's question." He went on to explain that the restaurant with the golden arches that was now a museum had been one of thousands of identical ones all over the world, owned by one big company. The company bought huge quantities of food for all its identical restaurants at very low prices, and shipped it cheaply to its restaurants thanks to the low fuel prices. And paid the workers in those restaurants very little because the work was simple and regimented and required few skills. And so the restaurant could sell its food more cheaply than practically any other restaurant around.

"And this system was applied to everything else that people bought in those days, class. Nowadays you walk down Mt. Shasta Boulevard and there's Barb and her husband who make your shoes, and Pete the Potter's shop who makes your pots and your plates, and . . ."

"And the candle maker," piped up Jeffrey Ramirez.

"Yes," said Mr. Thomas.

"And the *toy* store!" cried Susie Nagasaki.

"Right again," said Mr. Thomas.

"And the hat place," said Tony Manfredi.

"Yes," said Mr. Thomas.

"And the *candy* store!" cried Susie Nagasaki.

"Yes, yes, yes, very good," Mr. Thomas said. "Now, none of those shops existed 100 years ago. All of the things you mentioned, plus a lot more, were sold in one big store in Yreka, and it was brought there by all those trucks on the old highway. And people drove from all over, from Dunsmuir, Mt. Shasta, McCloud, Weed, to buy it. Like the restaurant, the folks who owned that big store had stores just like it all over the country, and they bought their stuff cheap and sold it cheap, which was a good thing, because they didn't pay their workers much, either."

Mr. Thomas ended the talk with a clever line he had made up himself: "So that's why we say the old system came from the dinosaurs and now it's *one* of the dinosaurs." Mr. Thomas looked around expectantly, but no one laughed or even chuckled, not even after he reminded them where oil came from. It was time to head down the mountain.

* * *

To the west the sun still blazed high above the Eddy mountain range as the two boys bicycled home from school. There had been a light spring shower the day before, and they were determined to splash through every puddle in the road. Jason amused himself for awhile by pretending that he was connecting the dots for a huge drawing—a drawing of a big, hump-backed dinosaur— that only a giant up on the mountain could see. He soon tired of this notion, however, and it was replaced by another image: that of an endless cavalcade of trucks marching down the highway, filled to overflowing with oranges, apples, tomatoes, shoes, candy, toys.

"Did you understand any of that stuff Mr. Thomas was talking about today?" Jason asked his friend.

"Yeah, kinda," Jeffrey replied. He lurched suddenly to the right to try and run over a lizard that had just skittered across the road. The lizard made it safely to an irrigation ditch at the side of the road as Jeffrey's rear tire caught some loose rock and skidded. Only a quick turn of the handlebars and some adrenalin-charged pedaling kept Jeffrey from joining the lizard.

"Yeah," he repeated, eyeing his friend surreptitiously to see if Jason had noticed his skillful maneuvering. "That's just the way they did things in those days. Nobody made anything themselves. They all worked in offices. They worked in offices all day, and then they went out and bought the stuff they needed. That's how they did things."

This seemed like a pretty satisfactory explanation to Jason; it was at least as understandable as Mr. Thomas's explanation. But it wasn't *entirely* satisfactory either, because it didn't explain *why* they did things that way. It didn't seem like much fun, sitting in an office all day, when you could be out in the fields like his dad and mom or, like Uncle Pete, working at a potter's wheel all day. (Shaping clay with your hands and spinning it into dishes and bowls was neat—Pete had even let him try it a few times.)

And another thing, why would anyone want to go into a restaurant that was just like thousands of others?

They reached Jeffrey's place. Before Jeffrey turned down the gravel road Jason asked, "Wanna come over and do somethin'?"

"Nah, can't. Dad's at the Yreka market so I gotta bring the sheep in." He said this in a tone of weary resignation, as if much of the responsibility for the farm's success, like it or not, rested on his narrow shoulders. Jason continued on his way, dutifully impressed with his friend's importance and wishing he had chores of his own to do that afternoon. But, alas, he had the rest of the afternoon to himself.

It was only a short distance to his own home—the two boys were neighbors—but Jason pedaled right past it. He knew it was empty; his mom and dad were also at the Yreka farmers' market today, and his sister Amanda had stayed after school for band practice. He continued on past the house down the narrow dirt path to his grandfather's place. As he had hoped, his grandfather was there, sitting on the porch.

"Hey Jason!" the old man called out as the boy leaned his bike against the oak tree. His craggy face broke into a wide grin. Since his wife had passed away last year, time passed slowly for the old man, and he was glad for the company of his grandson. To keep occupied, he was shelling walnuts. At his side were two five-gallon milk buckets, one with walnuts and the other already half-filled with shells. Next to that was a smaller bucket filled nearly to the top with shelled walnuts.

The boy bounded up on the porch and eyed the walnut operation. It would not be quite as good as herding sheep, but it would have to do.

"Need any help, Grandpa?"

"Why, sure, sure, son, help yourself," his grandfather replied, a little taken aback by the unexpected offer. He handed Jason the nutcrackers. In a businesslike way, Jason carefully arranged the three containers around the other chair on the porch and set to work.

"So how was that hike up Black Butte?" his grandfather asked.

"Oh . . . okay, pretty neat," Jason replied, not looking up, preoccupied with the task at hand. "You know, you can see all over, the highway and everything."

"Uh-huh. It's been awhile since I dragged these old bones up there, but I remember the view—you can practically see right over the Eddys to the ocean from up there."

You had to be careful with Grandpa, because he tended to exaggerate things. That was one of the reasons it was fun talking to Grandpa, but Jason knew from his geography class that the Eddys were at least as high as Black Butte.

"Grandpa?"

"Yes, Jason."

"Did you ever eat at that place that had the golden arches?"

"McDonald's? Well, when I was real young, even younger than you, I remember going to one of them in Sacramento. But by the time I got up here that place had gone out of business."

"Grandpa?"

"Yes?"

"Did you ever eat one of those oranges from Florida? Or a tomato from Mexico?"

"Oh sure, son, we had things like that in Sacramento and in the East Bay when I lived there. But things were different up here. We couldn't get that stuff because it cost so much to ship it. When I got here people were already growing most of their own food and making a lot of stuff for themselves. Things were a lot simpler up here, of course, 'cause they couldn't make everything that folks in the cities had—automatic dishwashers, for example, electric can openers, hair dryers. But we got along pretty well without all that stuff, anyway."

The old man and his grandson sat silent for awhile as the boy continued cracking walnuts. The old man was thinking of a conversation he'd had nearly a half century ago, and the words came back to him as distinctly as if they'd just been spoken the day before.

"You know, Jason," he said, "before people started making things and doing things for themselves, it was like the people here were living in a little box that somebody else, somebody outside this area, had put us in, you know, it was like they were sayin' 'You can't do this,' and 'You can't do that.'

"Now, understand Jason, nobody was sayin' we weren't *allowed* to grow oranges here, or tomatoes, or make our own shoes, but it's just that . . ."

"Everybody worked in offices and then at the end of the day they all had to go out and buy that stuff. That's what Jeffrey Ramirez says."

"Well yeah, that's about right. It all had to do with money. Somebody had figured out a way to make all that stuff cheaper than we could do it ourselves, and you could make more money workin' in an office than you could out in the fields, that's for sure, and people in those days thought making money was the whole point of life.

"But then there came a time, earlier in this century, when it wasn't profitable to ship all that stuff up here, and that kind of freed us to, as I said, start doin' things for ourselves, find out what we could do on our own.

"You know, Jason, I don't think folks realized what a tiny little box they'd been livin' in 'til they actually got out of it and stretched their legs and expanded their horizons, did a little *travelin'*, so to speak." Jess could see the old man just as clearly as on the day he had climbed the hill above Dunsmuir.

By now the smaller bucket was filled to the brim with walnuts. Jason had stopped working, but his grandfather hadn't noticed. His head had dropped down; he was off somewhere, Jason knew, as he was a lot of the time, so to get his attention Jason tapped him on the arm. His grandfather sat up with a jerk and blinked his eyes. Jason pointed to the full bucket.

"By God, Jason," his grandfather said, looking down at the bucket, "you're the best darned walnut cracker I've ever seen. You'll have to run and fetch another bucket. Let's see . . . can't use the mop bucket. Nope. Let's see . . . I think there's one up on the shelf above the workbench. Use that little stepladder in the garage to get up on the bench and then once you're on the bench you can probably reach up there."

Jason, still flushed from his grandfather's praise, jumped off the porch and dashed toward the garage.

"Careful, son," his grandfather called out to him. He's a live one, Jess thought to himself, just like his mom . . . and his grandma. That thought brought back memories, memories of the first time he'd seen her as she disappeared into the house next door and that first magic evening when he'd watched her ride her horse around the corral. The memories, the way she had looked and talked and acted at different times in their lives, overwhelmed him at times. Sometimes all he had to do was look up at the top of that mountain range and they came crowding in, more real than anything in present time.

Jason had rushed into the garage and grabbed the stepladder from a far corner. It was covered with dust, as was the workbench as he clambered on top of it. He had to stretch on tiptoe to reach the shelf, sending little wisps of dust floating downward as he felt around up there. His fingers brushed against a round metal object. By rotating the object slowly, he was able to nudge it toward the edge of the shelf, where he could just barely grasp it with both hands. As he gingerly brought the object down to eye level, he could see that it wasn't a bucket at all. It was made of some sort of tarnished metal. A fairly large orb of clear, hard plastic was implanted on one side. And the top was completely covered with the same tarnished metal. As he carefully replaced it in approximately the same position he had found it, he thought of his dad's comment that he hoped Grandpa lived forever because he sure wasn't looking forward to cleaning out that garage.

Jason resumed his blind search of the shelf and immediately grasped something that he knew wasn't a bucket. It was right next to where the weird metal thing had been but it felt very different, thin and cloth-like. Out of curiosity, he pulled it right to the edge. It turned out to be a pretty ordinary-looking old cowboy hat. But when he brought it down he noticed a couple of faded reddish blotches on one side of the brim.

Jason, with his fertile ten-year-old imagination, was experiencing a delicious feeling of guilt at his discovery of these mysterious objects that his grandfather had kept tucked out of sight all these years. He was in fact rather disappointed when the next object he retrieved turned out to be a solid metal bucket with absolutely no distinguishing characteristics. Oh well, he'd better get back to the porch before Grandpa started wondering what the heck he was doing in here.

Grandpa was back in his reveries, his eyes half-closed, when Jason got back to the porch with the empty bucket. Jason let him drift for awhile. Grandpa seemed to like whatever it was he was seeing behind the half-closed eyes, because he had a smile on his face and he gave a little grunt of pleasure every once in awhile.

He came out of it on his own, opened his eyes and was momentarily startled to see his grandson sitting there next to him, but then he saw the full bucket of walnuts and the almost-empty one and remembered what had happened before the memories had taken over.

The two of them sat on the porch until dusk, watching the sun gradually sink below the mountains, their conversation ebbing and flowing as Jason, still full of questions spawned by the day's field trip, asked them with his usual sense of wonder and curiosity. His grandfather tried to explain, as best he could, some of the strange and exotic practices of the ancient times he himself had lived through—when people had lived, and died, under plastic domes, and worked in offices and bought goods from all over, and the earth all around them was cracked and barren.

So the two of them shared the gift of companionship, as dusk settled in and a full moon rose over the surrounding fields. Jason had temporarily forgotten the strange metal object he had found in the garage, but the all-knowing moon cast its silvery light with equal measure on the tarnished metal face that peered through the grimy window in the garage, on the little bike under the oak tree, on the smooth face of the boy and on the wrinkled face of the old man.

What difference did it make to the moon? With its soft, caressing light, the moon bestowed its blessings on them all. The wise and patient moon, following the same stately course through the heavens on this night that it had in the years when the earth had shuddered and shriveled below. And when this night's course was run, as it sent its last shaft of light through the little window in the garage, and into the separate rooms where the old man and his grandson slept, it gave a passing nod to the orb that was sending its first glowing light over the pinnacle of Mount Shasta. The daily changing of the guard, the silent watching and nurturing.

More Quality Paperbacks From Suttertown Publishing

In *Old River Town*, Lloyd Bruno, who came to Sacramento in 1923, revels in the romance of its steamboats, its trolleys, and its vaguely Southern charm.

In this beautifully written, off-the-beaten track personal history, readers will learn of such long-forgotten but important Sacramento institutions as the McNeill Club and the X Club from someone who was an active participant in both. They will also learn more about some of Sacramento's more colorful personalities, including John Sutter, C.K. McClatchy and Belle Cooledge.

Must reading for natives and newcomers alike. $12.95

In *The Porch-Sitting Outlaw*, writer/journalist Tim Holt chronicles his adventures on the road and provides his whimsical obserations about small-town life in his new home, Dunsmuir, California.

Included among Holt's adventures are his attempted swim under the Golden Gate Bridge and his disastrous—and hilarious—bike ride from Sacramento to the South Yuba River.

Also included are profiles of Sarah Greenberg, one of the gutsiest ladies in New York City; Captain Jim Clove, skipper of a replica 16th century Spanish galleon; and the colorful denizens of North Beach when it was the center of the Beat Movement. $10.95.

In *The Pilgrims' Chorus*, a coming-of-age novel about a young dog who joins a wolf pack, you'll find the kind of enchanting characters that fill the pages of *Wind In The Willows*.

There's Barnabus, a wise old dog and the keeper of the book's great secret. And Dream Talker, the charming misfit of the wolf pack—a dreamer and a philosopher who speaks of his beloved woods and wilderness in the language of poetry.

A book for adults young and old who love a good story well told. $7.95.

Add $2 for shipping and tax for single book orders, $1 shipping and tax for each additional book ordered. No cash, please. Make check or money order payable to "Tim Holt," P.O. Box 214, Dunsmuir, California 96025. Phone number: (530) 235-4034.